The Thieves of Stonewood

Book I of the Stonewood Trilogy

Jeremy Hayes

I dedicate this book to my friend Mike Kotsopoulos (sunrise 1974 – sunset 1996), who is gone but never forgotten. Mike introduced me to the world of fantasy and the stories floating around in my head would not have been possible without him. Mike was an amazing artist and I was very pleased to have been able to incorporate one of his drawings into the cover of this book. This one is for you buddy.

The Stonewood Trilogy

Book I: The Thieves of Stonewood

Book II: The Demon of Stonewood
Coming Summer 2013

Book III: The King of Stonewood
Coming 2014

Northlord Publishing

Visit us at: www.northlordpublishing.com for news about upcoming releases or to contact the author.

Copy Editor: Daphne Lavers, M.J.
Cover Art: Mike Kotsopoulos
Cover Design: Robert Przybylo www.robpaperscissors.com
Website/Logo: Cody Kotsopoulos www.kotsysdesigns.com

Special thanks to Ed Greenwood for his sagely advice.

PROLOGUE

"Thief!" screamed the merchant's wife.

Harcourt momentarily froze in the doorway. The merchant and his wife were not due back home for another half hour. They never came back early. Harcourt had watched their routine for a week and they had never strayed from it. It looked as though bad luck had reared its ugly head yet again.

"Thief!" she cried louder the second time.

Harcourt reluctantly dropped his sack that was filled with a few of the fine cloaks the merchant and his wife were known for, and a small coin chest that had jingled with the sounds of heaven when he shook it. He darted around the older couple and sprinted across Leaf Lane for the closest alleyway. As he reached the mouth of the alley he felt as though he had run straight into a stone wall. Lying in wait was a burly city guard who dove out and tackled him to the cobblestone street. *Where did he come from?* the thief thought. He had done a sweep of the neighborhood prior to breaking into the merchant's home and did not find any patrols in the immediate area. Bad luck seemed to be the story of Harcourt's life lately.

Thinking that the thief was stunned and winded, the guard released his grip and attempted to stand. Harcourt kicked out and swept the legs from under him and the guard went crashing down onto his back. The thief was up and running a second later.

He sprinted down the dark alley and vaulted the low stone wall that separated this alley with the next. Behind him he could still hear the merchant's wife screaming "Thief!" Panic overtook him as he heard the unmistakable sound of the guard's horn being blown. Each guard in the city of Stonewood carried a small silver horn to be blown in the event of an emergency. Every guard in the vicinity that heard it would come running, including the special unit that was more heavily-armed and armored than the average patrol guard.

Harcourt skidded to a stop and peered out onto Dove Street, spotting four guards jogging in his direction. The thief was virtually invisible when he crouched in the dark shadows of the night and they had not yet seen him. Suddenly from behind, the guard that had tackled him was attempting to climb over the low stone wall, but his large stomach and chainmail vest were weighing him down and not co-operating. Huffing and puffing, he gave up and blew his horn again. Harcourt turned his attention back to the four on the street. One of the guards pointed to his alley and they all picked up their pace.

Desperation set in. This was not supposed to happen like this. He had been so careful this time. Harcourt backed up into the alley, his mind racing.

"Hold right there thief," the burly guard called from

over the wall.

Nowhere to go but up, he thought. Harcourt climbed onto an empty crate and looked for a way up the building wall. The thief had a knack for finding holes and crevices that allowed him to climb what appeared to be a sheer surface. Fortunately, this particular building was old and the stonework was in disrepair, so he scrambled up the side like a spider. The four guards ran into the alleyway and the fifth one signaled for them to look up. They were just in time to watch the thief's legs swing over the top and disappear onto the roof.

"Surround the building! Don't let him escape," he heard one of them shout from below.

Another horn blew. *Curses*, he thought, the entire garrison of the lower west district would be here soon. Harcourt knew he could navigate this district well enough, but if he could just make it back to the south district, he would be almost impossible to catch. He knew the south district, the poorest part of the city of Stonewood, inside and out. The thief was born there and had lived all of his thirty years there.

He ran to the southern end of the roof and without hesitation leaped across that alleyway to the next rooftop. This building was a row of six shops all attached together. When he reached the other end, there was nowhere else to go, the jump to the next building was much too far. Harcourt grabbed a hold of the sign for Marten's Meats and lowered himself over the edge, then dropped the remaining distance to the street below. He landed softly like a cat. "There he is," he heard off to his left, so he ran to his right as another horn blew.

The thief sped down the street dodging a few drunks

who had just left a tavern. The streets were fairly empty this night and two blocks ahead, he spotted three members of the special guards unit, their polished armor gleaming in the moonlight and their swords drawn. He took another right into the next alley and leaned against the wall to catch his breath. Perhaps he should make for the cemetery, he thought. He had spent many a night hiding out there. Most citizens and guards avoided the graveyard at night, fearing the dead would rise up and seize them. Harcourt, on the other hand, did not believe in ghosts or the walking dead, so he had little trouble hiding out there when it was necessary to avoid the authorities.

His thoughts were interrupted by a woman's voice from the street, "I saw a man run into that alley."

Time to move. To the thief's horror, the alley was a dead end. He attempted to scale the wall and was roughly dragged down and thrown to the ground. A tall lanky guard drew his sword and barked, "Nowhere to run now thief. Surrender."

The guard slowly advanced. Harcourt was stuck. He could not afford to get caught, not again. He dreaded returning to the dungeon, but most of all he would let down Jalanna. The thief needed to raise a lot of gold for the love of his life and tonight was supposed to be the first step in achieving his goal. It was an impossible goal, really, given that he was never granted a membership into the city's Thieves Guild. No crimes were to take place within the city without Guild approval, and without them getting their cut. Harcourt was desperate though and had no other choice than to bypass the Guild's rules.

He contemplated drawing his newly-acquired dagger but dismissed that thought. He was a thief, not a murderer.

Pulling a weapon on a guard would only make this situation even worse than it already was. Instead, he glanced behind the guard and gave a great big smile, then said, "About time you showed up."

Shocked, the guard turned his head, thinking the thief had an accomplice. Harcourt kicked his sword arm wide and then planted a fist square on the man's nose as he turned back. Harcourt stood nearly six feet tall with a lean muscular body. He had been fighting in the streets since he was eight, and could pack a punch. The blow sat the guard right down on the ground, dazed. Harcourt hurdled over the stunned man and ran back onto the street. The three special unit guards were almost on top of him and a strong hand clamped down on his shoulder from behind.

Harcourt dropped low causing a guard with a bushy black beard to lose his grip, and then rolled to his right. He was up and sprinting at full speed in the opposite direction from the special unit. Folk were beginning to gather in streets to watch the chase. Others hung their heads out windows after hearing the horns being blown, all wanting a glimpse at what had the guards all riled up.

Two more guards appeared from behind a wagon to block his path but the thief faked moving to his right and then went left around them and down the street beyond. A well-dressed man opened the door to the Red Horse Tavern to exit the establishment and Harcourt, seeing an escape, changed directions, running straight in. The tavern was packed with patrons and the thief shoved and weaved his way through the surprised crowd and vaulted the bar, disappearing into the back kitchen. The barkeep was too shocked to even react until the thief was gone. Before he could pursue the mysterious man, his attention was drawn to the two out-of-breath city guards who burst into the tavern. Guessing at why they were there, the barkeep gave a loud whistle and pointed to the kitchen door.

Harcourt passed two stunned cooks as they prepared a large meat dish that smelled delicious. He had not had a decent meal in days and his stomach growled at the aroma. He was out the back door and into the alleyway behind the building before they even had a chance to speak a word. The thief crept to the mouth of the alley and made sure the street was clear of guards. Harcourt had made so many twists and turns he was completely disoriented and lost his direction. He scanned the skyline for the tower of Fezzdin the Fantastic. The royal magician owned the tallest structure in the city. The cylindrical stone tower could be seen anywhere in the city as it seemed to reach up into the clouds themselves. After locating the tower, he allowed himself a faint smile as he realized he was closer to the south district than he originally thought, and there was no sign of any guards on Arrows Bend.

He heard a commotion coming from inside the tavern's kitchen and set off jogging down the street. He drew the attention of a few people but without any immediate pursuers he could have just been out for a cool evening run. Figuring out exactly where he was, he took a right and then a left, then entered into the city's south district.

It was easy to distinguish the south district from the others immediately as the stone road turned to dirt and the buildings were exclusively now made of wood. Everything was crowded and jammed together down here as the city tried to cram in as many buildings as they possibly could. Harcourt wondered why there were not any guards at this particular district border crossing. Had he been a guard, he would have set up a blockade at the various district entrances at the sound of the horns.

Harcourt spotted a familiar alley up ahead and he knew once he got there, he was home free. He took one more glance back to look for pursuers and was pleased to think he had lost them. He noted it was unusually quiet on this street; the south district normally came alive at night. Ignoring the warning signals, he ducked into the alley and took a mailed fist to the nose. His body went limp and fell to the ground, his head bouncing once on the hard earth. His broken nose spouted warm blood down the sides of his face as he dizzily gazed up to see the man who had leveled him.

Captain Dornell. He had been a thorn in Harcourt's side since the age of ten when the man first caught him picking pockets in the market. Each district had a captain of the guards, and Dornell was the south district's captain. He shook his head and gave the thief a very disappointed look.

Harcourt heard heavy footsteps approaching and rolled his eyes to see a brute of a guard he did not recognize lean over him. With an evil grin the guard said, "You are under arrest street urchin," then proceeded to stomp on the thief's chest, taking the wind out of him.

"Zorfal, that's enough!" Captain Dornell shouted. "Chain him."

For good measure, Zorfal kicked him once more in the head and Harcourt's world went black.

CHAPTER 1

Four Months Later

Harcourt heard the heavenly sound of the old iron key sliding into the keyhole, then the unmistakable click of the massive metal door as it unlocked. The guardsman who had unlocked the door gave it a shove, but it did not budge until he had put his shoulder into it using his full weight. The door creaked open and the morning sunlight bathed the archway with its brilliant radiance.

Harcourt was immediately blinded, his eyes stung and watered. The light he had been waiting so long to see now caused him pain. He had spent the last four months in the dimly-lit underground dungeons for the crime of thievery.

Harcourt was a thief. He had been his entire life. It was all he knew. He did not have any memories of his mother, and his father had died when he was only eight years old. He had no other family that he was aware of, and was left to fend for himself in the streets of Stonewood. Nothing came free in this city, so he had to learn to steal to survive. He was capable of doing any number of jobs if he had been given half a chance in life, but those were not the cards he was dealt. His path followed the only route open to him at the time.

As a thief, he was good. It was not surprising with all the years of experience he had. He felt his skills were second to none in the city, and yet he was never granted membership into the Thieves Guild. Every thief or criminal with any skill had to have a membership in order to operate in Stonewood. Smaller crimes could go unnoticed by the Guild but they did tend to be strict when dealing with non-members stealing or killing in their city. Some got off with a stern warning, and some were beaten. In severe cases, the offender just disappeared.

Harcourt's life would have been so very different if he had been allowed to join, but he had always been denied. While he thought he had no equal in skill, even he had to admit that he possessed an awful lot of bad luck. His luck was so bad that the Guild claimed he was too much of a risk to them.

Harcourt always went to great lengths to scout out a potential target before ever making a move. If he meant to burglarize a home or business establishment, he would spend days learning the patterns of the owners or employees. When they worked. When they slept. When they went to market. When did friends visit. How often would city guards patrol nearby. He never made a move until he was certain of everyone's schedule. He had little trouble getting into most of the city's buildings, there had not been a lock yet that he could not defeat. Yet something always went wrong. Much like his most recent trouble with the merchant and his wife, or the time before that when he came across private security in a shop that was not known to hire them. Just plain bad luck.

It seemed to be the story of Harcourt's life. It was little wonder that he had turned to the drink many, many years back to drown away his sorrows. Nowadays, most folk just saw him as the poor south-side homeless drunk, and not a thief of any success.

Four months in the dungeon had been hell. He would have preferred to eat the scraps he managed to get out on the streets over the filth that passed for food in there. Since his crime was not a violent one, at least he had been kept separate from the more vile and dangerous prisoners, but that did not make serving his time any easier.

Harcourt was still not able to open his eyes when the guard that had been standing behind him gave him a hard kick, sending him through the doorway out onto the cobblestone street. His arms flailed as he tried to keep his balance.

"See ye again soon, street scum," the guard with the keys taunted. "Yer escort awaits at the corner."

Through burning squinted eyes, the thief could make out three dark shapes standing just down the street, his armed escort through the city's north district. Despite the discomfort he felt from his eyes, Harcourt smiled. He was free.

* * * *

Since Harcourt could still barely open his eyes, he was shoved along the street by three city guardsmen. They wore their customary chainmail shirts, covered by a dark blue tunic which was the uniform of the city. Emblazoned on their chests and backs was the symbol of Stonewood, two grey trees standing beside a blue river. They were each armed with a long-bladed sword that hung from one hip, and a dagger from the other. A small silver horn hung from each of their belts.

These guards did not speak a word to the thief, just kept shoving him along. No citizen that did not reside in the north district could walk through there without an escort. The north district housed the city's castle, home to King Stonewood VII, the courts, the dungeons of course, and the city's wealthiest citizens. It was the only district that was walled off from the rest of the city and had only two entry points. There was a considerable guard presence in this area of the city, both near the gates as well as constant street patrols. Any visitor to the north district would need to state their business and destination at the gatehouse, and then would be accompanied by a guard to their destination. Harcourt, being a criminal, got an escort of three, and they watched him very closely.

The thief wished he could see clearly so he could admire the homes while they walked, and dream about how the other half lived. Most of the citizens of the north district were either nobles, from long lines of noble families, or the wealthiest and most successful merchant families. He could not even imagine what it was like to be rich. Harcourt did not have one copper coin to his name or a proper home to call his own. He lived in a small shack he had built himself in the poorest part of the city's south district. It had only three walls and a leaky roof. He slept on the ground. As bad as that sounded, he could not wait to sleep there tonight. Anything was better than that cold dark dungeon cell, listening to the wailing of the prisoners whose minds had gone mad.

Harcourt's vision gradually adjusted as they went along and passed the tallest structure in the city. He gazed upwards in awe as he did every time he passed by here. It was the tower of Fezzdin the Fantastic. It was a rather plain tower with very few windows which mostly dotted the upper reaches. The entrance was a set of large iron-bound double doors with a stone gargoyle perched above. Rumors said the gargoyle could come to life and punish any who did not have official business with the tower's resident.

Harcourt dismissed that as a fairy tale; he did not believe in monsters. He also did not believe in magic, which is what the city's royal magician was known for. It was said that Fezzdin possessed powerful magical abilities, although Harcourt had never met anyone who had ever witnessed any with their own eyes. It was always the second cousin of a friend's brother that told someone of some amazing thing the wizard had done.

Harcourt was a master of sleight of hand tricks and doing things with normal playing cards that others thought were magic, especially children. It did not involve any magic though; they were all just tricks he had learned. The thief believed Fezzdin was just the greatest conman in the city.

"Hey lowlife," smirked one of his escorts, a man with yellow teeth and in bad need of a shave. "I wouldn't stare too long at that tower if I were you. My friend's sister saw Fezzdin strike someone down with a bolt of lightning once. Fer just staring! He'd probably figure a no-good thief like you was lookin' fer a way in."

The other two chuckled and a second added, "I'd like to see him try to get in there. He'd go in a man and leave a frog."

Harcourt ignored them and turned his attention away from the tower and towards the gate they were approaching. This gate would lead him to the upper east district, and here his escort would leave him. As they reached the gatehouse, the guards posted there stared him down with suspicious eyes. They looked down on him as they usually did with that look of superiority that they always wore on their faces.

His arrival drew their gazes away from the foppishly-dressed young man trying to explain why he needed to cross into the north district. He was most likely there to court some rich nobleman's daughter, but he had phrased it, "meeting with an acquaintance." He smelled too flowery to be visiting with a chummy friend.

One very tall guard unlocked the gate and swung it open, but raised a hand for the fop to remain where he stood. One final shove from his escorts sent Harcourt stumbling through the gate. "And stay out," he heard one shout.

The gate slammed shut behind him, much to the dismay of the fop who started crying protests about being late for a special meeting. Harcourt took a deep breath, taking in the clean morning air, and set off without one backward glance.

It was early morning but there were a lot of folk about in the streets. He was in the upper east district, home of the market square. The market would be opening soon, so folk hurried about to get the good deals or the fresh food before anyone else.

The market was quite large with upwards of a few hundred stalls. Farmers sold fresh fruits and vegetables, butchers sold fresh meat, and the fishermen sold fresh fish caught that morning. There were merchants selling everything from clothing to jewelry to worthless trinkets. Harcourt spent a lot of time there as a youth. The market was busiest around high sun and the large crowds made it easier for small hands to snatch things. Also, by the end of the day, some of the kinder folk did not mind handing out some left-over food to a cute starving kid. As Harcourt got older, that option was no longer available to him and everything had to be stolen.

Without warning, Harcourt collided with a well-dressed, overly-obese man who jingled when he walked from the many chains he wore around his neck.

"See here man, watch where you are going! Get your damned head out of the clouds and pay attention," the man said in disgust at coming into contact with an obvious resident of the south district.

Harcourt's clothes were torn and dirty, his hair was long and unkempt, and he was in need of a shave. The thief just strolled passed him and said, "It would help if you didn't take up most of the street."

The obese man's jaw just hung open at the blatant insult and was rendered speechless with anger. Harcourt turned a corner onto Fairway Court and once he was out of view of the man, he opened his right palm and admired how the sunlight sparkled on the two silver coins he held there. He thought the man might have had more than that in his pockets, but he would eat and drink well with these tonight.

The thief stuffed the coins into a secret pocket sewn into the inside of the ripped shirt he wore. Being a thief himself, he knew the importance of keeping your coins where sneaky hands could not reach them. He would need some new clothes soon since the ripped pants and shirt he wore now were all he owned, and identified him as a south district beggar. He would worry about that later and steal a new set from someone's clothes line. His boots would do fine for now since he had stolen those only a few weeks before he was locked up. To Harcourt, that was practically brand new.

A very wide and deep fast-flowing river cut the city of Stonewood in half. The river flowed from east to west and there were four bridges that linked the two halves of the city together. Each half consisted of three districts. North of the river there was the north district, the upper east and the upper west. The upper east, of course, had the market and most of the shops, where the upper west housed most of the merchants that worked in the upper east. The cost of things tended to be a little pricier north of the river.

South of the river was the lower east district, the lower west and the south. The lower east contained shops that catered to the more middle-class and working-class citizens while the lower west housed most of those people. The city's cemetery could also be found in the west district, separated again by the river. Depending on which side of the river you dwelled on determined which side of the graveyard you would be buried in. Even in death, those of the north did not want to mingle with those from the south.

The south district was the poor district. There were smaller shops and houses spread around this area for those who could afford them, and shacks and tents for those who could not.

Stonewood had a large homeless population and the

city was constantly fighting the rising crime rate that went hand-in-hand with that. The average citizen would never venture into the south district and if they did, they kept their coin purses and jewelry well hidden. There was less of a guard presence down there, with the Thieves Guild running things for the most part. Only the toughest and most seasoned guards patrolled the south, and even then never alone. They were always in groups of two or more.

For years, the city had wanted to regain full control of the south district but it was a battle they were losing. As the districts' population grew, it was increasingly more difficult to control. The thieves in Stonewood were cunning and resourceful, they operated everywhere. One never knew just who was a Guild member and who was not. They were so secretive that even most members did not know who the other members were, aside from a contact person they liaised with. It was said only the senior members knew all of the Guild hideouts and the location of their headquarters. Harcourt had dreamed of being in that elite group since he was a young boy. The members he knew of always had fine food and drink, nice clothes, and coins in their pockets.

Stonewood was a large city and a wealthy city, so there was much to plunder for those allowed to do so. The city was located near the center of this region, so merchants from other cities tended to flock here with their goods to sell, or at least pass through on their way to another destination. It was said that anything could be bought and sold in Stonewood.

Harcourt reached the bridge that led across the river to the lower east district and had to dodge a few horse-drawn carts on their way to the market. Even with the sun high in the sky, there was two guards posted at each end. Given the time of day, they did not pay the thief much mind. Were it at night, they might have stopped to question him, although Harcourt was difficult to spot at night when he did not wish to be seen.

The sturdy stone bridge was wide, maybe thirty feet, and spanned fifty feet across to the other side of the river. The water moved swiftly. Someone falling in would be swept away by the current, but it did slow down on the outskirts of the city where the children liked to swim and fish. There were large fish in the river; fresh seafood was a good business in Stonewood. Harcourt had never been any good at catching the fish, nor could he often afford buying it, but he sure loved the smell of them cooking. The thief loved the view of the city and river from the bridge. The bridges all arched up over the water offering a nice view from the center.

When crossing to the south side of the river, the first thing people tended to notice was the architecture. The buildings in the north were large beautiful stone structures, or a mixture of stone and wood. Many of the homes were gated and surrounded by low walls. The wealthiest employed private security forces. South of the river there were fewer stone buildings and more wooden structures. The lower east and lower west still had their fair share of nice homes but they were smaller and less extravagant.

The tallest structure south of the river was a temple located in the heart of the lower west. It was a massive building with exquisitely-detailed architecture. It was dedicated to what some believed was the one true god. There were smaller temples to other gods but the majority of Stonewood's citizens believed there was only one god, and they referred to him as such.

Harcourt never really cared much for any of the gods as they seemed not to care too much for him. The thief had trouble believing in anything that he could not see with his own eyes. He always wondered how a being as all-powerful as a god was always in need of coins, as the priests were always asking for more. What could the gods be spending it on?

There was even a cult of demon worshippers in the city. They preyed mostly on the weak and desperate in the south district. Many disappearances and unexplained deaths were blamed on the cult. Most of them were probably true, and some might have been the Thieves Guild trying to divert blame from themselves. Who better to point a finger at than the loathsome demon worshippers? Harcourt had run into the occasional cult member from time to time and preferred to keep his distance from that lot. He may not have believed in demons either, but he did know the cult was capable of making human sacrifices for some demonic rituals. Fools all, but dangerous fools.

The cult was the one thing on which the city and the Thieves Guild both saw eye to eye, and both wished to be rid of them. The cult, though, was dug in deeper than the Guild. There had been arrests over the years but never a senior member. There were not even any suspects as to who might be leading them.

Harcourt made his way through the labyrinth-like streets, twisting and turning but never once losing his way. A visitor to the city could easily become lost. The easiest way to get your bearings was to find Fezzdin's tower, then you knew that direction was northeast.

The thief suddenly stopped dead in his tracks. The most fabulous aroma filled his nostrils and he knew without even turning his head where it had originated from.

"Shelda," he muttered to himself.

Shelda's bakery was famous south of the river, and could also tempt those in the north to make the trek down. Shelda was a jolly plump woman with a knack for baking breads and sweets. Because she was so good at baking, and loved to do it, it was no small wonder that her husband and three children were just as plump as she. That family ate well. As a youth, Harcourt would press his face against the window near closing time and put on his most pathetic look. The jovial baker who always wore a smile would come out and give him a sweet. Oh, they were good! The thief's stomach growled. There was already a line-up inside waiting for the fresh batch of whatever she was making.

Harcourt played with the two silver coins in his hidden pocket for a moment then set off again down the street. He was going to need those if he wanted a decent meal today along with some much-needed ale. It had been four months since the thief had a drink and his hands shook at the thought of a tall mug of foaming ale.

A little while later, he finally stepped onto the dry dusty road and knew he was home as he passed the Southside Armory. It was a mid-to low-quality weapons and armor shop and the beggars that sat outside of it were a sight for sore eyes to the thief who had been away for too long.

CHAPTER 2

The south district was a crowded place. Shops and homes were packed closely together to fit in as many as they could. Many of the homes consisted of only one room. Harcourt considered them lucky; he did not even have that. Taverns were the most successful businesses down here since everyone loved to drink their problems away. Drunken bar brawls and street fights were an every-day occurrence.

It was easier to navigate the narrow streets at this time of day as the south district mostly came alive at night. Harcourt noticed some clothes hanging on lines from a few house windows. As badly as he needed a change of clothes, the thief never stole from anyone in the south district. He would just take a trip north a little later on.

As the thief passed Briar's Lumber Yard, two small grubby children ran up to him and began jumping up and down with excitement. "Harcourt, is dat really you?" a little girl with long curly brown hair asked.

She could not be more than six years old. Her

brother, a scrawny little thing with messy brown hair, was probably about eight. That was the same age as Harcourt when he was alone in the streets. For the life of him, he could not remember either of their names, but he knew they were from the local orphanage.

Not long ago, a woman named Dahleene opened an orphanage in the south district. It was not much more than an old rundown ramshackle building, but it kept a roof over their heads. That was a lot more than Harcourt had when he was a youth. Dahleene's heart was in the right place but she was very poor herself and could not provide the children with much.

The shack Harcourt lived in was not far from the orphanage and often the children would drop by and ask him to show them some magic tricks. If he was not too drunk at the time, he always obliged them with sleight of hand and card tricks (if he had any cards). It never failed to make him laugh when one of the kids would comment that he was probably as powerful as Fezzdin. He probably was just as good as the magician when it came to parlor tricks, but somehow Fezzdin managed to make a fortune with his.

"Yes, my darling it is me," the thief said while patting her on the head.

"Where have you been?" she asked.

"I went on a little trip for awhile, that's all. But I'm back now," he replied.

"I heard the guards took you away. Did they lock you in the dungeon?" the little girl's brother inquired.

"No, they just asked me a few questions about someone else and then I was on my way," Harcourt lied. "I went to visit a friend in Blueburrow," he added, referring to the next closest town north of Stonewood.

In truth, Harcourt had never ventured anywhere outside of Stonewood. He had never felt the urge to explore the world as some people did. He figured if life was hard here, it would be worse anywhere else. At least here, everything was familiar to him.

"We missed your tricks," the girl said with a big smile.

"Aw well, Uncle Harcourt will be back around to stay now, don't you kids worry."

The two of them looked pale and deathly skinny. He wondered how long it had been since they had last eaten, and remembered how many days he spent starving at their age.

"Ok now, I have to get going but I've got time for one magic trick," the thief said.

"YAY!" both kids yelled in unison, hopping around in circles.

Harcourt rolled up the sleeves of his shirt and held his hands out in front of him, turning them both over to show the kids they were empty.

"Alright, as you can see there is nothing in my hands. But wait, what is that behind your ears?"

The thief reached out with both hands and produced a silver coin from behind each of the kid's ears. "Wow, look at that. You were hiding these all this time?"

Their faces shone with amazement. Firstly, at how he made the coins appear from their ears, and secondly at the sight of real silver coins. "Here you go, one for each of you," he said as he dropped the coins into their tiny hands.

"You are giving these to us?" the little boy could not believe his eyes.

Harcourt smiled and replied, "No, they were yours

already. I just found them behind your ears."

"How come I never knew it was there before?" the girl asked.

"Well, you cannot see behind your own ears can you?" Harcourt replied.

That logic made sense to the little girl. The thief then crouched down to their level and took on a serious tone. He closed their palms around the coins and held their hands and said, "You hold onto these tightly and do not let anyone see them. Ok? Now run along over to Bettina's tavern and get something to eat."

He gave them each a playful swat to send them on their way. The little girl punched her brother in the arm as they ran and said, "Why didn't you tell me I had a silver coin behind my ear, we could have ate yesterday."

Harcourt chuckled to himself and made a right down the next street. His own stomach growled again reminding him how hungry he was, but he would worry about himself later. Those kids deserved a decent meal, and those two silver coins would get them at least two days worth. Bettina was a fine cook and always gave out extra helpings, especially to the hungry kids.

The thief picked up his pace feeling excited as he got closer to his destination. Soon he would see the love of his life, the real reason he was so happy to be out of the dungeon. Jalanna. She meant the world to him. The dark-haired beauty was a barmaid at the Ogre's Den Tavern. The Ogre's Den was Harcourt's hangout and where he usually drank himself into a stupor on any given night he could afford it.

Jalanna had started working there five years past, and captured the hearts of every man that beheld her. She was a few inches shorter than Harcourt, and a stunningly beautiful woman with shoulder-length raven colored hair and exotic brown eyes. She was not a native of Stonewood or the surrounding areas, which was evident from her olive-colored skin. Her family had come from a far away land but she had little memory of it. Jalanna could have had any man in the city and yet for some reason she liked him.

Harcourt had spent the first few years after she arrived being afraid to even speak with her, she seemed so out of his league. To his surprise though, he found that she was very fond of him. She was a kind soul, and saw the best in him when nobody else could. The irony was that he felt very lucky to have her in his life, but at the same time, that was when all his other luck ran out. He was sure he was on his way to a Thieves Guild membership but then it had all gone sour. He tried to find some link between the two events. Was his love for Jalanna clouding his mind when he should have been concentrating on his jobs? Was she causing him to slip up where he had not before they met?

Jalanna had also run into some very bad luck of her own. Three years past, she and her family had been trapped in the famous south-side fire. Forty-two homes were destroyed and thirty-seven people had died. The fire just spread so fast. Conspiracy theorists claimed the fires were set deliberately by order of King Stonewood to drop the population in the south district and hopefully wipe out some thieves in the process. Harcourt never believed that. Three city guards had also died that night trying to save people. Jalanna and her parents were trapped in the fires that engulfed their home. Only Jalanna had escaped, but not unscathed. She suffered severe burns to her face and body. Her once beautiful face was now difficult to view by most if it was not covered. She wore a veil to cover her face similar to those worn by exotic dancers from her homeland. Many of the men that used to flock to the Ogre's Den for their chance to flirt with her ceased to come.

Harcourt could look beyond the scars and still loved her just as much and stuck with her. She was just as beautiful inside as she had been on the outside. Initially, the scars took some getting used to but he knew it was still the same woman underneath. They only bothered the thief now because they bothered her. She had never gotten used to them, or to the way people looked at her now.

Harcourt had heard tales before about priests performing miracles and healing folk of all kinds of afflictions. While the thief did not believe in magic, even divine magic, he was willing to try anything to help her. They sought out a priest who had said he could heal her of all her scars, but for a price. That price was five thousand gold pieces! Harcourt had never owned more than thirty pieces ever at one time, and this priest wanted five thousand.

Priests always liked to claim they were there to help, looking after the good of the people. They simply did not say out loud that their help was not free. With the healing by the priest no longer an option, Jalanna fell into a depression for quite some time. Losing both her parents did not help her situation. Two other barmaids at the Ogre's Den also lost their homes in the fire, so the tavern owner Wulfred, allowed the three women to live in the tavern's attic. It was not much, but it was still better than what some had in the south district, Harcourt included.

"Harcourt, my lad, been awhile," someone called out from a narrow alleyway between a used clothing shop and a bakery that sold stale left-over goods thrown out by shops in the other districts.

The thief turned to see old Kan lying on a thick brown blanket with his tin cup sitting next to him. Kan was a one-legged beggar as old as the hills. His real name was too difficult to pronounce so folk just called him Kan for short. He claimed he had been a soldier of Stonewood long ago and lost his leg defending the city from an invading army from over the western mountains. The invasion was common knowledge, but whether Kan had ever participated in the city's defense, nobody could verify. Most people just dismissed it as the ramblings of a senile old man.

The meaner kids in the area had invented a game called "kick the Kan," where they would kick the old man and run away laughing because he could not chase after them. He would just wave his walking stick and shout at them.

"Aye Kan, it has been awhile. Business a little slow I see," Harcourt commented after peeking into the empty tin cup.

"Same as always, lad. You know, when I was a soldier all my meals were provided for by the city. I never had to pay for food and drink."

Oh oh, the thief thought. Once he started with these old stories he did not stop. "I hear ya. In a hurry right now, Kan, but we'll share a drink soon, I promise."

"Ah bless you lad."

Harcourt turned to go and found his way blocked by

a city guard, with two more he noticed approaching from behind. The one in front of him was none other than Captain Dornell, the one who caused Harcourt the most trouble. Dornell was taller than the thief and had wide thick shoulders. He was in good shape for a man who had to be somewhere in his fifties. His salt-and-pepper hair was closely cropped with a neatly trimmed beard of the same color.

They had first met when the young guard had caught Harcourt picking pockets at the age of ten. He had been arresting him ever since. Dornell, who was the captain of the south district's guard, had dedicated his life to upholding Stonewood's laws and he did it very well. Being the captain of the south district was no easy job, and not a position most other guards aspired to.

"Well, if it isn't my old friend Harcourt," the captain said. "I figured you would be out soon and back to haunt my district."

"I did my time Captain. Now I just need some food and drink, that's all," the thief replied.

"And how do you plan on paying for that? You been picking pockets on the way down here boy?" the captain accused.

"No, sir."

"Then you won't mind a quick search then will you?"

Harcourt was relieved he gave away those coins. Good luck for a change.

"No, sir."

"Great. Harcourt, meet Zorfal. Zorfal, meet Harcourt. Zorfal has been assigned to the south district. You've met briefly before, and I am sure the two of you will become very familiar with each other soon enough."

Zorfal stepped towards Harcourt with an evil grin. He was a brute of a man. They stood about the same height but Zorfal was much heavier and more muscular. He had a crooked smile and was missing a few teeth. His nose was almost flat to his face and his bald head sported many scars. Harcourt could not get over the size of the man's forearms; he must have the grip of a bear, he thought. The thief suddenly recalled seeing this man the night he was locked away; he had been the reason for the splitting headache he awoke with in a dungeon cell.

Before Zorfal grabbed the thief, he asked, "You wouldn't happen to be armed would you?"

Harcourt recoiled as the guards breath smelled strongly of onions. "No, sir."

"Hope not. I don't want any surprises," and with that, the guard spun the thief around roughly and proceeded to search him for weapons and coins.

"Don't forgot the inside of that rag he calls a cloak. Our little friend here has hidden pockets all over," Captain Dornell mentioned.

Zorfal did have a vice-like grip and gave Harcourt a very thorough search. When finished, he held the rogue tightly by the front of his shirt and leaned in close.

"You might be clean now, but once a thief, always a thief. I am going to keep an eye on you. By all accounts, you are a horrible thief. Next time you slip up, I'll be there."

The old beggar shouted from the alley, "In my day, the soldiers didn't bully innocent citizens."

"Shut up old man and mind your own business. You wanna keep your one good leg?" Zorfal growled.

"That's enough, Zorfal," the captain said in a stern

voice. Then he added, "Harcourt, I can only hope that this time you've learned your lesson. I am sure you don't want to return to the dungeon, but break the law again and you can be sure we'll be there to send you back."

Zorfal shoved the thief back a few feet.

"We don't have to send you back in one piece either. Keep that in mind," he threatened.

"Zorfal, enough of that," Dornell commanded. "Let's go."

"Hey Zorf, don't forget these, you might need them," Harcourt said, holding up an iron ring full of keys and jingling them teasingly.

The guard quickly reached for the set of keys that he wore attached to this belt and found them missing.

"Why you little…," he was too angry to finish his sentence and stormed over and snatched his keys back.

Before he could turn to go, Harcourt held up the guard's dagger and said, "Might also need this."

Zorfal's face turned red with anger and embarrassment. He grabbed his dagger back with his left hand, and struck Harcourt square in the mouth with his right. Harcourt staggered back and somehow managed to stay on his feet. He felt like he just took a club to the head. Bright dots of light shimmered in front of his eyes and his mouthed filled with the coppery taste of his own blood.

"Enough!" shouted Dornell. "There will be no more of that Zorfal. And you, Harcourt, keep your hands to yourself."

"Nothing to see here, folks. Go back about your business," said the third guard who had remained silent until now.

A crowd had gathered to watch the exchange.

Harcourt spat blood onto the dirt road and watched the three guards walk away. Zorfal turned back to glare at the thief with hatred. Harcourt made a mental note that he would have to watch out for that one. He sensed the guard was trouble immediately, but still could not resist playing around with him to make him look foolish.

With a salute to Kan, the thief continued on his way. He received a few nods of approval from some that observed what just took place, and admired him for standing up to the guards. After a couple more twists and turns past shops and homes, he finally stood in front of his destination, the Ogre's Den tavern.

CHAPTER 3

Like most properties in the south district, the Ogre's Den tavern was not much to look at from the outside. It was not fancy like the taverns and inns of the other districts. The sign out front was crooked and looked as though it was just waiting for the next big gust of wind to come along and blow it down. The paint was chipping and the face of the grinning ogre was now missing half of its forehead. It was one of the bigger structures in the south district though, and the only one that Harcourt cared to frequent. He always found the place warm, cozy and inviting.

Harcourt, excited to finally see Jalanna after so long, hurried inside. The main room of the tavern was quite large. It could fit about seventy people comfortably, and a few times in the past, had been host to a lot more than that. A fireplace stood on one side of the room to warm those coming in from a cold night. Of course, it was not necessary for this time of the year but still added a nice elegant look to the room.

The walls were mounted with carved heads of various animals, some were real species and some mythical. The tavern owner, Wulfred, preferred hand-made heads over real ones, but one could hardly tell the difference from looking at them. They seemed to stare right back at you, their eyes eerily following your every move. Right above the bar hung Wulfred's favorite, the head of a great dragon. He liked to tease people, telling them the dragon's head was real and that he had slain it himself.

Wulfred had been a bit of a traveler in his younger days, a mercenary working for many different people and places. He was from the far north and tired of deathly cold winters and eventually settled in Stonewood where the weather was much more tolerable and snow was seldom seen. Wulfred was a large man with a loud booming laugh. His stomach had expanded quite a bit over the years but he could still move fast when it was required. He was patient and kind but when a situation called for it, he had little trouble tossing out an unruly patron himself.

Wulfred was believed to be in his late forties and was as strong as an ox still. Below the dragons head hung his mighty battle axe, in case strength alone was not enough. Generally, if someone was getting out of hand, all the tavern owner had to do was reach for the axe and things would settle down.

The people of the south district loved to drink, it was their favorite hobby, so business was good for the northman. Maybe too good, since it drew the attention of the Thieves Guild. Once a month, a Guild representative paid a visit to the tavern to collect an operating tax. At first the proud northman resisted, but after weeks of random damage done to the property and threats made against patrons, he was forced to give in. Wulfred could not fight the whole Guild by himself. The tax was not too much, he still made a great deal of profit, but it was the principal of it that bothered him.

Harcourt found the tavern fairly empty in this late hour of the morning. The place really filled up in the evenings. He first spotted Wulfred at the bar wiping down the already-spotless table for lack of much else to do. He stood out in a crowd with his large distinguishable handlebar moustache.

In a far corner sat two middle-aged men Harcourt did not recognize, eating breakfast. One of the other waitresses, the fiery-haired Deelia, was taking the order for a young couple seated near the doorway. Harcourt knew the young man to be a street sweeper who worked for the city, the woman was his girlfriend. Not far from them sat Whitemane by himself, enjoying a morning mug of ale. Whitemane was an older man, a gravedigger in the cemetery.

He was called Whitemane because of his long pure white hair. The strange thing was that it had gone white overnight. One day it was black, the next pure white. As the story goes, he was digging a grave late one night and came face to face with a ghost. He escaped the encounter unharmed but was frightened to the point of his hair turning color. Now Harcourt did not believe in ghosts, but the hair thing was a mystery.

Seated close to the bar, also by himself, was Harcourt's good friend Andil. He was probably the best friend the thief had next to Jalanna. Andil was a few years younger than Harcourt but looked about ten years younger. He had a baby face and a skeletal body. The man was so thin it was like skin stretched over a skeleton. All of his bones were visible. Despite that, he was deceptively strong. He was a good wrestler, very slippery and difficult to hold onto. Andil was not very effective in a straight-up fight, but had saved Harcourt on a few occasions with a bottle to the head of an opponent from behind.

Like himself, Andil was a thief and also not a very successful one. He had a lot of connections and seemed to know much about what went on in the streets, but he too was never given membership into the Thieves Guild. Andil survived by petty scams here and there and was a decent pick-pocket. The other rogue's face lit up at the sight of his friend. Harcourt gestured that he would be there in a moment and approached Wulfred at the bar.

Wulfred looked up from his work and gave a big warm smile.

"Harcourt, it is good to see you again. You are looking a little thin. Dungeon food still not to your liking huh?"

"The rat is not half bad when you get used to it, but nothing beats your stew and ribs," Harcourt replied returning the man's smile.

"Well, what can I get you my friend? I know they don't serve no ale in the dungeon," the tavern owner said while reaching for a clean mug.

Harcourt tried to stop him before he poured the drink. "No no, Wulfred, maybe a little later. First I need to sort a few things out then I'll be back later for a drink and a proper meal."

"Is that because you've no coins?" Wulfred asked.

"Well," Harcourt was always embarrassed about his financial difficulties, "yes, but as I said, I'll sort that out and be back a little later."

"Nonsense." Wulfred proceeded to pour a tall mug of foaming ale that made the thief's mouth water. "Anyone spending that long locked up in the dungeon deserves a little something. This drink here, and your meal are on the house. You come back later for another drink and a meal. Today you don't pay. Sound good?"

Harcourt took the mug handed to him and almost did not hear what the man said as he stared intensely at the ale and licked his lips. He really did hate free handouts from friends. As a child, he did not care how he got a meal but as an adult it bothered him that he could not pay for one. "You are the best, Wulfred. I'll pay you back I promise, just as soon as I can. Where's Jalanna? She not working this morning?"

"She's upstairs asleep. It was a long night last night, the place was very busy. Want me to tell her you're here?"

"No thanks. I'd rather she not see me looking like this anyways. I'll get cleaned up and see her later tonight when I come back."

"Alright then. Go join your buddy and I'll send some food over in a moment," Wulfred said clapping the thief on the shoulder.

Harcourt thanked the man and walked over to take a seat opposite Andil. The two rogues raised their mugs and clinked them together.

"Four months in the castle. You and King Stonewood must be best of friends by now, eh?" the skinny thief jested.

"We might have been if I hadn't been kept in the guest quarters underneath the castle," Harcourt returned.

"So it's been four months already? I lost track of the

time."

Harcourt winced. "Yeah I lost track of the time too but for me it felt like years."

"Oh, right. Sorry. Hey, old Gaptooth still handing out those beatings he's famous for?" Andil asked referring to a particularly mean dungeon guard who was called Gaptooth for obvious reasons.

The grizzled old guard was sensitive about his teeth and administered beatings to anyone calling attention to them. "He's still there and misses you, I think. Asked when you were coming back for a visit?"

Andil laughed, "Never if I have my way."

"How's Jal doing?" Harcourt inquired, changing the subject from his four-month nightmare.

"She's been ok. Misses you. Talks about you all the time telling everyone you'll be out soon."

"I thought she'd be mad at me."

"She was at first. Didn't talk to anyone for days. But she knows you were just trying to survive. Just some bad luck on your part, that's all."

"Yeah, I've got some bad luck alright. I don't understand Andil, I studied this place for a week and swept the whole area before I went for it. Then it just all went wrong, like the rest," he took a mouthful of ale and savored every drop. "I don't know why this keeps happening to me."

"Speaking about that," Andil's voice lowered and he lost his smile. "I think you need to just lay low for awhile. The Guild wasn't happy to hear about you trying to pull off that job."

"What am I supposed to do?" Harcourt said with anger in his tone. "They won't let us join but we have to survive somehow."

"I know, I know. Just stick to small scams and jobs like me, I fall under their gaze. They don't give a damn about me. You keep crossing them and you'll be floating down the river soon, mark my words."

Harcourt sighed. "It's not fair. We are good at what we do aside from the rotten luck I've developed. And you've only been to the dungeon once. What's their excuse for not allowing you to join?"

Andil thought on that for a moment then replied. "I don't really know. Maybe because I wasn't born here. Maybe someone just doesn't like me. Maybe it's my association with you. Who knows how they make their decisions. What I do know is that we cannot pull off anything big without a membership. So if we want to live a long life we need to adhere to their rules. Got it?"

Harcourt's mood brightened a little when Deelia brought over a steaming bowl of stew and a half rack of marinated ribs, placing then down in front of him. "Welcome home, Harcourt," she leaned in and kissed him on the cheek. "Jal will be so happy to see you."

"Hey, where's my kiss and ribs?" Andil asked pouting.

The waitress rolled her eyes and ignored the skinny rogue. "Want me to go get her for you?"

"No thanks, Dee. I want to change and clean up. I'll be back here tonight to see her."

"Ok, handsome, we'll catch you later. Enjoy your meal," she said strolling away back to the bar.

Andil's eyes followed the redhead all the way back. "You know how long I've been wanting a kiss from her? Do I have to get locked up again to get one?"

Harcourt did not even hear his friend as he dug into his food. By all the so-called gods was it ever good he thought. He had forgotten what real food tasted like. The only time he stopped shoveling food into his mouth was to wash it down with ale. Andil let him finish before continuing where he left off.

"Look, by trying to steal from that merchant you not only broke the city's laws, but you broke the Guild's laws. Now the city punished you already but the Guild hasn't. Don't think that because four months have passed that they have forgotten. Just keep a low profile for a little while, alright?"

"Low is the only profile I know how to keep."

Andil did not find that funny. "I am being serious here. Try not to steal anything for the next few days. Take these," the skinny thief slid four silver coins across the table.

"I can't take that," Harcourt said pushing them back.

"You can and you will. Don't worry, it's not charity, I'll want them back eventually. Just don't steal anything for awhile," Andil replied.

"Since when do you have extra coins to give away?" the older thief asked finishing the last drop of his ale.

Andil's eyes followed Deelia around the room and when he glanced back at the table the silver coins were gone. Damn that Harcourt was fast, he thought. "No such thing as extra coins. But I've a few to loan if I know I'll get them back."

With that Harcourt thanked his friend, and Wulfred, for the meal and set off to take care of some business.

*　　*　　*　　*

Harcourt felt very refreshed. He spent a little of Andil's loan at the Siren's Retreat where he had a much-needed and long-overdue bath, shave and haircut. The rogue preferred to keep his hair very short. Also he could not very well have gotten cleaned up and put on the same rags he was wearing, so he stole a new set of clothes prior to visiting the bathhouse. The grey pants were a little worn in the knees but otherwise in good shape and the black shirt was missing two buttons. They were clean and that was Harcourt's top priority. He would "shop" for some better clothes in the next day or two.

After his bath, he dropped a few copper coins in old Kan's empty tin cup and headed for the shack he called home. The afternoon was getting late and the streets of the south district were starting to get busy. He had to dodge many horse and donkey-drawn carts as well as avoid the street merchants hawking their wares.

He turned down his alley off Sailor Street and never thought he could feel so happy to see his shack. This alley was nestled between two warehouses and Harcourt shared it with three others who were worse off than him. There was not anyone around at the moment so Harcourt figured his neighbors were off somewhere begging for coins. His home consisted of three pieces of wood he had attached to the warehouse wall with an old bed sheet he could pull across the empty side like a curtain when he needed some privacy. It was just tall enough to sit up in, and long enough to lie down in.

The thief was happy his neighbors were not about since he could use a good nap before heading back to the Ogre's Den this evening. Only problem was that he was sure his blanket would have been stolen during his absence and he would be sleeping on the ground.

He pulled the sheet across and to his surprise there was a blanket and pillow inside with a piece of wood laying on top. Carved into the wood was a message. "Wulcom hom Harcart." The thief smiled. It must have been from the kids at the orphanage since the spelling was so bad. Harcourt was never formally educated but his father had taught him to read and write before he died. The pillow and blanket were obviously second hand but would feel like clouds from the heavens above to the thief after his recent accommodations.

He climbed into his shack and removed a loose board from the warehouse wall and pulled out a dull, rusted dagger. This was the only weapon he had left since the guards did not return his other one when he was released. He had had this dagger since he was a kid, it was his father's. The years had not been kind to it though and the dull and worn blade had begun to rust. He slid the weapon under his pillow and laid down. After only minutes, he drifted off into a deep sleep.

*   *   *   *

Harcourt was jolted awake by a solid kick to his stomach. He did not know how long he was asleep but it was now dark outside. Before his eyes could focus he took a boot heel to the nose. "I am awake already," he sputtered reaching under his pillow to grip the handle of his dagger.

A moment passed without another strike. When he could finally make out the silhouette of the person in front of him he lunged forward with his dagger. With great speed his attacker drew a short-bladed sword and slashed him across the top of his hand sending his dagger spinning out onto Sailor Street. Harcourt fell back into his shack clutching his wounded hand. When he looked back up he could finally see the man's face that was standing in front of him, Randar.

Randar was the Thieves Guild's top enforcer. He was a mean man as hard as a stone wall and had the reputation as one of the most dangerous men on the streets of Stonewood. Harcourt had never had any personal dealings with the thug but he had seen him at work on more than a few occasions, and was more than happy to stay out of the man's way.

Randar crouched down in front of the shack's opening and pressed the tip of his sword into Harcourt's chest. The thief winced as it dug into his skin and drew a trickle of blood. Harcourt had never been this close to the enforcer before and even in the dark alley he could see the patchwork of scars that covered the man's face and shaved head. Thieves Guild members did not wear any patches or symbols so he was clad in simple black clothing.

After an uncomfortable silence Randar spoke. "I am assuming from the description I was given that you are Harcourt."

The thief just nodded. He was thinking how he survived four months in the dungeon only to be slain right here on the day he got out. It would be just his luck.

"You have been a very naughty boy I am told. Trying to rob a merchant behind the Guilds' back? That wasn't very nice of you," Randar said leaning forward pushing the sword tip deeper into Harcourt's skin.

Harcourt gritted his teeth in pain but did not try to

move away. "This isn't the first time either," Randar continued. "You are lucky to still be breathing. Good thing for you that you are a terrible thief. But let's put a stop to this eh? You are not a Guild member and are therefore not permitted to conduct thievery in this city. Now either move someplace else or find a new line of work. This is your last warning boy. You hear me?" and with that the thug slashed his blade upwards drawing a red line from Harcourt's jaw to his temple.

Randar sheathed his sword and casually strolled away fearing no retaliation from the thief. Harcourt refused to cry out in pain, he just held his shirt to his face to absorb the blood flowing down. The thief wished he could have wiped that smug look off Randar's face. Harcourt liked his chances if they were on even terms, being no stranger to fights. This was not the time nor the place though. He knew Randar would have impaled him on that sword if he gave him any excuse to do so. Given the enforcer's reputation, Harcourt was actually lucky to come away with his life and only a few scratches. He did not like being bullied though; that did not sit well with him.

He was also not happy about his sleep being interrupted either, but he figured it was time to get up now anyways. It had been too long since he had seen Jalanna.

CHAPTER 4

It was mid-evening when Harcourt returned to the Ogre's Den. He had stolen a new shirt and wrapped his wounded hand with a strip from the old one. The gash on his face had stopped bleeding but there was no hiding it.

The tavern was busy tonight. Almost every table was filled with patrons and Wulfred had not stopped pouring drinks for hours. These were some of Stonewood's poorest folk and yet they always had a coin or three to drink. The thief fit right in here; when he was down to his last coin he would also spend it on a drink. It was not always like that, but years of hardship and misery had taken their toll on the man.

Several patrons flashed him big smiles and gave him slaps on the back, congratulating him on his release. Down here no one was judged or shunned for being a thief or a criminal, everyone did what they had to do in order to survive. In fact, many of the thieves were seen as heroes.

After he was stopped many times, Harcourt eventually made it over to Andil's table and sat down. His friend immediately noticed his face. "By the demon god, what happened to you?"

"Randar happened to me," he replied.

"Randar? See, I told you the Guild wasn't happy. How did you escape that?"

Harcourt told the story of his brief encounter with the Guild enforcer. Just as he finished, he found himself locked in a choke hold from behind. The rogue relaxed when he realized the person was not very strong and smelled of perfume. His favorite perfume as well, called "Love in Stonewood." He gently broke the hold and jumped to his feet. "Jal!" he shouted.

Jalanna stood there with her hands on her hips, eyes a little glassy and said, "I was wondering when you were planning to come see me."

"I was here earlier, but you were still sleeping. I didn't want to disturb you," the thief pleaded his case.

"Oh my god, what happened to you?" the woman cried, just then noticing the wound on his face. She reached over to gently run a finger down his cheek.

"Ah this? Just a scratch, nothing to worry about."

Jalanna gave him a worried look, then wrapped him in the tightest hug possible and whispered in his ear, "You better not leave me again like that. I've been worried sick about you."

It was great to see her again. Harcourt felt nervous during the walk over but seeing her eyes light up and feeling her arms wrapped around him was just like old times. He wished he could just stand there in her embrace for days. Her face was veiled to hide her burns but her exotic eyes were stunning. The tight-fitting clothes she wore to work really showed off her wonderful figure, and of course helped bring in tips.

Most folk who frequented the Ogre's Den knew she was taken but still flirted anyways. With the veil hiding her scars, she looked like any other attractive barmaid.

"You look fantastic," Harcourt said, "thinking about seeing you again was the only thing that kept me going in the dungeon."

Jalanna blushed behind her veil. "Wulfred has some food for you. After you eat, let's take a walk. Ok?"

"Of course," he answered, "as it turns out, I have the whole evening free."

The dark-haired woman chuckled and punched him in the arm. "I'll be back soon with your food."

Harcourt watched has she disappeared into the kitchen, then turned to Andil, "I am going to see Serdic tomorrow."

The skinny thief shook his head in disbelief. "Serdic? Are you a fool? The Guild just sent Randar with a message for you and you are going to go seek them out? Stay away from them! How many times do I have to tell you?"

Serdic was a senior member of the Thieves Guild. Very few of the senior members were known but Harcourt had lived in the city his entire life and got to know a little about the who's who. Every time Harcourt had petitioned to join the Guild he had gone to speak with Serdic. He was a fair man and seemed to get along well with Harcourt.

When Harcout did not reply right away, Andil continued. "You just did four months in the dungeon for a failed thieving attempt. They never wanted you before so why would they want you now?"

"I did four months and never named any names. I did my time with my mouth shut even though I was presented many opportunities to give up names and make things easier on myself. That has to count for something. And I am good, Andil. I don't know why things always get messed up the way they do but if I had Guild inside info maybe that would change everything," Harcourt reasoned. "And besides, I have no other choice. I need that membership to survive."

"I suppose. Just don't be surprised if Serdic's goons chase you out of there. You've got a better shot at joining the demon cult. At least they are always looking for new recruits," the skinny thief said, then emptied his mug of ale.

"They are still up to no good?" Harcourt inquired.

"Three more people have been found butchered and missing their hearts since you've been away."

Harcourt screwed his face up in disgust. "Those sick bastards. How is that I always get caught and yet those despicable murderers have been getting away with this for years?"

"If you ask me, some high-ranking city official must be a cult member, or leader, or something," Andil said looking around for a waitress to flag for more ale.

Jalanna brought over a large plate of sizzling hot steak with vegetables for Harcourt along with a tall mug of ale. Harcourt dug in while Andil ordered more to drink. Not long after the thief had devoured every morsel on his plate, Jalanna came back and announced she was taking a break and the two left together for a walk in the fresh night air.

It was quite a fair distance from the Ogre's Den but the lovers walked to one of the two bridges that connected the lower east district with the upper east. They had always loved the view and the sound of the river here at night. It was their favorite place to sit, and the first place they had kissed.

"This was too far," Jalanna said. "Wulfred is going to want me back soon."

"Don't worry about him. He knows we haven't seen each other for awhile. He won't mind if you take an extended break."

Wulfred was always good to the girls that worked for him, treating them like they were his own daughters. Jalanna knew Harcourt was right but she always felt badly taking advantage of the northman's generosity.

The bridge was a popular place at this time of night. Other couples were scattered across the bridge in their own little spots and the occasional city guard would patrol past. After staring out at the fast flowing waters, holding each other's hands, Jalanna finally spoke again

"You should not have tried to rob that merchant. You never told me you were going to do that. Harcourt, these last four months have been torture for me." Tears began to stream down her face.

He wanted to say they were not so pleasurable for him either but held his tongue. "I was desperate, Jal. I need a lot of coins and there is no other way for me to earn that much."

"Need them for what?" she asked. "I can make enough to feed the both of us from the Den and you could always work with Jardo in his warehouse. So what if it doesn't pay much? It is safe and it is legal. We have each other and that's all that should matter. And you cannot get locked up in the dungeon for doing honest work."

Harcourt put his arm around her. "I know we could be happy like that, but then we could never raise enough gold."

"Enough gold for what?"

Harcourt paused then said, "You know, for the priests' help in healing you."

"I thought we were through discussing that," she said, her voice getting louder. "Harcourt, that is just a dream. You and I both know that neither one of us will ever see five thousand gold pieces in this lifetime or the next. I have accepted that. You are all that I need to make me happy."

"You might be happy with me, but you are far from happy with yourself. If you cannot be happy with yourself, then you can never be truly content."

"Is that just your way of saying that you need the priest to heal me in order for yourself to be happy? I know I can be hard to look at, you can just be honest about it," she accused.

"Don't be foolish," he countered. "My love for you has never lessened because of your scars, you should know that. But you are not happy, I can see it in your eyes."

"Of course, I am not happy about it. If my face is not covered people can't stand the sight of me. That is something I will never get over. But at the same time, I've accepted that this is my fate and there isn't anything that you or I can do about it. You are all that I have and if you get locked away in the dungeon again because of me then I will just die."

"I am not ready to give up just yet. I will do anything to see you truly happy again. I am going to see Serdic tomorrow and beg, if I have to, for a Guild membership."

"Harcourt no! Look at what they did to your poor face. I already spoke to Jardo earlier this evening. He is willing to have you. He knows you are strong and would be a good worker. He'll be expecting you tomorrow at the crack of dawn at his warehouse. Ok? Forget the stupid Guild, forget the priest. Let's just move on with our lives. This last time you were locked away for four months, but what about the next time? A year? Two years? Harcourt, I couldn't handle that."

The thief did not answer, only stared out at the river in deep thought. "Harcourt, I have to get back to work. But first promise me you'll go see Jardo tomorrow. Ok? Please? Forget Serdic. Get a real job with Jardo and we can even save for our own place. I've already been putting coins aside. Maybe in a year we could get a one room apartment over on Snake Street. Wouldn't that be great? I can finally get out of the Den's attic and you can finally get out of that alley. Please? Go see him tomorrow. For me?" Jalanna pleaded.

After a moment of silence Harcourt spoke. "Alright. For you, I'll go see Jardo."

"Thank you! You just made me so happy. Don't forget the crack of dawn." She gave him a giant hug and kiss. "Now walk me back to work."

*   *   *   *

Harcourt's eyes finally fluttered open at the sound of one his neighbors shuffling through the alley. His head pounded and his mouth was dry. *What time is it?* he wondered. How did he even get back to his shack? He remembered walking Jalanna back to the Ogre's Den last night, then Andil insisted he stay and have a few drinks with him. He told the other thief about his early morning appointment with Jardo but Andil refused to drink alone and kept on buying. Since he kept buying, Harcourt kept drinking. Jalanna would periodically stop by the table to remind him not to have too many and not to be out too late. Three drinks turned into six and then his memory ended there.

Trying to shake the cobwebs out of his head, he pulled open his curtain door to look up at the sky. *Curses*, he thought. It was midday already, and with the way he felt, it could have been days later. Jalanna would kill him for missing that appointment with Jardo. He staggered to his feet only to stumble across into the other wall and slide back down to the ground.

A toothless old man laughed at him from outside his tent down the end of the alley. So this is what his life had come to, being the amusement for toothless beggars. What had Jalanna said? If they both worked, in a year they could get a small apartment on Snake Street? In a year? No, Jardo can keep his warehouse job. Harcourt was a thief, it was the only life he had known. It was time to visit Serdic again. He needed a lot of gold and joining the Thieves Guild was the only way he could ever get it. They needed to know that his skills surpassed those of the other members, bad luck aside. He could not imagine that even Serdic was a better thief than he.

It was decided then, he had to try and reason with the man one last time. First he would visit the orphanage and thank Dahleene and the kids for the pillow and blanket. Then he would need to steal some new clothes to make himself more presentable.

Andil could be right though, he thought. Given his recent run in with Randar, Serdic could be less hospitable this time around. He figured he should grab his dagger from its hidden spot then remembered that the thug had sent it flying into Sailor Street yesterday. When he had gone later to retrieve it, it was nowhere to be found. The last of Harcourt's real possessions were gone. The clothes on his back were stolen and the two silver coins in his pocket were loaned to him. This needed to change.

He forced himself up on unsteady legs, gave a rude gesture to the toothless beggar, then set off to find some water for his parched throat.

CHAPTER 5

As the sun began to set that evening, Harcourt made his way through the busy streets of the lower west district to arrive at the Lonely Traveller Tavern and Inn. This was Serdic's hangout. He purposely took the long way to avoid passing the area of his most recent thieving failure.

He had found a new set of clothes that fit him, including a cloak, and to his joy, all were black. He had parted ways though with his last two coins and was now officially broke again.

He visited the orphanage earlier and the kids were all happy to see him back and asked to see some magic tricks. Being short on props, he had produced the last two coins from behind two other kids' ears, and told them all to share and get some sweets. Dahleene struggled to keep the kids fed each day by working three jobs. She told Harcourt she was trying to get some funding from the city but to date, not one copper coin had come. It was no wonder the thief was always broke, every time he had some coins, he found someone to give them to. He figured he wanted to give the kids chances that he was never provided. When he was young, he did not have anyone around to give him coins; he was forced to steal everything.

With his pockets empty, he was hoping he would not be expected to buy a drink at the inn. Harcourt took a deep breath, then followed three fishermen into the Lonely Traveller. The first thing that always hit the thief when he had visited the inn was the smell of pipe smoke as he entered. Pipeweed had to be imported from the lowlands in the south and was not cheap. Therefore, it was not very common in the south district. Harcourt had lifted a pipe with some of the weed off a wealthy individual once and had given it a try. It was not to his taste.

The common room was busy with patrons, most of them traveling merchants or other visitors to the city. The inn was situated closest to the western city gate, so it was the first inn that visitors saw when they arrived through there. It was believed that Serdic actually owned the place and that it was a front for Guild activities. None of that had ever been proven, even though the man did have an office in the cellar.

Harcourt could feel eyes on him sizing him up as he walked towards the bar. He knew Serdic had men spread throughout the room. The thief took a seat on a stool next to a man with a long grey beard and signaled for the barkeep. The middle-aged man wearing a white apron strolled over. "What can I get ya?"

"I'd like to see Serdic," Harcourt replied trying to keep his voice low.

The barkeep nodded then gave a short whistle and motioned to the thief with his eyes. A moment later a hard-looking man with an extremely flat nose walked over to the bar. Harcourt had never seen this one before. The man spoke with a gravelly voice. "What's your business here?"

"I just want to speak with Serdic. I won't take up much of his time."

The man looked the thief up and down. "Do you see him here? No. Just leave me your message and I'll get it to him."

"I know he is here, maybe in his office? Look, he knows me. My name is Harcourt. Just tell him I need a moment of his time," the thief said.

A flash of recognition crossed the man's face. "Harcourt eh? Follow me."

The thug gave a hand gesture and a short stocky man stood up from a nearby table and opened the door leading down to the cellar. "Harcourt to see Serdic," the first man said to the second with a smile.

"After you two," the shorter one said waving his hand towards the stairs.

Harcourt and the first man started down the stairs with the other following and locking the door behind him. The thief suddenly had a bad feeling as the warning bells were chiming in his head. As he descended the stairs there was a third man, equally as hard-looking, in the room below guarding a set of doors. This man wore a mail vest and a thin-bladed sword hung from his belt.

When they all reached the bottom of the stairs, the two men behind the thief fanned out to form a triangle around Harcourt. The flat-nosed man with the gravelly voice spoke. "You got a lot of nerve coming in here, Harcourt the renegade."

Panic then set in. Harcourt knew this was not going

to end well. He should have listened to Andil. Three against one and he was unarmed, he did not like those odds. "I just need to speak with Serdic. He's known me for a long time."

"You broke Guild laws. You've got to pay for that," said the short stocky man.

The thief pointed to the cut on his face, "I've already been visited by Randar. I've been punished."

"That was Randar, not us," the flat-nosed man said as he stepped in and threw a right cross.

Anticipating some form of attack, Harcourt easily side-stepped the punch and gave the thug a nudge, his momentum sending him right past the thief. The shorter man burst into action putting his head down and charging the renegade thief to bowl him over. Harcourt brought his right knee up in time to meet the man's nose with a crunch. The thug's head snapped upwards from the impact and Harcourt planted a left hook across his jaw sending him to the floor on his back.

The swordsman grabbed Harcourt from behind with his left hand and spun him around to throw his right hand. The thief immediately crowded the man to neutralize the punch and then launched his forehead towards his nose. The swordsman pulled back just enough to take the head-butt in the mouth splitting his lip.

By instinct, Harcourt threw a left hook to the body but stopped short remembering the armor that the man wore. In his moment of hesitation, the flat-nosed man landed a fist to Harcourt's liver almost dropping him to his knees. Luckily the swordsman shoved the thief away from him which took Harcourt out of range for the other's follow up shot. He recovered quickly and made a break for the stairs. The flat-nosed man was right behind him so when Harcourt made the third step he turned and kicked his pursuer right under the chin staggering him backwards.

Knowing he would never reach the top before being caught, Harcourt elected to leap off the stairs and tackled the swordsman who was charging forward. The pair hit the floor hard with the swordsman on the bottom losing his breath from the impact. Harcourt came down with his right elbow splitting the man's face open above his left eye.

The flat-nosed thug hauled the thief off the swordsman and tossed him aside. Harcourt tripped over the short man he had dropped earlier and sprawled to the floor. The short thug, having regained his senses, rolled on top of the thief and pressed his meaty forearm down on Harcourt's face grinding his head into the stone floor. Desperately, Harcourt managed to shift his head just enough to clamp down on the man's arm with his teeth. His teeth sunk in deep and the man howled in agony, rolling off.

The flat-nosed man came in with a boot to the head that Harcourt just narrowly avoided. He swept out the thugs' legs from under him and crashed down beside him.

"Enough of this!" bellowed the swordsman, his face now a mask of blood.

He drew his sword and advanced. "You made a big mistake, you should have just taken your beatings like a man."

As the flat-nosed thug tried to rise, Harcourt dove and pulled a dagger free from the man's boot. The thief shot up behind the man pressing the blade of the weapon to his throat. When he attempted to break free, Harcourt pressed the dagger harder drawing a trickle of blood. In his gravelly voice the flat-nosed man said, "You fool! You won't be getting out of here alive."

"Neither will you if your friend with the sword here takes one step closer," Harcourt countered, stopping the swordsman's advance.

Now he was in a jam. His mind raced. How was he going to get out of here in one piece? Then his thoughts were interrupted with a familiar voice. "Well, isn't this an interesting situation."

One of the doors stood open and Serdic was surveying the scene before him. An amused look crossed his face. "Jenson, what are you doing on the floor?"

"The bastard bit me," the short man said, lying on the floor holding his wounded arm with blood flowing from his nose.

Harcourt spoke up, the dagger still firmly held to his captive's throat.

"Serdic, I only came here to speak with you, not cause any trouble. I am only defending myself."

"This scum is a renegade and an enemy of the Guild. Let's just gut him here," suggested the bloodied swordsman.

"You forget, he has poor Dolan here captive," Serdic said calmly, then added, "and I don't recall ordering any visitors to be assaulted."

"He is…."

Then Serdic cut off the swordsman. "I am well aware of who he is. And your orders are always to inform me if I have a visitor and not lay your hands on them. Am I clear on this matter?"

"Yes sir," the thug grumbled, sheathing his sword and wiping the blood from his face.

Serdic smiled. "Seems that if I want to feel safe, I should be firing you three and hiring the thief here. So Harcourt, how can we settle this without any further blood spilled? On the part of my men that is."

"I am not looking for more trouble, Serdic. Tell your men to back off so we can talk in your office. That's all I want," Harcourt said maintaining his hold on Dolan.

"Deal," Serdic replied. "No harm will come to you. You are my guest. Now toss the dagger aside and let poor Dolan return to his post upstairs."

"I'll let him go, but I think I'll hang onto the dagger for now."

"Suit yourself," Serdic said. "But try and use it and you really will not be leaving here."

Harcourt pulled the blade away from Dolan's throat and shoved him. The flat-nosed thug gave him a nasty look and trudged up the stairs rubbing his neck with Jenson in tow.

"Horus will remain here outside the door if you don't mind," Serdic said referring to the swordsman.

"By all means," Harcourt replied following Serdic into his office.

The two men sat in comfy leather chairs opposite each other, a beautiful oak desk between them. The small cool room was bare otherwise. Harcourt never took his eyes off the other man, watching for any hints of a trap. Sensing this, Serdic said, "Relax will you. No more trouble, you've got my word. I apologize for their behavior."

Harcourt believed the other thief, he had always been fair with him in the past. Serdic was about ten years older than Harcourt with hints of grey creeping their way into his short dark hair. Like himself, Serdic had also been a thief his entire life. Serdic's father had been a member of the Thieves Guild and his son followed in his footsteps. But unlike Harcourt, Serdic always had gold in his pockets. The older thief was not a physical man and relied on his cunning and his gold that bought the thugs he surrounded himself with.

"That was brave of you showing up here, given your reputation as a renegade," Serdic pointed out.

"I don't want to be a renegade. I want to be in the Guild, you know that. I'll do whatever it takes. Please give me a chance. I am a thief and always will be. If the Guild orders me to stop thieving, you are essentially giving me a death sentence. Serdic, you know I have the skills. I could be a great asset if you'd give me a chance."

"Harcourt, we've had this conversation many times. The decision is not mine to make. I've brought you up to my superiors and they have chosen to deny your requests. Doing four months in the dungeon for a failed theft that was not approved by the Guild does not exactly add strength to your case."

"Bad luck, that's all. Totally unforeseen," Harcourt said.

"Bad luck surrounds you. The Guild thinks you are too dangerous and will draw unwanted attention. Right now, we have our hands full dealing with the city cracking down on crime. Then we have the demon cult stirring up more and more trouble. They don't want sloppy thieves. Now tell me you'll hand over the ingredients for those poisons that you are known for, and just maybe there will be a chance."

There it was again. The one thing the Guild wanted from him was the one thing he was not willing to give.

Harcourt had a knack for mixing different ingredients to create potent poisons. He inherited the skill from his father who was a barkeep for a long time and known for his unusual drinks. The thief turned that knowledge to thievery and invented a few concoctions that could achieve unusual effects. His best creation was a liquid that if ingested or injected into an individual would cause them to pass out for hours. Another could cause temporary paralysis. Once by accident, he had mixed a chemical that stole his voice leaving him mute for several hours.

The thief was never willing to part with those secrets. He was sure in the hands of the Guild they would end up being used for some very vile purposes. Most of Stonewood's underworld did not share the same code of ethics that Harcourt had. He would have preferred that nobody even knew about this but a drunk Andil had let it slip out to a Guild member. Serdic always brought it up anytime they spoke. While it could help him gain membership, it was a topic that he was not willing to negotiate on.

"I haven't mixed poisons in years. I am sure I have forgotten how," Harcourt lied.

"I don't know what else to say then. It will be extremely difficult to sway the minds of my superiors," the older thief stated.

"Just please try again. I need this Serdic. I will be an asset I guarantee it. I was even beaten and then offered incentives to give up Guild names, I never once talked."

Serdic sat there rubbing his chin in thought. He let out a sigh then said, "Alright I will try one more time. I guess I owe you that for not killing any of my men. For your own safety though, don't come back around here.

When I have news I'll get a message sent to you. Now do you think you can leave without hurting anyone on your way out?"

*   *   *   *

Serdic passed through the gambling room where various thieves and thugs played games with dice or cards. Gold and silver coins were stacked tall at some of the tables where the stakes were high. He liked a good game of cards but tonight he was here on business. This gambling house was one of the Thieves Guild's many secret hideouts, and here he was to meet with Trascar, the current leader of the Guild.

Trascar was younger than Serdic by a few years and was known to be a very cruel man. He rose through the Guild ranks quickly and assumed leadership when the former Guildmaster, Mormek, suddenly disappeared. Mormek had led the Guild for nearly fifteen years and then vanished without a trace. Rumors surrounding his disappearance were many. Some thought the city was close to catching him so he had fled. Some thought the city did catch him and he was locked in a cell in the dungeon. Some others thought he was abducted by the demon worshippers and sacrificed. Then there were some, and they did not think this out loud, that thought Trascar played a part in it. Serdic was one of those. Not wanting to be buried somewhere next to Mormek, Serdic knew when to keep his mouth shut.

Regardless of where Mormek was, Trascar was next in line and seized control. Under Trascar's command, the Guild went into new directions that Mormek would never have allowed. They now offered assassins for hire and extorted businesses for payments in order to remain open. The Guild was now more profitable than ever but it drew even more attention from the city. King Stonewood vowed to see them crushed for good. Serdic missed the good ole days of just running gambling houses and robbing wealthy merchants and nobles. "You're late," he heard Trascar say in his typically miserable voice.

Serdic turned to find the Guild leader getting up from a game of cards, his dirty blond hair a mess as if he had been pulling at it in frustration. "Lose a few hands did you?" Serdic asked but had already guessed the answer.

"I wouldn't have if you'd been on time," the grumpy man replied. "So you owe me seventy gold."

"Maybe this will help your mood," Serdic said shaking a satchel he wore over his shoulder.

"Right this way," Trascar indicated to a door close by, his mood already changing.

Trascar always seemed to be in a miserable mood unless he was counting gold. It was one of the few times you could catch the man smile. The pair went into a small private room furnished with expensive leather sofas and sat down. Serdic strained to drop the heavy satchel between them. "I was just retrieving the last of it. That's why I was running a little late."

The Guild leader opened the bag and gave a nod of approval. "Even some gold bars in there I notice. Good work. No trouble in collecting it from all the merchants?"

"There were a few who needed a little extra persuading. But all in all it went smoothly," then he added, "this time."

He could see Trascar doing a quick count so he

continued. "I will admit I am a little concerned about this. What happens when we cross a merchant that will not pay our vending tax and goes straight to the King? I don't want any attention on the Lonely Traveller. I am running a very successful legitimate business there and wouldn't want to lose it because of some unnecessary risks."

For the last six months the Thieves Guild had been hitting foreign merchants with a vending tax the moment they arrived in Stonewood. This fee must be paid each and every time they visited the city to sell their wares. Since many of these visiting merchants stayed at the Lonely Traveller, Serdic had been worried that this would all come back to haunt him in the end. The senior Guild member was a thief and was involved in many illegal activities, but he was always proud of his one legitimate business, running the inn and tavern. The inn also gave him something to fall back on in the event of some unforeseen tragedy with the Guild.

Trascar looked up from his counting. "I wouldn't worry about that. The merchants are terrified of crossing us. Especially since Randar paid a visit to that loud-mouthed Meldor and made an example of him. They know that Stonewood is too profitable for them to jeopardize. And it is too profitable for us to abandon."

Serdic knew there was no use in arguing with the Guild leader. If something brought in gold, he would not give it up, so he changed the subject. "I'll tell you what the merchants and citizens are terrified of more than us - that cursed demon cult."

Trascar's miserable face returned and he immediately jumped up to pace around the room, waving his arms in anger. "How is that we have eyes and ears throughout this entire city, and yet we know nothing, NOTHING about this cult?"

Serdic regretted bringing up the cult the second he finished his sentence. The Guild leader continued his rant. "Mormek was too passive with them when they first started their nonsense. He let them dig in and get a hold on the city. He should have run them out from the beginning. Mark my words, Serdic, I will run them out of Stonewood. Minus their hearts. I can play their game too."

A knock came at the door and a stunningly beautiful blonde woman stuck her head into the room. At least it was blonde tonight. Feylane was the Guild's top assassin and her hair styles and colors changed as often as the wind.

"Excuse me, boys," she said. "Trascar, Minold will be expecting you at the Thirsty Trout in an hour."

"Thank you, my dear," the Guild leader replied. "Please go and tell Randar I have a delivery here for him to make," he added, motioning to the satchel of gold.

The woman gave a wink and shut the door as she left. Serdic got up to leave and remembered one other thing. "Oh by the way, Harcourt dropped in to see me today."

"And what did that lowlife want? To file a complaint about Randar's visit?"

"Not exactly. He came looking for work again."

Trascar shook his head in disbelief. "I hope you punished him for his stupidity."

Serdic laughed. "Funny thing about that. Three of my men tried to do just that and he made fools of them all. Dolan nearly lost his head."

The Guild leader once again fumed with anger. "I suffer that wretch's existence because he is a nobody. But he is coming very close to floating down the river."

"So I take it the answer is no again?"

Trascar just blinked, unable to form a response.

"Allow me to at least hire him at the inn. The man is good in a scrap," Serdic said.

"NO!" Trascar yelled. "He will never have anything to do with us. That is final."

"Why do you hate him so much?" Serdic asked. "Didn't you grow up in the same neighborhood there around the Ogre's Den? Did you know him?"

"That man has always been a loser. Then and now. Same with that scarred whore of his."

When Trascar did not elaborate further, Serdic knew the conversation was at an end. *Oh well*, he thought, *waste of talent*. The thief left the room and then could not resist sitting down at a table for a few rounds of cards.

CHAPTER 6

Midday was the busiest time of day at the market. There were many permanent stalls but hundreds of merchants came each morning to pick out an empty spot to set up for the day. These were usually the foreign merchants just passing through. This was the one place in the city where the very rich and the very poor all mingled together for a common purpose, to shop. Or to steal, as was the case for Harcourt this sunny afternoon. The midday crowds offered excellent cover and distractions for a thief.

Harcourt made his way around behind a stand belonging to a jewelry merchant while Andil did his best to keep the merchant distracted. The two men were currently arguing over the price of a gaudy necklace in which Andil had feigned interest. In his haste to make a sale with Andil, the merchant had dropped his coin purse not too far from the foot path behind his stall. The stall consisted of four rectangular tables that surrounded the merchant, with his jewelry spread out across three of them. The table behind the merchant was empty since he did not have eyes in the back of his head, for which Harcourt was happy since he moved into position leaning up against the empty table.

The thief faced the crowd, scanning for anyone that may have been looking in his direction. To his satisfaction, everyone went about their business as if he did not even exist. In one hand Harcourt held a walking stick, which was common enough in Stonewood, only his was not used for walking. On the tip of the stick was a small hook, about the size of the average fish hook. When Harcourt was positive that no eyes were on him, he crouched down as if had dropped something, reached under the empty merchants table with the stick, and hooked the coin purse that was resting on the ground. In the blink of an eye, the thief hid the purse under his cloak and disappeared into the crowd.

The weight of the purse made the thief smile while he wove his way through the market, putting as much distance as he could between him and the jewelry stall. He wanted to peek inside but you never stopped to count your score. Suddenly his progress was halted as somebody seized his arm. "Slow down there fella, what's the hurry?"

Harcourt turned to regard one of the shortest city guards he had ever seen. The man was shorter than Jalanna, around the five foot mark. Yet for such a short man, he had a strong grip. The thief just stared down at the hand holding him, then back to the guard.

"I said what's the hurry, fella? Leaving the market already? But you haven't even purchased anything yet," the guard said looking to Harcourt's empty hands.

"Does your father know you're wearing his uniform?" Harcourt could not resist saying.

"Alright, you're coming with me smart guy," the

guard replied with an angry tone.

Then from behind they heard a panicked voice shouting, "Sir! Sir! Please sir we need your help."

Harcourt was relieved to see Andil running up to the pair. "Mister guard sir, quickly, a woman has fainted just over there by the vegetable cart. She's struck her head. Please, she needs help."

Forgetting Harcourt was even there, the guard let go and leaped into action. "Where did you say?"

"Straight ahead and to the left, next to the easterners' vegetable cart. Hurry!" Andil replied, sounding positively frantic and out of breath.

As the little guard sprinted off to save the day, the skinny thief turned to Harcourt and in a very calm voice said, "Come on, let's get out of here."

The two thieves did not stop moving until they reached the bridge to the lower east district, then decided to take a little break. Satisfied that they had not been followed, Harcourt pulled out the coin purse to inspect its contents. "Not bad," he said to the other thief, "exactly twelve gold pieces and ten silver. Easy to divide."

He pocketed his half of the coins, handed the other half to Andil, then tossed the purse into the river. "Nice little invention," he said, handing the walking stick back to his skinny partner.

"Does come in handy, doesn't it?" Andil replied. "So what are you gonna spend you half on? Couple of bottles?"

"Well," Harcourt paused to do a calculation in his head. "Now I just need four thousand, nine hundred and ninety-four gold pieces to pay the priest to heal Jal."

Andil shook his head. "You can't be serious about

that still? You'll never come up with that gold and how do you even know that priest can do what he says?"

"I've never believed in any divine magic but people swear those priests perform miracles all the time. If there is a chance to make Jal really happy again, I'll take it," Harcourt replied.

"Jal is happy my friend. She's gotten over that tragedy. If you find her hard to look at, then just admit it's you and not her that's unhappy. Nobody would fault you there."

"It's not me," Harcourt grew annoyed at the accusation. "I love her either way. She still hates herself. She puts on a fake smile for everyone else. You don't see the way her eyes still tear up when she catches a glimpse of her reflection in the river. She'll never be really happy unless she is healed."

"Speaking of Jal, have you seen her yet since missing that job appointment?"

Harcourt let out a long sigh. "No. I have been putting that off. But I am heading there now."

"Alright, well I've got some business to take care of elsewhere so I'll see you back at the Den later. Don't get too drunk 'til I get there." Andil slapped the thief on the back and headed off north.

Harcourt went the opposite direction towards the south district. Lost in thought over what to tell Jalanna, he was nearly run over by a horse pulling a cart full of goods on its way to the market. Then a sweet smell from Shelda's bakery drew his attention back. With coins in his pocket, he treated himself this time to a delicious pastry, and bought an extra one for Jalanna.

When he reached the corner of Jerkel Street and

Maple, he noticed a familiar face and shouted, "Serdic!"

Brushing powdered sugar from his cloak, the thief excitedly rushed over to the senior Guild member. "Hey Serdic, just wondering if you had a chance to speak with the bosses yet?"

Serdic said plainly, "Maybe you should think of a different line of work. Do security somewhere or join Stonewood's army, the pay isn't too bad and you get a roof over your head."

Harcourt felt like he was stabbed with a knife and his shoulders slumped. "They said no again?"

Serdic nodded.

"If they think my luck as a thief isn't great, then I could work for you at the Traveller. Come on, I am better than those goons you have working there now," Harcourt pleaded with the older thief.

"I know you are good but the decision is not mine to make. I tried. You are not well-liked in the Guild. They'll never accept you anytime soon. I am sorry."

Serdic said something else but Harcourt never heard him. He felt numb all over and just walked away. He did not know why he had felt this time would be different. All he had done was fool himself. He was a fool indeed, he thought to himself. A fool for thinking the Guild would accept him. A fool for thinking he could raise enough gold for Jalanna. A fool for ever thinking that his life would improve. He was a homeless lowlife from the south district and that was all he would ever be. Scraping up just enough coins to get through the day. Sleeping on the ground in a shack with a curtain for a door. He wondered then what Jalanna ever saw in him. She must have been as big a fool as he. Instinct guided him back to the south district as he walked in a daze of self-loathing.

Suddenly and without warning he was roughly pulled into an alleyway and shoved hard against a wooden building wall. The smell of onions assaulted his nostrils as Zorfal spoke. "You think you can just make a fool of me and get away with it? Huh, street urchin?"

Harcourt was limp in the man's iron grip, almost lifeless. He did not resist, he did not care. "What? No smart comments now?" Zorfal growled.

The thief's silence seemed to enrage the brutish guard even more. Zorfal slammed him again into the wall. "You will slip up again and I cannot wait to drag you back to the dungeon for good. Just don't make me wait too long."

The guard landed a powerful punch to the thief's stomach, doubling him over and sending him to the ground in a heap. Gasping for air, Harcourt was powerless to stop Zorfal from searching him. The guard found his coins in a hidden cloak pocket. "Been thieving again already eh? Well I am just gonna have to confiscate these," Zorfal said depositing them into his own pocket.

Zorfal gave the thief a hard kick in the back and strolled away eating Jalanna's pastry. Harcourt did not know how long he laid there but night had fallen by the time he found the strength to get up. Instead of making his way to the Ogre's Den to see Jalanna and Andil, Harcourt did something that was low for even a thief of the south district. He robbed a homeless man of a bottle of Zordian brandy and went back to his shack to drink it.

*   *   *   *

Harcourt was jolted awake, but this time it was from a

bucket of cold water splashed onto his face and not a Guild thug's boot. His head pounded with a monstrous headache. Zordian brandy was great going down, but you suffered for it the next day. He squinted and made out what looked like Jalanna. *Am I dreaming?* he thought.

"You selfish bastard!"

It was definitely Jalanna.

"I waited four months for you to get out of that dungeon. Four months! I worried about you every single day and couldn't wait to see you again. I even forgave you for pulling that job that got you locked up without discussing it with me first. All I wanted was for you to get out of there safely and return to my arms. You promised me the other day you'd meet Jardo and work a real job. For us. For our future. You promised! Then not only do you NOT meet with Jardo, but you do NOT even come see me for two days! You've been avoiding me? Me, who waited four months to see you? Do you even care about me? I have to come looking for you and I find you drunk and passed out here in your precious little home? Don't you want to get out of this stinking alley once and for all?"

The thief winced as her shouting only made his head hurt even more. She had it all wrong but his brain could not formulate a response quick enough. All he could manage was, "I was doing everything for you."

At first she looked too angry to reply, but then she did. "You were doing everything for me? What's everything? Getting drunk by yourself and avoiding me for two days? Gee, that's so wonderful. I don't even know how to thank you for that. You are so thoughtful."

"I wasn't referring to that," he replied.

"You know what? I don't care what you were

referring to." Tears started to stream down from her beautiful exotic eyes. "I give up. I am tired of this. Ever since we've been together, you keep getting into trouble and keep getting locked in the dungeon. And each time it gets longer and longer. I never cared that you were a thief. I loved you no matter what. I can see the kindness in your heart. You are a good man, Harcourt. You know how rare that is in these parts? But your thieving skills, or lack of, has been interfering with our relationship. I told you before it was time to do something else or this would drive us apart. Guess what? It finally has. And this drinking a bottle of brandy," she kicked the empty bottle, "was supposed to do what exactly? Make you a better thief? Improve your skills? Help you find a job? You are heading right back to the dungeon again. I can see it coming. And this time, I will not be here waiting for you to get out. I never want to see you again!"

Jalanna stormed off, sobbing uncontrollably. Harcourt wanted to drag her back and explain things properly but his body would not co-operate and he collapsed back down on the ground. Now he truly had lost everything. He had hit rock bottom. If Randar, Zorfal, or Dolan happened by now he would not care if any of them ran him through with their swords. At least the pain would be gone, permanently.

Harcourt eventually forced himself to stand up. He noticed that same toothless beggar sitting down the alley grinning at him. He must have overheard the whole exchange with Jalanna and found it amusing. The thief gave the beggar another rude hand gesture and set off to find another bottle to empty.

CHAPTER 7

The next two days were a blur to Harcourt. For the few moments that he was not drunk, he managed to gather the wherewithal to pick enough pockets in order to buy stale bread and more drink. Every so often, he found a new bruise or cut somewhere on his body and could not recall where they had come from. At the moment, his right hand throbbed. He must have punched something or someone, but what or who? Since he had a small lump on his head, he figured he must have been in a fight. *I hope I won*, he thought to himself as he stumbled down Snake Street in search of a drink.

Night had fallen on Stonewood and the residents of the south district started to emerge in search of their respective places to drink or steal. Nobody paid the thief any mind since a drunk staggering down Snake Street wearing dirty rags was quite common. "There you are," the thief heard somebody say from behind.

He turned to see Andil standing with his hands on his bony hips, looking him up and down.

"You look horrible," the skinny thief said shaking his head. "What's happened to you? You never came back to the Den that day after the market. Jal said she didn't know where you were and didn't care. You guys fight?"

"Something like that."

"Come on, join me for something to eat. I am buying. Let's just go over here to Edmond's," Andil said, pulling Harcourt along behind him.

Edmond's was an old storage warehouse converted into a makeshift tavern. The tavern was spacious but never full so it was a place where you could have a private conversation with very few people sitting nearby. Andil picked a table near a corner, the farthest away from everyone else. He ordered two quarter roasted chickens and a tall mug of watered down ale for each of them. The food was cheap here, and the quality reflected it.

"What's gotten into you?" Andil asked.

"I failed Jal. Serdic told me I'll never get into the Guild which means I'll never raise the gold for Jal. And now I've lost her anyways."

"Jal doesn't care about that gold, you idiot. Go and apologize to her and make up," the skinny thief said as the food arrived.

Harcourt did not realize how hungry he was until he smelled the chicken. "She deserves better Andil. I can't give her anything. I can barely even take care of myself. She'll be much better off without me around to drag her down."

"I think you are making a mistake but you are an adult," Andil replied then attacked the chicken before him.

Folk getting sick after eating the food at Edmond's was not a rare occurrence at all. That did not stop the pair from devouring their meals and downing their ale in silence. Andil ordered two more drinks, then pulled his chair in close to the table and lowered his voice.

"Get this. There is a huge shipment of gold coming into the city next week. Some duke from Milbury is buying up a lot of property. There is a large unit of soldiers bringing in a fake shipment as a diversion. The real shipment is coming in afterwards, quietly with little protection."

Harcourt sounded very disinterested. "Well, I am sure the Guild will be happy with that score."

Andil chuckled. "Actually, the Guild won't touch it. The duke has made some arrangements with the Guild so the gold is off limits to anyone. Can you imagine? All that gold with virtually no protection. It's almost a crime not to steal it."

"How much gold are we talking about here?" Harcourt inquired with a raised brow.

"Tens of thousands," Andil replied looking around for eavesdroppers.

Harcourt took a sip from the ale that the round barmaid just dropped off. She winked but he never noticed. "Hired security or city guards?"

"Hired mercenaries are bringing it a quarter mile outside the city, then a couple of guards are taking over and bringing it in to a warehouse in the lower east," Andil answered.

Harcourt sat silent, processing all the details, then asked, "How do you know all this?"

The skinny thief gave a big smile. "I hear things. It's a talent of mine."

Harcourt returned the smile. "Alright then, so how

do you want to do this?"

"Do what?" his friend asked.

"Steal the gold," the thief whispered matter-of-factly. "You wanna hit the mercs outside the city, or the guards inside?"

"Whoa, whoa, whoa," Andil said, taken by surprise. "I was only sharing gossip with you. I just told you that gold is off limits. The Guild won't allow anyone to touch it."

"Well, we are not Guild members, are we? We don't need to follow their rules."

"We do if we would like to live a little longer. Are you out of your mind? If the guards catch you, you'll do at least ten years, and if the Guild gets you first they will behead you. And that's only after they've tortured you for days!" Andil said, looking around and suddenly feeling very paranoid.

Harcourt sat silently thinking, and rubbing the several days growth of hair on his chin. Andil continued to try and reason with his friend.

"A job like that you can't do alone, and don't think that I will help you. I happen to enjoy living. Just forget about this. Besides, even if you got away with it, good luck spending that gold. The city, the duke and the Guild would not rest until they caught who did it."

The truth in Andil's words finally sunk in and Harcourt slumped back in his chair feeling as miserable as before. "You are right, I am a fool."

"You are not a fool, you are just human. I'd be lying if I told you that thought didn't cross my mind as well. But like I said, I happen to enjoy living. Now I gotta meet a couple of toughs in a few hours and I don't trust them. So meet me later and come with me. I'll give you a cut of the deal."

"So now I've become just a bodyguard?" Harcourt said finishing the last of his awful ale.

"You know I don't think that. But yeah, tonight I need the muscle. As you know, I don't intimidate," Andil said flexing his skeletal arms in a comedic pose.

The skinny thief tossed Harcourt a small coin pouch. "Here, get yourself cleaned up and get some new clothes. Meet me outside Londo's shop in three hours."

Andil stood up to leave then pointed at his friend. "Don't spend that on drinks. We do this deal tonight and I am buying when we are done."

Harcourt thanked his skinny friend and wandered out of the tavern shortly after. A young couple passed him by holding hands and giggling to one another, just as he and Jal had used to do. He turned down the next street to see another couple making out on a door step. Everything was reminding him of her.

Harcourt took his friend's advice and went for a hot bath and a shave. He bought a clean set of used clothes but with his remaining silver pieces, he bought three bottles of fire water. Fire water was a particularly potent drink that got its name from the burning sensation it left when going down, and lingered long after. It was the cheapest of the strong drinks that one could buy. Harcourt did not care about quality right now, only potency.

The thief made his way towards Londo's shop, but then cracked open one of the bottles and took a detour instead. He didn't feel much like working tonight.

*   *   *   *

Halfway through a bottle of fire water, Harcourt collapsed on the step of a closed shop somewhere in the bowels of the south district. This area was full of little shops and quite empty at this hour of the night. Shops closed early for fear of being robbed. At the moment, the thief was alone and it was just the way he wanted it. Alone to wallow in his misery. He had felt bad for not meeting up with Andil but the fire water had silenced his nagging conscience.

Harcourt leaned his head back against a shop wall and was about to close his eyes when he was startled by a dark figure standing next to him that he swore he never saw approaching. The gaunt man was dressed in a long black overcoat and had a face as pale as a ghost, if there were such things. He had sunken eyes and protruding cheek bones. There was something unnerving about the man but the thief could not figure out quite what it was.

"You seem lost, my friend," the eerie man said in a gentle melodic voice which did not seem to match his appearance.

"I have lived in this cesspool my whole life, I am not lost. And I am not your friend," the thief replied with a slur to his speech.

The pale man smiled. "Not yet anyway. And I was not referring to your physical location, but to your emotional state. I believe you have lost your way. You lack a purpose in life. The city has held you down and stripped away your humanity."

"You know nothing about me," Harcourt said taking a mouthful of fire water and shaking his head as it burned.

"Ah, but you are mistaken. I can tell a lot about

someone when I first meet them. Your eyes tell me the story of your life. You have given up. Something you've held dear is now gone, and you are unsure about how you can get it back. I can also tell that you have a lot of potential in life but the oppression of the city holds you firmly in the muck of the south district. But there is hope, my friend. There is always hope. With strong friends by your side, you can rise up out of the filth and find new purpose in life." The man put his hand on Harcourt's shoulder and thief swore his skin tingled from under his shirt.

"Join me tonight in a meeting of like-minded individuals. Lost souls like yourself, seeking friendship and direction. Together we can all cast aside the chains of tyranny placed on us by King Stonewood and prepare for the arrival of the great Lucivenus who will save us and usher in a new era of prosperity for all."

Lucivenus? Where have I heard that name before? the thief struggled to wonder. The fire water had clouded his mind. *Lucivenus?*

"Our Lord Lucivenus will come to Stonewood," the pale man continued, "and topple the regime of evil that now controls us all. Lucivenus will reward his friends handsomely I can assure you."

Then it hit Harcourt like a club. Lucivenus was the demon lord that the fanatical cult members believed they would one day summon forth to wreak devastation on the city. He pulled away from the man's hand in absolute disgust.

"Get away from me. I'd like to keep my heart right where it is."

There were a lot of horrific unsolved murders

throughout Stonewood linked to the demon worshipping cult. The poor victims were always missing their hearts.

"I do not presume to know what you are referring to but perhaps you will change your mind. Here, please take this and think this over when your head is clear. Remember, there are friends waiting to help you," the eerie man handed the thief what appeared to be a small child's wooden whistle.

Harcourt snatched the whistle then took a step back and examined it. It seemed to be unremarkable without any visible markings. A common whistle.

"It's just a child's whistle," he said looking up and noticing the pale cult member was gone.

Harcourt scanned the dark street but there was no sign of the strange man. *He could not be that fast*, thought the thief. He just vanished. Harcourt wondered if he was hallucinating but he was still holding a very real whistle. Oh well, he thought, at least the man was gone and his heart was still beating in his chest where it belonged. The thief tossed the whistle aside and left to find someplace else to drink.

*　*　*　*

It was the dead of night, only hours from dawn, and Harcourt stumbled down a dusty street. The only folk out at this time were drunks like himself, or thieves like himself. It was a miracle the man was still standing, let alone walking after the amount of fire water he had consumed.

His vision was not very clear but he thought he saw two men step out of an alley to block his path. When he halted and swayed back and forth trying to remain upright, one of the men approached him.

"Let's make this easy. Just hand over anything of value," said the man whose face was hidden with the hood of his dark cloak.

Truth was Harcourt had nothing of value save two nearly full bottles of fire water stuffed inside his own cloak. He was not about to give those up freely without a fight.

"You gotta do this the hard way," he tried to say but it came out incoherently.

Harcourt reached back for a dagger that was not there and a third man stepped up and struck him in the back of the head with a blackjack. The world spun as Harcourt fell to the ground and blacked out, luckily not landing on either of his two bottles.

*   *   *   *

Harcourt's eyes shot open at the piercing sound of a horn. At first he found himself staring up at the stars not realizing where he was, but then he heard the clang of steel on steel which told him he was in potential danger. He attempted to prop himself up on one elbow and a searing pain shot through his head.

He was able to make out a cloaked man engaged with a city guard in a sword fight. Suddenly everything came back to him and he remembered being surrounded by a group of thugs, then one had hit him from behind.

Before the guard could blow his horn a second time another thug slashed him from behind with a wicked-looking knife. He dropped his horn to concentrate on the fight which now included two opponents, one wielding a short sword and the other a knife.

Harcourt thought he recalled there being three thugs, when suddenly a rock flew by and just grazed the guards head. Taking advantage of that distraction, one of the thugs rushed in thrusting his sword for the guard's belly but it was easily knocked aside. It was clear the guard was the better swordsman but he was outnumbered. He swung his blade wildly just trying to fend the thugs off while he attempted to manoeuver closer to a building where he could get his back to a wall. The man with the knife flipped the weapon into the air catching it by the blade. He lifted his arm back to throw but suddenly dropped to one knee grunting in pain, a crossbow bolt protruding from the back of his leg. Reinforcements had arrived.

The thug with the sword turned his head for a brief moment to take note of the arriving guards when the one he was battling slashed down at his sword arm and took his hand off at the wrist. His hand, still gripping the sword, fell to the ground as he let out a blood-curdling scream.

The rock-throwing thief sprinted away but was intercepted by the brute Zorfal who put an elbow into the man's mouth, knocking out several teeth. For once in his life, Harcourt was relieved to see city guards. Captain Dornell arrived and issued orders to the three guards that stood with him. He shouted at Zorfal who decided to rough up the thug he caught a little more than was necessary. Zorfal and the others dragged away the three thugs, one of them still screaming. The brutish guard flashed Harcourt an evil grin before departing.

"Don't forget his hand," the thief called after him and one of the other guards trotted back to retrieve the hand

and the sword.

Harcourt had an immense headache but the blow had somewhat sobered him up. He reached back and felt blood caked all over the back of his head. Suddenly in a panic, he looked around for his bottles of fire water which were no longer on his person.

"I think what you're looking for is over there," Captain Dornell said, pointing to the bottles lying on the ground a few feet away.

The thief was relieved to see both were still intact. He attempted to rise but a flash of pain and a nauseating wave of dizziness forced him back down.

"I'd stay down there for awhile if I were you. You took a nasty blow to the head," said the captain.

"Every other time, you boys would be right on time, but you arrive late when it's to help me," Harcourt replied rubbing his aching head, his speech still a little slurred.

"I wouldn't say that. You'd be dead right now if we hadn't shown up. I'd call that good timing," Dornell countered.

"Yeah, well I could do without this headache."

"Poor you," the captain said with no sympathy. "How does it feel being the victim for a change? Not very fun is it? How many people have you put in this position?"

"I've never assaulted an innocent on the street," the thief said.

"You mean we haven't caught you doing it yet. And you are far from an innocent on the street. A thief being robbed. I like the irony there," the captain chuckled to himself. "I grow weary of having these run-ins with you. How many times have I arrested you, boy?"

"Too many," the thief said.

"Too many, you are right. I've patrolled this district for a very long time. I know how things work down here. I know that you can't be a member of the Thieves Guild, or you wouldn't be so down and out all the time, or getting mugged in the streets. I don't know what you've done to keep yourself excluded from that lot, but I do know Guild justice. You continue with your life of crime and they will kill you, if we don't lock you up first. And as you are aware, I've got no problems in doing that. I love ridding the streets of poison like yourself. Even if it's only temporary," the guard captain lectured.

"I hate you," Harcourt replied. "I hate you and everyone else who looks down us in the south district because we are not as privileged as you."

Captain Dornell crouched down, putting his face to the thief's.

"You made your choices, boy. You and you alone. When you were young, I could understand. I was always lenient on you the first couple of times I caught you breaking the laws. I knew you didn't have any options then. But you are an adult now. You know the differences between right and wrong. You could have changed."

"Easy for you to say," the thief muttered, turning his head.

Angry, the guard captain turned Harcourt back to face him. "Easy for me? What do you know of me? I am going to tell you a little something, boy. I too grew up here in the south district after both of my parents died of a disease when I was young. I had nothing and nobody gave me anything in life. I lived in a stable with the horses I looked after for whatever coins I could get. I chose to work, and do any job available to survive. I chose NOT to become a thief. So don't tell me I don't know what it's like on the other side."

Harcourt had no answer to that. He just continued to rub his head in silence. Captain Dornell stood up then walked over to the bottles of fire water. "And these things here only speed up your spiral downfall. You think they are helping you but all they do is more damage." He then crushed both bottles with the heel of his boot.

"Noooooooooooooooooo!" Harcourt shouted.

Ignoring the pain in his head the thief managed to get to his feet and lunged at the guard in rage. He had no coins and that was all he had left to drink. Dornell was surprised by the sudden attack, not believing the thief could even stand. Harcourt collided with the guard captain hard, tackling him to the dirty street. The thief threw a right cross at Dornell's head but the guard blocked it with a mailed forearm. The guard seized his arm and bucked the thief off while twisting the arm behind his back. Harcourt, knowing that Dornell could break his arm with little effort, laid still, spitting curses.

The guard captain was thankful the thief had been injured and intoxicated or this would have been a very different fight. He shackled Harcourt's wrists behind his back and hauled him up to his feet. "Now I know it was just the drink that caused your outburst here, so be happy I am just throwing you in the drunk cell 'til you sober up," Dornell said, then dragged a staggering Harcourt down the street.

An elderly woman had watched the scene unfold from her window above a fabric shop. She hung her head out and shouted, "That's right, you drag away that lowlife scum and get those thugs off the streets!"

Harcourt suddenly felt very ashamed of himself, then he vomited.

CHAPTER 8

Harcourt awoke again and when he opened his eyes this time, the scenery still had not changed. He still lay on the cold stone floor of a small prison cell. He had hoped it was just a nightmare he was having but this time he was sure it was real. He had drifted in and out of sleep for the better part of a day. He did not remember much of the night before but his body ached and his head was killing him. He had attacked Dornell, that much he recalled.

Harcourt hated the captain but had never before attacked the man, no matter how much he had wanted to. His nemesis was right though, it was the drink and it was doing him damage. He would not last much longer at this rate. You could not survive on stale bread and alcohol forever. He needed to change his life around, and he knew exactly how to do it. Steal the duke's gold.

The thief did not care that the Guild put the gold off limits to everyone. They did not want him as a member, so he would not play by their rules. If he actually got away with this, he decided he would leave Stonewood for good.

He would have Jalanna healed and take her with him if she would have him back. If she did not want him back, that was ok; he would still have her healed to thank her for all the years she put up with him. But of course, he was hoping she would. He could only be truly happy in life with her.

If he failed in this attempt, the Guild would not matter since he would spend a very long time in the dungeons. He figured it was worth the risk. There was no way he would ever get that much gold anywhere else if Andil's intelligence was correct. He could not let this opportunity pass him by.

The only problem was how? It would be better to hit the duke's hired mercenaries outside the city he thought, but that put him completely out his element. Harcourt had rarely ever ventured outside the city walls in his life, and it had been many years since the last time. As beautiful as the countryside was, Harcourt was simply not comfortable unless surrounded by the walls of the city. It made him feel safe, even though the city was not always a safe place.

That meant he would have to deal with the city guards when they brought the gold inside the walls, and that would not be easy by any stretch of the imagination. Killing the guards would be the simplest plan, but that was not his way. Robbing them and keeping them alive just made the job a lot more difficult.

Harcourt figured it was time he gathered together some ingredients to mix up some of the sleeping poison he had perfected many years back. If he was lucky, he could use a blowgun with poisoned needles to take out the guards before any of them became aware of an attack. He had to be sure that none of them got the chance to blow a horn.

The thief needed a few more details from Andil to finalize his plan. He winced when he remembered that he had failed to meet his friend last night, opting instead to get drunk. His cell door flung open and he frowned when he saw Zorfal's hulking form fill the doorway.

"What's wrong, scum? Not happy to see me?" the guard said with a wicked smile.

"I must be still sleeping. I am having a nightmare that some hideous river troll has come to eat me," Harcourt said, bracing for the assault that would surely follow.

Zorfal cracked his knuckles and stepped inside the cell. "Just get him outta here, Zorfal," Captain Dornell shouted from outside.

"I'll be seeing you later," the nasty guard said, roughly pulling him up and shoving him out of the cell.

* * * *

Harcourt spent the remainder of the day resting and recovering in his alley home, then when darkness fell he went in search of Andil. He found him in his usual haunt, the Ogre's Den. There was an awkward moment when he entered the tavern and passed by Jalanna who was working. It hurt when she just looked away and stormed off without a word. Soon though, he thought, soon he would make things right and see that smile she had lost long ago.

The thief did not want to bother her further and so convinced an angry Andil to talk with him elsewhere. They found an empty alley just down the street and Harcourt explained that he could not meet the skinny thief the other night because he had been arrested along the way. Most of the tale was true, just the timing was off. When it appeared that his friend bought his story, he laid out his plan for the duke's gold.

"You are insane," Andil repeated several times.

"You are probably right," Harcourt replied. "But be that as it may, I am still going through with it. So I need you to pick up a few things for me. If I succeed, I'll pay you back a hundred times over. If I fail, consider it a going-away gift since you'll probably not be seeing me again."

The thief then ran down a list of items he knew the resourceful Andil should be able to acquire for him. Andil just kept shaking his head in disbelief the entire time. "There is supposed to be three guards, you realize that right?"

Harcourt nodded. "Yes, that's what the blowgun is for. I figure if I shoot one with a needle, he'll go down before the others know what happened. By the time they check on him, I can have the second one down with another needle, then I should only have to deal with one guard."

"Still, that will be one guard that is armored and armed with a sword. You remember what a sword is, don't you? That really really long dagger?" Andil said.

"One I can handle no problem," Harcourt answered confidently.

"Alright, your insanity is contagious apparently," Andil let out a long sigh. "I am going to help you. You are going to need a lookout. I am not going to engage anyone though. Got that? I will be nearby and alert you if anyone is coming but that's the extent of it. I can't bear the thought of you getting killed. Or spending all that gold all by yourself."

"What happened to not wanting to cross the Guild?" Harcourt asked.

"Well, this might actually work as crazy as that sounds. And if it does, I don't mind burying my cut until this all blows over. I have patience," Andil reasoned.

Harcourt smiled. He would be lying if he said he wanted to do this alone. He did not mind doing all the physical and dangerous work, but having an extra set of eyes on a rooftop would be invaluable. They had never failed when working together in the past. They had four days to prepare according to Andil's information. This really might work after all Harcourt thought.

*   *   *   *

Harcourt lay on his blanket inside his tiny shack deep in thought. He had run over the plan a million times in his head the last four days. Andil found out that the gold was being brought into the city at midnight, and that was now only a few hours away. A nervous excitement had been building for days and was now reaching its climax. This was the fateful night. Either way, it would be the last time he laid in this home of his.

Harcourt did not know why that thought made him feel sad in a strange way. It was a shack he shared in an alley with homeless beggars. But it was his shack. It had been his home for over ten years. He spent his entire life dreaming about something better, dreaming about a change, and now that it was almost upon him, he feared venturing away from familiar ground. A small part of him said to just forget about this plan and return to the life he knew. Then images of Jalanna would chase those thoughts away.

The thief finally rose and dusted off his new clothes, a midnight black outfit with a matching cloak that Andil was able to acquire for him. He stuffed his old clothes and cloak in his little hiding spot in the wall. *Maybe the next person to occupy this spot might find them and make use of them*, he thought.

Harcourt did a quick inventory check. He had two daggers strapped to the back of his belt in an "x" pattern, and a small hollow tube which was his blowgun, tucked into a cloak pocket. Also attached to his belt in a pouch, was a handful of needles and two vials of a powerful sleeping poison he had concocted the day before. It had been quite some time since he had made any so he tested it out on the toothless beggar at the end of the alley. The thief was satisfied when the man snored for several hours.

There was just one more last minute thing he needed but he would pick that up before he met up with Andil. Harcourt had not had one drop of alcohol since his stay in the cell. He did not even have the time to think about it. His every thought had been consumed with this plan.

Harcourt considered going to see Jalanna one last time, just in case things went horribly wrong, but he talked himself out of that idea. He needed to concentrate tonight and not have any distractions. This was going to be his biggest and most dangerous job ever, and his recent track record was not a very good one at all. The thief was at peace with his decision though. For good or ill, he was going through with it.

CHAPTER 9

Harcourt crouched on the roof of a shop facing East Gate Road. From here, he would be able to watch the gold shipment arrive and note which street they turned down. Andil knew the general direction they would be heading but not the specific streets, so Harcourt had studied all their possible routes and formulated a plan for each.

He looked to the roofs across the street, scanning for his partner, but Andil could not be seen. That, of course, did not mean he was not there. Harcourt figured that the other thief could not see him either. It was a cloudy night making the city even darker than usual. It was slightly windy but eerily silent.

Andil had been surprised by Harcourt's last minute decision to wear a mask. Harcourt had startled the skinny thief by showing up in a black and white mask resembling a skull. He explained that he could not risk any of the guards recognizing him or getting a description. The skinny thief tried to tell him that it would hinder his vision, but Harcourt felt it was necessary.

Waiting for the shipment to arrive was the worst part. The thief was anxious to get this all over with. The longer he sat perched on the roof, the more he thought it was a bad idea. Breaking into homes and shops was one thing but robbing city guards of a duke's gold shipment was a different league entirely.

Harcourt watched two street sweepers make their way down the street, then spotted what he had been waiting for. From around the corner, three blocks away, came a horse pulling a covered wagon surrounded by three armored city guards. One was in front leading the way, one was to the left of the wagon, and one followed behind. Each looked about nervously, their eyes peeled for danger.

The guard in the rear carried a large crossbow, the other two just their customary swords hung from their belts. Each wore that dreaded horn. Harcourt figured he should take out the crossbowman first. He watched patiently as the trio of guards slowly made their way towards him then turned left onto Denniz Street. The thief had chosen his spot well and did not have to leap across any buildings yet to shadow the shipment.

Harcourt's full attention was on the guards, trusting in Andil to keep watch for anyone else. They had a series of whistle codes that would allow Andil to specify how many people approached, and from what direction. He could even specify if it was a guard or not. So far, no whistles. This area of the city was asleep, thankfully.

Harcourt allowed himself a smile when the shipment made its next turn onto Ortis Lane. That street was long and narrow with many alleys to strike from and he could easily get ahead of them from the rooftops here. He stayed low and moved as quickly as possible to position himself in the perfect spot. The thief lay down near the ledge of the roof and pulled out his blowgun and needles. He got into a comfortable position and waited for the wagon to approach. He would get the crossbowman first, then the guard on the left.

The wind started picking up as the trio got closer and that worried the thief. The needles were light, and the slightest breeze could ruin his aim, especially at this distance. The armored guards gave him little to work with, having only their necks and faces exposed - an impossible shot with wind. Harcourt cursed silently to himself. The wagon was almost below him and still the wind blew. *Damn*, he thought, he would have to get closer. He wanted to be on street level in case things went awry, and he felt the building walls might provide some shelter from the wind.

He sped along the roof then dropped down an alley about a block ahead of the trio. A large rat gave him a start as it scurried away from him. The thief hid at the mouth of the alley, blending in perfectly with the shadows. Thankfully, the wind was no longer an issue here and he felt he could not miss a shot from this range. His heart was pounding now, nearly exploding from his chest.

The clip-clop of the horse's hooves grew louder as he spotted some movement from an alley across the street. Was it Andil? The skinny thief had said he would not get close to the action and remain on rooftops only. There it was again. Definitely someone in the alley, and not Andil. Whoever it was did not possess very good skills at hiding, but in the darkness it was difficult to make out who it could be.

Then Harcourt saw a glint of metal as the moon

poked through the clouds momentarily. Armor! There was a guard in the alley. Why had Andil not alerted him? No wait, there were two guards. The bigger of the two stuck his head out to peer down the street and there was no mistaking that ugly head. Zorfal! What was he doing here?

Despair hit the thief hard, the dream was over. He had to abort the mission. Before he could move, another guard walked through his alley from behind and stopped right next to the thief without even noticing he was there. The thief froze in horror; he thought even his heart stopped beating. He had to get out of here, and now.

When it did not appear that the guard was going to move anytime soon, Harcourt rose from his hiding spot and shot the guard point blank in the neck with a poisoned needle. He dropped the blowgun and drew both of his daggers. In one quick motion, he cut the horn from the guard's belt and it fell to the ground out of reach. The guard then spun around reaching for the horn that was no longer there. He drew his sword and attempted to say something, then stopped. He blinked his eyes and took a shaky step forward. The poison was working. The guard opened his mouth again, but his eyes rolled back in his head and he fell. He could have fallen any number of ways but to Harcourt's dismay, he went straight back and crashed to the street landing in front of the gold wagon that had just rolled up.

"What in the name of…" he heard one the three guards shout, followed by a blast from a horn.

And there it was, he thought. His bad luck had come to pay him a visit once again. Four days of planning and preparing had unraveled in a heartbeat. Why did this always happen to him? Where was Andil? Was his friend captured? Did he flee? Harcourt could not waste time pondering the fate of his friend, it was time he fled. If Andil was still around, he would have to fend for himself.

He turned to leave out the opposite end of the alley but found his way blocked by another guard. The guard had his sword in hand and shouted, "Over here!"

Harcourt ran at the guard full speed and threw one of his daggers at the man's thigh. The guard yelped and did his best to leap aside just barely avoiding the spinning blade. With his defense down, the thief jumped up and planted a boot square in the man's mailed chest sending him sprawling to the ground. As the thief ran past, he bent low and slashed the man's boot cutting through to the flesh of his ankle. Not a serious wound, but one that would keep this guard from pursuing him.

Harcourt scooped up his other dagger and dashed down the street making a quick left as two more horns blew. The thief heard voices from around the next corner and ducked behind an empty cart out front of an apothecary shop. Four heavily armored guards jogged right past the cart. He thought he could make out the words "thief" and "gold" as they disappeared from sight. Another horn blew. This was bad. Very bad. He stood up and glanced at Fezzdin's tower off in the distance to get his bearings. He was not too far from the south district but they were waiting for him there the last time. This time, he would flee north of the river and find somewhere to hide out for the night.

Harcourt crept down the street sticking to the shadows, pausing only when the occasional person passed by. He drew the hood of his cloak over his face concealing his skull mask as two northmen passed by singing a tavern song, then took the next street leading north.

Hearing more footsteps approaching, the thief turned to face the wall of a building and pretended to be relieving himself after a long night of drinking. He heard a voice from behind, "Hey, what are you about there?"

The thief kept up with his act. "You there stop that. You are not a dog. Go someplace..," but the voice was cut off as a guard entered the street and shouted, "Stop that thief!"

Harcourt spun with daggers in his hands and saw that it was another guard who had been standing behind him. The thief took off in a run and the guard drew his sword and gave chase. Unfortunately for Harcourt, this guard was in pretty good shape and did not seem to be weighed down by his chainmail vest. He was actually gaining on the thief and demanding that he stop. Figuring the guard would not be expecting him to do just that, Harcourt came to a dead stop. The surprised guard clumsily thrust his sword forward and Harcourt used both daggers to deflect the blade aside, then smashed his elbow into the guards face. The blow stunned the guard and bought Harcourt some time to sprint away and get some distance between them. Another horn blew as he heard, "Over here! Over here!"

Harcourt zigzagged down the next few streets as fast as he could, trying to maintain a northerly direction. Luckily he passed very few citizens but he was getting the strange feeling that someone was shadowing him. He had first gotten the feeling a few streets back and wondered if it was Andil.

Finding a narrow alley, he slipped in and stopped for a moment to catch his breath and think about how he was going to get across the bridge into the upper east. At this time of night, there would be at least a guard or two at each end.

His thoughts were suddenly interrupted when his shadow finally decided to reveal itself. Randar stepped into the alley from the other end with short sword in hand while shaking his head.

"Attempting to steal gold from the duke is the same as attempting to steal gold from the Guild. You've got to be the most foolish person in this city, Harcourt."

Harcourt? The Guild enforcer said Harcourt? But how? I am wearing the mask, the thief thought. Dread overcame him. If the Guild knew what he was attempting to do tonight then he had to flee the city or die. There were no other options. Randar was here to ensure the latter took place. Since it no longer mattered, Harcourt pulled off the mask and tossed it away. Randar advanced with an evil grin.

Harcourt had been in many fights in his life, and many that could have meant the death of him, but this would be his toughest yet. Randar was one of the most feared men in the city, for those that knew of him. Harcourt could not even imagine how many deaths the enforcer had to his credit. He knew there would be no way to escape him and so decided to meet him head on. At least this time, the thief was not drunk or hung over.

The pair closed on each other, Randar with his sword in hand, Harcourt with his two daggers. Randar gave a few teasing feints causing Harcourt to react each time. The thug laughed, he was so calm. Randar favored the shorter-bladed swords for just this kind of close quarters combat. This time, the thug committed to a thrust aimed at Harcourt's chest but the thief managed a parry with one of his daggers. Another thrust, another parry. Randar was testing his defenses, and skills.

Harcourt had never learned to fight with a sword, never owned one, but he was a master with the dagger, favoring a two-weapon style. The third thrust he parried with his left and countered with his right. He did not have the range though and Randar stepped back away from the strike, smiling. For all of Randar's arrogance, he still did not just rush the thief; he was playing it careful, looking for the right opening.

The thug feinted a thrust and this time when Harcourt's arm moved in to parry, he came right back slashing the thief's forearm, drawing a long gash. Harcourt grimaced and backpedaled a few steps. "First blood's mine," Randar taunted.

Harcourt made the motion that he was going to throw his left dagger. Randar positioned his sword up in defense and the thief lunged with amazing speed, slicing the thugs left arm with his right dagger. Harcourt backed away smiling, while Randar's face turned to a scowl.

The thug rushed forward with a growl bringing his sword chopping down at Harcourt's head. Harcourt held both daggers in an "x" position and blocked the strike. The force of the blow sent sharp pain down both his arms, then Randar kicked him in the stomach, sending him skidding backwards. The pair ended up in the middle of Peach Street, circling each other slowly.

Harcourt glanced around nervously for any city guards but the two of them were alone on the dark street. He needed to end this quickly and get out of the city as soon as possible. He could never return to Stonewood. Randar's blade nicked him on the shoulder and he brought his concentration back fully to the fight.

The thug came in with a series of slashes backing Harcourt up towards the window of a shop that sold wines from around the world. Desperate to keep Randar off him, he launched his right dagger into the thugs shoulder, then tossed his left dagger over to his right hand. Randar grunted in pain. He pulled the blade out and threw it aside, blood flowing freely down his arm from the nasty wound. He hissed through his teeth and came in with a wide arcing slash, forcing Harcourt to leap back and suck in his stomach to avoid having it cut open. Randar then stepped in with a powerful kick to the off-balance thief, sending him straight through the shop window. Harcourt landed on his back showered with glass. Luckily his cloak was thick enough that no shards had penetrated his skin. Randar reached the shattered window and stopped as a nearby voice shouted, "Hold right there."

Harcourt heard the sound of several armored men jogging their way closer. As Randar turned to look, Harcourt grabbed a bottle of wine from the floor, jumped to his feet, and smashed the bottle over the thug's head. Randar dropped to his knees dazed, blood streaming down his face. Harcourt ran through the shop and disappeared out the back door.

CHAPTER 10

It was not easy getting across the river. The water flowed too swiftly so swimming was not an option and there were two guards posted at the ends of each bridge. Harcourt had grabbed a few bottles of wine from the shop to use as distractions. He threw one bottle down a street causing the two guards at one end of the bridge to leave and investigate the noise. The thief stealthily crossed the bridge and used his second bottle to rid himself of the remaining two at the other end. He passed them by like a ghost in the night.

Harcourt now sat against a tree in a large park north of the river. He was still bleeding from his forearm and shoulder, but it was much better than being dead, he thought. Surviving his encounter with Randar might have actually been the easiest part of this night - getting out of the city would be the hardest part. Leaving through one of the city's two main gates was out of the question. He would have to find a spot to scale the city's defensive wall without being spotted or find a way through a sewer tunnel. The south district did not have any sewers so Harcourt was not familiar with the underground labyrinth.

Then, of course, came the problem of where to go if he did manage to get out. The thief had no food, no water, no coins, and no horse. As far as he knew, the next closest town was a two-day walk. He let out a long sigh, wondering why everything had gone so horribly wrong.

Then from the corner of his eye he spotted a shadow moving from tree to tree. He slipped behind the tree he was resting against and sat motionless watching for more movement. There it was again. It was a cloaked figure all in black, similar to what Harcourt wore. As far as he could tell, he had not been spotted. It had to be a member of the Thieves Guild he thought. They must be searching for him and tracked him to the park. Harcourt laughed to himself thinking that he should be considered the greatest thief ever should he actually survive this night.

Harcourt crouched low and made his way to some thick bushes near a large pond. A few water birds floated around but paid him no mind. The bushes provided a good hiding spot if he wanted to wait until dawn, but it would be much harder to escape the city by day. No, he thought, it had to be tonight.

Just then two men arrived at the edge of the pond next to the bushes, both clad all in black. One whispered to the other, "Have you seen anything?"

The other answered, "Nope. Saw him enter the park but lost him after that."

"He will run out of places to hide soon enough. He is not going to see another sunrise."

"Sure isn't. You stay here. I am going to look around and see if can flush him out for you. And watch yourself.

This guy held his own with Randar tonight."

With that, one of his would be assassins crept away. He had to get out of this park. Silently Harcourt crawled from the bushes towards the assassin left behind. He slipped his arm around the man's throat and covered his mouth while dragging him to the ground. The assassin struggled but the thief held him tight. Harcourt then stuck a poisoned needle into the man's neck and did not let go until the assassin drifted away into unconsciousness. The thief dragged the sleeping man into the bushes and sped off.

Harcourt vaulted a low iron fence that surrounded the park and felt a sudden sting in his right leg. When the thief landed his leg gave out and he tumbled to the cobblestone street. He looked down to see a small crossbow bolt lodged in his leg and in the distance another assassin was dropping down out of a park tree. *Hell of a shot* he thought, and he was a moving target too.

Wasting no time, he gritted his teeth, pulled the bolt from his leg, then got to his feet. Harcourt drew his remaining dagger and hurled it with precise accuracy at the charging assassin's upper left thigh. The assassin went down in obvious pain but did not shout out or make any sound at all. He knew that a good assassin is trained to remain silent, even under excruciating pain. Seems the Guild had sent out their best tonight.

Harcourt hobbled down the street as quickly as his wounded leg allowed. He tore off a strip from his cloak and tied it tightly around his leg to staunch the flow of blood. This situation had just gotten worse, which he grimly thought was not possible. He was now weaponless and could no longer run. His next encounter was most likely going to be his last.

He was unfamiliar with the street he was on but caught sight of a portly man leaving a tavern. Glancing up he read the sign that said "The Last Stop." *How fitting*, he thought. The thief did not have any coins to spend, but he had to get off the street and think of a plan. A pair of city guards appeared from a corner not far away and stared at the thief. One of them called out, "Excuse me, sir. We would like a word with you."

Pretending that he did not hear them, Harcourt quickly entered the tavern and desperately scanned the main room for a way out. It was very late and the tavern was nearly empty save for a few people sitting in dark booths. The grey-haired man at the bar was startled awake by the thief's entrance. He had dozed off with his head resting in his palms. Surprised by the appearance of a man who had obviously been in some kind of fight, he asked, "Uh, are you looking for someone?"

"Well..I...ahhh....," Harcourt was at a loss for words. He was wounded and exhausted and just could not think fast enough.

"Ah my good man, you finally made it," called an elderly gentlemen sitting alone in a dark booth. "I was beginning to think you wouldn't show. Come on and take a seat."

The thief eyed the man suspiciously, but really had no choice but to play along. Perhaps the old man could not see very well and mistook him for someone else. Harcourt did his best to walk over to the booth without too much of a limp and sat down across the table from the old man. Before he had a chance to say anything, the two guards entered. They spotted Harcourt and walked over. The taller of the two spoke.

"Didn't you hear us calling? We'd like a word with you."

The elderly man noticed the worried expression that crossed the thief's face, then said, "Ahem, good gentlemen. My nephew here has travelled five days and is a little exhausted at the moment. You'll have to excuse him."

The guard's face turned red when he realized who the speaker was.

"Begging your pardon, sir, I had no idea he was with you. There has been strange activity about tonight."

The guards nodded their heads to the old man and turned to leave. Harcourt spoke up. "You might want to check out the park. I noticed some suspicious characters lurking around when I passed by."

"Thank you, sir," the taller guard replied and they rushed back out into the night.

For a long moment, Harcourt and the old man sat in silence sizing one another up. Harcourt was grateful for the help but could not figure out why this stranger would have done that for him. In his experience, people only helped when they wanted something from you. As far as he could tell, he did not recognize the man. He looked to be in his seventies and was dressed in the finest blue shirt Harcourt had ever seen. A thick gold chain hung from his neck and on his left hand he wore three bejeweled gold rings. The thief could not see his other hand but imagined more rings there as well. Whoever this person was, he was extremely wealthy, that was evident.

The old man finally broke the silence. "I take it you must have tangled with these suspicious characters lurking in the park?"

"Perhaps I did," Harcourt replied feeling blood running down his leg again. "I'd like to thank you for covering for me. Why did you?"

"You looked like someone in need of help and I was lonely this night. I could use the company," the man replied.

"Well, unfortunately I cannot stay long. If you don't mind, I just need to rewrap my leg here. I caught it on the park fence while trying to elude those bandits," Harcourt said.

"By all means, go ahead. I don't want you bleeding to death at my table. But I insist you stay awhile. What are you drinking?"

"I am afraid those evil men in the park have robbed me of all my coins so I won't be imposing on you for long," Harcourt said, wiping blood from his leg and wrapping it again with a fresh strip from his cloak. By all the gods, it hurt.

"Nonsense. Filbur, bring us over a bottle of Andollian whiskey. And not that ten-year old vintage you tried to sell me earlier, I want the fifty-year old bottle," the old man said to the barkeep who had almost dozed off again.

Fifty-year-old Andollian whiskey? That bottle was worth more than all the coin Harcourt had ever owned put together. "You really don't understand. It's not that I am ungrateful but I really need to go. Truth is, I need to leave the city before the sun rises."

"Why? Are you a vampire?" the old man chuckled. "You are in no shape to leave the city tonight."

"Agreed, but I've no choice in the matter," the thief replied.

"Now this sounds like an intriguing tale. You'll have to tell me all about it over a drink."

Filbur brought over the bottle and two glasses, then returned to the bar to shut his eyes. Harcourt sighed. "I am sure it would be an exciting tale to one such as you. I don't imagine you've ever stepped foot in the south district before. I've made some powerful enemies tonight and it's time I leave Stonewood for good."

"Crossed the Thieves Guild have you?" the man inquired.

Harcourt narrowed his eyes in suspicion. He suddenly got the feeling this old man was not the pampered noble he first mistook him for.

"I am sorry, I didn't catch your name."

"Warden," the old man said. "Warden Smalldain."

Harcourt laughed out loud. He was glad he had not taken a mouthful of the whiskey yet or he would have risked spitting it all over the table. "That's funny. Did anyone ever tell you that you have the same name as Warden Smalldain, the One-Handed Bandit? The most famous thief in Stonewood?"

The old man smiled and lifted up his right arm, which was missing a hand. "I generally don't use my real name with most people."

Harcourt's jaw dropped open in absolute shock. He was speechless. He was sitting across the table from a living legend. Well, except that nobody knew he was still living. Everyone in Stonewood, from the beggars right on up to the King himself, knew of the One-Handed Bandit. The man had robbed the city blind for decades and was never caught. Then about fifteen years ago, he vanished and his crime spree ended. Rumors said that he had died.

Every thief young and old idolized the man but nobody had ever duplicated his success. It was even told that he was so skilled, he had stolen the King's favorite jewels from the King's own bedchamber in the castle. Many folk considered that tale to be just that, a tale, but people could not deny that the King no longer wore those same jewels. "This is unbelievable," Harcourt said. "Everyone thinks you are dead."

"Makes life easier for me," Warden replied. "I am getting too old to keep evading bounty hunters and treasure seekers after my fortune."

"I am assuming those guards that were just here do not know you as Warden Smalldain then," Harcourt reasoned.

Warden smiled a warm smile. "Surely not. They know me as Lord Erigol, a wealthy nobleman from the far south who comes here on business."

Harcourt could still not believe he was sitting here with the One-Handed Bandit. Then he asked, "Meaning no disrespect, but how is it that I have two hands and can barely scrape together a couple of copper coins for a meal, and you have only one hand and became the most successful thief that ever lived? How?"

Warden chuckled and took a sip of his whiskey with his one good hand, motioning for the other thief to drink up too. "Looks can be deceiving. If there is one bit of knowledge I can pass on, it is that you should never believe everything you see," he said cryptically. "Now what is your name?"

"Harcourt."

"Harcourt what?"

"Just Harcourt. I don't have a last name, or at least I

don't remember what it is," he replied, taking a sip of the finest drink to ever touch his lips.

Since this could be his last night, he might as well indulge. Surprisingly, he found that it did not taste all that different from other whiskies he had drunk. Wealthy people were mad, he thought, to spend this kind of gold. "I never knew my mother, and my father died when I was very young," he continued.

"So what brings you here tonight, Harcourt? To this quiet little tavern so far from the south district?" Warden asked.

The younger thief felt that he had nothing more to lose tonight and so proceeded to tell Warden an abbreviated version of his relationship with the Guild and the events that led him to the tavern.

"So there you have it. I must leave the city for good or the Guild kills me. You must have led the Guild at one time, did you?"

The old thief shook his head. "I was never a member either."

"But how is that? How did they let you live?" Harcourt asked.

"Don't think they didn't try to catch me, but they can't kill what they can't catch. The Guild and the city tried for thirty years to find me, to no avail," Warden said.

Harcourt could not believe that. "I know Stonewood is a big city, but how is that possible? The Guild has eyes everywhere and there cannot be too many wealthy one-handed people around."

"They first have to know what they are looking for."

Harcourt waited for him to continue but that was all he said. Another cryptic answer. Harcourt really needed to get out of the city soon but he found that he did not want to leave the table. The two sat in silence for a few moments sipping their drinks, then the younger thief asked, "What's it like to be wealthy?"

Warden paused, then said, "Lonely." After another sip, he continued. "You see, I was a greedy man having no time for anyone but myself. I have shared the company of many in my time, but they were people attracted to my wealth, not me. I have lived a happy and exciting life, don't get me wrong, but I am lonely in my old age."

There was another long moment of silence before Warden asked, "Tell me, Harcourt. If you were to stumble across a dragon's treasure horde, what would you do?"

Harcourt chuckled. "Everyone knows that there is no such thing as dragons."

"Not all myths are myths, my young friend. The world is a vast place full of strange and wondrous things," Warden said. "But forget about that then, let's use something else. Let's say that you stole the duke's gold tonight. What would you have done with it?"

"Firstly, I would have Jalanna, the woman I love, healed of a certain condition she has. A priest in the city claimed that he could do it, but only after a five thousand gold piece donation is made. That was the whole reason for my attempt on the duke's gold. After that? Hmmm. I guess I've never really given much thought to what I'd do after that. I've never really imagined reaching my first goal," Harcourt answered.

"She loves you? This Jalanna?" the old man asked.

"Yes. I don't know why she does, but she does. Or did. I have messed it all up," the thief suddenly felt very sad. "I don't suppose I shall ever see her again now."

Warden gave a warm smile. "That's what I was missing from my life. This Jalanna loves you when you have nothing to give save yourself. I am jealous of that."

"The One-Handed Bandit is jealous of me?" Harcourt laughed. "You must have more gold than you can spend and you can have anything you want."

"Except for the love you share with Jalanna. I cannot buy that. When I was younger, I didn't care, but now I do. I will die a lonely old man. Wealthy? Yes. But lonely."

All that did was make Harcourt feel worse since Jalanna was lost to him now and he was most likely going to die the same way. "Harcourt, meet me outside the city in an hour. I too am leaving Stonewood for good and had come in here for my *last stop* as the sign reads. I have something I'd like to give you."

"Well you see," Harcourt said, "that's my problem. I am not sure how I will get out of the city. Guards and Guild assassins alike are looking for me."

Warden smiled again. "That is no longer a problem. In the cellar of this fine establishment, you'll find a tunnel leading outside the city. I will let them know here that you are welcome to use it. Take one of the lanterns hanging on the wall down there, you'll need it. I'll follow shortly and meet you by the large oak in an hour."

Harcourt felt a giant weight lift from his shoulders. Perhaps this was just prolonging his eventual death but he would take any aid he could get.

"What could you want to give me? You've already done enough to help."

"Just a parting gift. Something I won't be needing any longer."

CHAPTER 11

Harcourt sat with his back against a large oak tree about a half mile outside of Stonewood. He was far from any of the main roads and all he could hear was the sound of the crickets chirping. He hoped Warden would hurry up, it was almost dawn and he needed to put as much distance between himself and the city as possible. His cloak was now destroyed as he cleaned and redressed his wounds. He was not sure how long it would take him in his current state to walk to the next town but he had little choice in the matter. Fortunately, he had filled a water skin and found some bread in the cellar that he brought along with him. He left the lantern down in the tunnel so as not to attract attention.

Looking back at the wooden door that covered the tunnel's entrance, he wondered what other secrets laid beneath the city. Just then the door flipped open and out climbed a young man with a thick black beard. It was not Warden as the thief had expected. He instinctively reached for his daggers but of course they were not there. He flew to his feet thinking something must have gone wrong. The Guild must have tracked him here.

"Who are you? Speak quickly," the thief demanded.

"It's your friend, Warden. Don't you recognize me?" the man said, smiling ear to ear.

Harcourt was exhausted and in pain. He was not in the mood for another fight. This man looked to be about twenty, and had two hands. He could not see any visible weapons but that did not mean the man was unarmed. "I am too tired for games. Where is Warden?"

"But I am Warden."

"And I am not in the mood for games I just said. You are not Warden."

"Harcourt, I thought I told you earlier not to believe everything you see. That things are not always what they appear to be," the bearded man said.

The thief was now very confused. Those were Warden's words, and the man even had Warden's voice. But how? Seeing the thief's obvious confusion, the man laughed out loud. He whispered something under his breath, then to Harcourt's utter shock, he peeled away his face. Peeled away his face??? The form of the bearded man shrank slightly into the fragile frame of an old man, and there stood the Warden that Harcourt had met earlier. Grey-haired, beardless, and missing his right hand. Harcourt just stared. *The old thief must have drugged the whiskey,* he thought, *and I am hallucinating. Maybe this was all a trap set by the Guild!?*

Warden sensed the other thief's thoughts and laughed again. "Easy my boy, you are in no danger here. This is the gift I spoke of. Here, I want you to have this," he said tossing over......his face.

Harcourt jumped back letting the "face" fall to the grass in front of him. He had no desire to touch whatever that was. "What did you put in the whiskey?" he asked.

"Nothing at all," Warden replied. "You are not hallucinating."

"Well, I just saw a different person standing there a moment ago. Your face and your body just changed right before my eyes. The only time I've ever seen anything as crazy was when I had eaten some wild mushrooms. So you've done something to me, this I know."

"It was magic, my boy," Warden stated.

"There is no such thing as magic," Harcourt countered.

"Are you so sure?" Warden asked raising an eyebrow.

"Of course I am. Magic is what I tell the kids I can do when I make coins appear out of thin air. Magic is when I mysteriously find the playing card that someone else was thinking of, but did not tell me. None of that is real magic though, there is a trick to it all," Harcourt answered.

"There is no trick here my young friend. Just magic. Real magic. I told you earlier the world is a vast place filled with many wondrous things. That mask there, is one of those wondrous things. Don't ask how it does what it does. It just does it," Warden said laughing, then repeated, "Just magic."

Harcourt did not know what to make of all this. He knew what he saw and he did feel fine. He did not feel drunk or drugged. He was tired but his head was still clear. The thief flipped the "mask" over with the toe of his boot and a blank, featureless, flesh colored face stared back up at him. It looked similar to a party mask, like the skull-faced one he wore earlier.

"Go on, pick it up," Warden implored. "We don't have all morning."

Harcourt knelt down and grimaced as a sharp pain shot through his injured leg. He reached out to touch the mask then stopped short. "Go on, would you. It's not going to bite," he heard Warden urge.

The thief picked up the mask and found it to be as light as a feather. It felt hard but he could not quite guess the material. He inspected both sides closely and found no visible markings. Wait. He did find something. Some very tiny symbols etched into the back where the mouth was. They were not like any symbols he had ever seen before.

"It's from the far east."

"Pardon?" Harcourt said looking puzzled.

"The writing there, the symbols. They are from the far east," Warden explained, walking over to stand next to the thief. "Translated it says, Argon Dol."

"What's Argon Dol?"

"The command words."

"Command words for what?"

"To release the mask."

"Release the mask from what?"

"Ok, ok, slow down here," Warden waved his hands in the air. "You hold the mask to your face and the magic within binds it to your skin. In a sense, it becomes your face. Then you concentrate on how you wish to look, and the magic alters your appearance. Creates an illusion if you will. You can alter your hair color or length, your eye color, give scars, remove scars, add or remove facial hair. When you wish to remove the mask, you speak the command words, then pull it off."

"I saw your body change as well."

Warden nodded. "Yes, you can give the illusion of a slightly different body but not by too much. A little heavier or a little skinnier. A little taller or a little shorter. Though creating the illusion of bigger muscles will not make you stronger. And appearing taller does not actually make you taller, it's just the illusion created by the mask."

"You aren't kidding, are you?" Harcourt asked having a difficult time wrapping his head around the notion of actual magic.

"You saw it for yourself," Warden said.

"So this is how nobody could ever catch you? All those years you were wearing other faces?" Harcourt asked amazed.

"Now you know the secret of the One-Handed Bandit. You and I alone are the only ones who know this. You see Harcourt, I never really was a good thief. After all, I lost my hand in a middle eastern city for pickpocketing. It was this mask that made me a legend. It comes in quite handy as you can imagine. But I was told by a wise magician long ago, not to wear it for more than three days at a time."

"Or else what?" Harcourt inquired.

"Don't know. I was told not to and I listened."

"Why are you giving this to me? You don't even know me. This must be worth a King's ransom," Harcourt asked.

"Harcourt, like you I am a thief. I've spent my entire life taking things that did not belong to me. So this is me finally giving something back. And I am not just giving someone the mask, I am saving a life. Two actually, because I don't want your Jalanna dying of a broken heart because you are gone. Use the mask to get her healed, my boy, and live a happy life together. Don't end up lonely like me. I am old, my thieving days are over. The mask is of no more use to me," Warden said, patting the thief on the shoulder.

"May I ask where you found this treasure?"

Warden began walking away. "That, my boy, is a tale for another time. We both should be moving along now."

"Where are you going?" the younger thief asked.

"To Suldarn, a beautiful coastal city in the far south. I have a mansion there overlooking the ocean. You should come visit me sometime and we can trade stories. I am too old to be travelling back and forth now. I will spend the rest of my days there, I shall not be returning to Stonewood again." Warden stopped and turned back. "Use this tunnel whenever you like, just leave a tip for Filbur when you do. Filbur is an old smuggler and can be trusted. He has no affiliation with the Guild and they know nothing of the tunnel. Oh, one more thing before I depart," Warden threw Harcourt a set of keys. "That is for forty-two Birkdale Road. Lord Erigol has been renting the place for his visits to Stonewood. You can say that you are my business partner and will now be my Stonewood representative. Rent is due in a few weeks, and I trust by that time you'll have enough to cover it."

"I really don't know how to thank you for everything," Harcourt said.

Warden just waved the comment away and said, "Practice using the mask for awhile first until you are comfortable with it. It is going to take some getting used to."

The sound of horses could be heard from over a nearby hill.

"Ah," Warden said. "My escort awaits. Farewell my young friend. Wish Jalanna well for me." Then the old thief closed his eyes and held his fingers to his temples as if in deep concentration. "Wait. I see something, it's the future. I see you are going to be a more famous thief than the One-Handed Bandit."

Warden winked at the thief and then disappeared over the hill. Harcourt stood like a statue staring down at the mask in his hands long after the sun had risen.

CHAPTER 12

Lord Mornay picked up the pace as rain started to fall in a light drizzle. He pulled the hood of his expensive forest green cloak up over his head and adjusted the large leather satchel he carried on his shoulder so he could shield it with his cloak. It had been a long night and he looked forward to getting home and relaxing. Perhaps he would even slip in a drink to help unwind before getting some sleep, he thought.

He turned onto his quiet street and opened the iron gate that led up to his front door. Mornay lived in a cozy little stone bungalow in the upper west district. A fence surrounded his house but his gate, always unlocked, was more for decoration. His front door, however, was a different story. It took three separate keys to open the door and each locking mechanism was highly-sophisticated. The Lord was paranoid about thieves and went to great lengths to secure his home against them. He hurried into his house as the rain began to fall much harder.

His living room was dark but the man had little trouble navigating his way around until he managed to light a lantern. The tired man hung up his wet cloak and placed the satchel on a small table. Lord Mornay stopped in front of a mirror to inspect his blood-shot eyes. He had bright green eyes that stood out, but they were in desperate need of sleep. The lord was in his late thirties and was considered a handsome man. Some speculated as to why he was not married yet, but he was simply a busy man. Always on the go.

Mornay leaned in closer, looked deeper into the reflection of himself and just shook his head. He whispered the words, "Argon Dol" and then peeled away his face.

A month had gone by since Harcourt had that fateful meeting with Warden, and he still could not get used to looking into the mirror and having someone else stare back at him. The illusion was flawless. Like Warden, he could not even begin to fathom what made it work, but it worked. Harcourt often wondered that if magic created this mask, then what other wondrous things were out there? Were there other masks? Were other people walking around wearing different faces, just as he was? Or was this it, a one of a kind treasure?

The thief knew the night he went out to steal the duke's gold that things would never be the same again, but this he could never have imagined. In the span of a day, his life was completely altered. He woke up that morning in his south district alley, and slept the next day in this house that was now his. His house!

It took some time before he could believe it, that it was not some crazy dream or mushroom-induced hallucination. He had stared at the mask for a whole day before getting the courage to put it on. It did take some time before he was able to properly use it. Now he had it down. Harcourt could walk into an alley wearing one face, and come out the other end with a different face.

The face he wore most often was that of his creation, Lord Mornay. Lord Mornay was ostensibly a nobleman from the south, and business partner to Lord Erigol. Erigol had returned south and Mornay took over his import/export business in Stonewood - well, mostly export. Harcourt exported stolen goods to Filbur's smuggler contacts. The thief had just returned from one such transaction.

He opened the leather satchel and placed two hundred gold pieces worth of gold bars onto the table. The first few weeks, his hands trembled each time he handled the gold, but he had finally gotten used to being around so much of it. He no longer dropped any while counting it.

Harcourt wished Jalanna could be here counting it with him, sharing drinks and some laughs while they lounged on the comfortable sofa, living together in this house. The thief thought for her own safety though, that he should avoid her for now. It was best if everyone believed that Harcourt was gone. The Guild might still be looking for him and they would be watching Jalanna closely to see if he showed up. He had not even visited the south district since that bizarre night a month past. He was positive that the rumors were that he must have fled the city and was long gone. Many times he wondered what happened to Andil that night. His partner's disappearance was almost the end of him.

Harcourt walked over to the cabinet where he kept

bottles of some of the most expensive drinks in Stonewood. He did not indulge much, certainly not like he used to, but he poured himself a glass of very expensive shir, a liquor from the far east. The thief finally understood why the wealthy bought these kinds of drinks. It was not that they tasted any better than other brands, it was because they could.

He poured himself a glass, downed it quickly, stored the gold away in one of the hidden rooms below the house, then retired to his warm comfortable bed.

Harcourt had never before slept on a mattress in his entire life. For the first week, he slept on the floor beside the bed until he could get used to it. Now he could never go back to the cold ground. He never slept so well. The thief drifted off to sleep with thoughts of Jalanna.

*   *   *   *

"Jalanna?......Jalanna?"

The second time Wulfred called her name, she awoke from her daydream. "Table three needs more ale," her boss said.

He gave her a kind smile, he was not angry. Wulfred understood that she was not herself, she had not been for quite some time. She missed Harcourt. He was the only one she had ever loved and she knew he had loved her back. Jalanna possessed a gift for seeing into someone's soul, she got "feelings" about people which were almost always dead-on. Her mother had been a fortune teller with some minor mystical abilities, some of which were passed onto her daughter. Despite his tough exterior, Jalanna knew Harcourt had a pure heart, a gentle soul who had just been molded by his surroundings. She simply could not handle him disappearing all the time. It had been killing her inside. At least when he was locked up in the dungeon, she knew he would be coming back eventually. This time though, she was not so sure.

It had been just over a month now since she last saw him leaving the Den with Andil. They had not spoken that evening. Then she had heard something about a run-in with the Thieves Guild and the rumors claimed he was dead. It tore her up inside to hear that but she did not want to believe it was true. Now though, she was beginning to wonder.

Neither Andil nor Wulfred had seen or heard from him in all this time. His shack in the alley was abandoned. There was no sign of him and that was not like Harcourt, he had nowhere else to go. She would forgive him for everything if he would just walk through that tavern door, and she would give anything to be able to hug him once more.

Jalanna brought table three some more ale and there was the usual flirting by the drunk patrons. One even slapped her behind. It came with the job, she knew. She did receive good tips though, and that was surprising given the city's poorest folk drank here. At one time, every male that ever visited the Den, and some females, had tried to hit on her. That was before the great fire. Now all the regulars who knew what she looked like beneath her veil, kept their distance. A nod or a pity-filled hello was usually what she received now. The non-regulars, like the four men at table three, flirted because they did not know her. They saw a beautiful body with an exotic veil that revealed incredible eyes, but not the scars she went to great lengths to conceal. Once they caught a glimpse of those, they would avert their eyes in disgust like most everyone else.

Her mind wandered back to Harcourt. He never cared about the scars. She had expected him to leave her but he never did. He loved her for who she was, and not so much for how she looked. She desperately wanted to know where he was.

Jalanna passed by table three again and the ugliest of the quartet in a stained shirt grabbed ahold of her wrist. "Come 'ere, me pretty," he slurred.

She tried to break away but the man was too strong. "Please sir, I am busy working," she pleaded with him.

"Then just give 'ole Haig a kiss for now, then. We'll discuss the rest later."

His three companions roared with laughter at the spectacle of the woman trying to squirm away. Jalanna tried with all her might to get free but to no avail. He pulled her in closer, puckering his lips, then THUNK! Wulfred's great battle axe that hung on the wall slammed into the center of the table. Everyone jumped and nearly fell from their seats.

"She said she was busy," the former mercenary said with a low growl as the entire tavern went silent. "Time to leave."

One of Haig's friends, a scrawny weasel of a man, spoke up. "Leave? You should watch how you speak to us. Now be a good lad and bring us some more to drink."

"I will speak to you however I wish," Wulfred growled.

"Perhaps you would change that tone if you knew who we worked for," the weasely man said arrogantly.

"I don't care if you work for King Stonewood,"

Wulfred said threateningly, "This is my place and you play by my rules. Now leave, you are no longer welcome here."

The four men looked furious but said not another word as they rose from the table and left.

"I am sorry you lost customers Wulfred," Jalanna said.

"Didn't want them here anyways. Why don't you go take a break?" he said, dislodging his axe from the table and returning to the bar.

"No thanks, I think I'd rather keep working."

"In that case, how about bringing me some ale then," said a man seated by himself behind her.

Jalanna did not remember him coming in, nor had she ever seen him before. "I am sorry sir, I hope you weren't waiting too long?"

"No worries, my dear. I think you were, ummm, tied up a moment ago when I arrived," the man replied.

Jalanna blushed. "You'll have to excuse that situation, Wulfred rarely takes his axe off the wall. It's a pretty safe place to drink. So just an ale then?"

"Yes please, just an ale, and a moment of your time," he smiled. "I could not help noticing your eyes. You are not from Stonewood, are you?"

"Very observant, I see. No, I am not from here. My family and I came from a distant land."

"I am not from around here either. Just passing through actually. I noticed you looked nothing like the locals here. You really stand out in a crowd."

Jalanna blushed and smiled from under her veil and went to retrieve the man's drink. When she returned she asked, "So what do you do that brings you through here?"

The man took a mouthful of ale first, obviously very

thirsty, then replied. "I am a mercenary for hire. Always moving around and looking for work."

Jalanna could believe that. He did look quite strong and wore an impressive-looking sword. He was rugged-looking but handsome.

"Well it was nice to meet you, but I should see to my other tables," she said.

"Wait. When are you off work? I could use a tour of the city from someone who knows their way around. Someone beautiful is even better," the mercenary said.

"I am sorry. I am flattered but I would not make very good company. And it's not safe to walk around the city too late at night," Jalanna replied.

"Maybe tomorrow then? Before your shift? You might feel better by then."

"I doubt that very much. I have to decline, I am sorry."

"Is it something I said?" the man wondered.

"Not at all. Truth is, sir, my heart belongs to someone and I am very worried for this person right now. It's a long story. Shout if you need a refill, my name is Jalanna."

Jalanna went back to waiting on the other tables and the mercenary slowly finished off his mug of ale. The next time she passed by, he asked, "What do I owe you?"

"Five copper sir."

He dropped a gold coin on the table and said, "I don't have any change so just give that to Wulfred."

"But I can make change sir, it's no problem."

"No, don't trouble yourself . Best drink I have had in awhile. The scenery makes all the difference. And this is for you," the mercenary said, putting a fifty gold piece coin on the table and sliding it over closer to her.

Jalanna's eyes nearly bulged from her head. "Um, um that is a bit much, sir," she stammered.

"Don't be foolish, my time here was worth that and more," he replied, getting up to leave.

"I thank you very much, you are very kind," Jalanna said. "But beware carrying that kind of coin around here."

"Thanks for the advice. And don't worry about whatever is troubling you. I have a feeling it will all work out," the mercenary said, then left the Den.

Jalanna stood for a moment holding the coin in disbelief. She had a strange feeling that she had met that mercenary somewhere before, she just could not place him.

*   *   *   *

After the mercenary left the Ogre's Den, he crossed the street and entered an empty alley. Once he was sure he was alone, he sat on the ground and leaned his back against a building wall. He whispered the words, "Argon Dol" and removed his face. Harcourt sat there running over the whole encounter with Jalanna in his mind. He badly wished he could have told her it was him. He wanted to reach out and touch her. Soon though, he thought. He had already raised half of the five thousand gold pieces that he needed. Harcourt was already a highly-skilled thief and combined with the mask, he was confident that he would have the rest very soon.

The thief knew his little crime spree was starting to get noticed and the Guild would be scrambling around to find out who was behind it and put a stop to it. He was already noticing businesses and homes beefing up their security.

Harcourt was surprised not to see Andil at the Den this evening. He was hoping his friend was alright. The thief figured it was about time to head back north. He hated the thought of leaving without Jalanna, but he knew she was in good hands with Wulfred until he had everything ready.

Harcourt heard two people enter the alley from the far end. Not having enough time to put the mask back on, he hid his face in his knees, appearing to be sick from too much to drink. Then he heard a young girl's voice. A scared voice. "Please don't hurt me," the girl pleaded.

"It's not going to hurt, much," said a man who held her roughly.

The girl tried to scream out but he clamped a meaty hand over her mouth. His voice sounded familiar to the thief. Harcourt peeked over and noticed it was the same trouble-maker that grabbed Jalanna in the Den. He was about to enter that altercation but Wulfred beat him to it. It seemed this man found it difficult to keep his hands to himself.

Harcourt tucked the mask under his shirt and drew one of his shiny new razor-sharp daggers. The thief made not a sound as he walked towards the pair. Too focused on the struggling young girl, the man never noticed the thief until Harcourt cleared his throat directly behind him. The man known as Haig did not even turn around. "Bugger off. You can have her when I am finished."

"Actually," Harcourt replied, "I am more interested in you, big boy."

The thief kicked Haig hard in the back of one knee buckling him, then brought his elbow across to connect with the back of the man's head. Momentarily blinded and dazed, Haig released the girl. Using one of Dornell's tactics, Harcourt twisted Haig's left arm around behind his back and lifted up slightly causing a squeal of pain to escape from the grotesque man. He could break his arm easily with this hold. "Haven't you learned that no means no, my ugly friend?" Harcourt taunted.

"You are gonna regret this," Haig spat. "Just for this, I am gonna gut the girl."

The young girl standing nearby trembled and paled with fright. Harcourt lifted the man's arm up even higher, making him grunt.

"How about you never touch a girl from around here again? I don't want to hear that you even laid one finger on another girl, Haig. In fact, starting tonight, I am going to take a finger from you for each girl you touch."

Harcourt, already holding the man's left wrist in place, took his dagger and sliced off a finger. Haig howled in pain and dropped to his knees. Harcourt let him go and kicked him over onto the ground. Haig rolled around shrieking and clutching his wounded hand, blood spurting all over.

"Remember what I said," Harcourt threatened. "Touch another girl and lose another finger." He turned to the girl, "Come on, I'll walk you to your home."

As the two left Haig wailing, a large rat emerged from the shadows of the alley and made off with the severed digit. Harcourt and the girl walked away at a swift pace, and the thief was careful to keep his head down whenever anyone passed them by. He could not risk being recognized. "Where do you live?" he asked.

"Don't you remember? I live at the orphanage. And

you are Harcourt," the girl answered, still shaken up.

Harcourt stared at the girl but there was no recognition. She was a pretty little thing with long brown hair, but young. Just a teenager. "What is your name?"

The girl gave a disappointed sigh. "You've asked me that every time we've met."

"Sorry, girl. I've lost a lot of my life and my memories to the drink. Wicked stuff. I apologize, but I don't recall you."

"Krestina," she said, sounding heartbroken.

"Well, Krestina, I can promise I will remember your name the next time I see that pretty face of yours."

That seemed to brighten her mood and made her blush. "Thank you so much for saving me from that monster. I really thought my life was over tonight," Krestina said.

"It was my pleasure. You were just lucky that I was in the neighborhood," Harcourt replied.

"I don't believe in luck. You were meant to save me tonight."

"I don't know about that. I've plenty of luck, though most of it's bad. Just be thankful you possess some of the good kind," he said.

"No. There is more to it than that, I think. There has to be," she reasoned.

The rest of their walk passed uneventfully. Harcourt stopped when the orphanage came into view. "When can I see you again, Harcourt? Tomorrow?" Krestina asked.

"I am afraid I won't be around here very often. You see, some very bad people are looking for me. It's not safe for you to be seen with me," Harcourt replied.

"I don't care about that. It's never safe around here

anyways," she countered.

The thief could see a certain sparkle in the young girl's eyes. "Krestina, how old are you?"

"I am not a little girl anymore. I will be seventeen soon."

The thief laughed at that. "You are right, you are not a little girl anymore, but still you are a lot younger than me. And it is very dangerous to be seen with me these days. We'll run into each other again soon, I am sure." As Krestina began to pout, he continued. "I have an important favor to ask of you. Are you up for it?"

That brightened her mood a little. "Of course, anything for you."

Harcourt pulled out a coin purse and dropped it into Krestina's hands. It was heavy. "Alright, there is a lot of gold in there. I need you to take that to Dahleene. Just say it's from an old friend and there is more on the way. Also, you must not mention to anyone that you have seen me tonight. Can you do this for me?"

Her hands trembled at the thought of holding so much gold. "Y-y-yes, I can do it."

Harcourt messed her hair. "Good girl. And this one is all for you, ok?" he handed her a fifty-piece gold coin. "You buy yourself some nice new clothes with that, maybe some jewelry. But don't tell anyone."

Krestina was speechless, she could not believe her eyes. Then the thief added, "Don't mind the teeth marks on the coin. Somewhere in that coin's history, someone must not have believed it was real gold."

Krestina pulled on his shirt and Harcourt leaned over. She gave the thief a kiss on the cheek, blushed, and ran off to the orphanage on her important mission.

Harcourt shook his head chuckling to himself. Before heading back to his house, he made one more stop. He found old Kan sound asleep on a street corner, and filled his cup with coins.

CHAPTER 13

"So we have no idea who is behind all these thefts? Is that what you are all telling me?" Trascar asked angrily.

Randar, Serdic, and a weasely man with dark eyes named Zenod, sat across from the Guild leader in his private office. None of them responded to his last question.

"The Guild is taking all the blame of course, but we are getting none of the coin," he continued. "They have all been big jobs, carried out flawlessly. No witnesses. No clues. Whoever is behind this is good. My guess would be one of ours doing side jobs. But who?"

Serdic finally spoke. "That is a lot of coin and merchandise to hide and I have not seen any of it on the market. If it's being moved around, they are not using Guild contacts or I would know."

"The King is quite angry. He has doubled night patrols making our own jobs increasingly difficult. I've had to cancel three this week," the weasely Zenod said.

"So we are losing gold while some renegade is piling

it high?" Trascar looked ready to explode. "I can't have this! I want this man hung from the center of the market square for all to see."

"I'll catch him and make a good example of him," Randar said.

"Oh? You will, huh? Like you made a good example of that loser, Harcourt? And how's that search going? Coming up on two months yet?" Trascar fumed. "If we cannot even catch that lowlife scum, how are we ever going to catch this skilled thief?"

"It shouldn't take too long," Serdic answered. "It's not like we are dealing with the One-Handed Bandit here. This guy is bound to make a mistake."

"Get out, all of you. I don't want to see any of your faces here until you have some good news for a change," Trascar had had enough. "Zenod, tell Feylane to come in here if she is still out there playing cards."

The three men rose and left the office. Trascar was still fuming inside when the beautiful assassin Feylane, her hair a chestnut brown, entered and shut the door behind her. "You said one of your agents injured Harcourt in the park that night he was chased, didn't you?" the Guild leader asked.

"Yes, he did. Put a crossbow bolt in his leg," she replied.

"Yet the man still got away."

"Yes, but he's a clever..."

Trascar cut her off. "What's his name? Your agent?"

"Dargat."

"I want Dargat dead by tomorrow. I will not tolerate failure. Do you understand?"

"Yes sir."

*　　*　　*　　*

Jalanna was exhausted; it had been a long night. She had been doing double shifts lately for the extra coins, and to help Wulfred out while he searched for another serving girl. The added hours and that generous tip from the mysterious mercenary was just what she needed to finally get her own little one-room apartment on Snake Street. It was about time she moved out of the Ogre's Den attic she shared with the other barmaids, but she would always be grateful to Wulfred for allowing her to stay there.

She did not like the walk home though, at this hour. The area around Snake Street was a dangerous neighborhood, but then the whole of the south district was one big dangerous neighborhood. She did know a lot of the folk around here, as they frequented the Den, but she touched the hilt of the dagger stuck in her belt for reassurance.

The dagger was fairly dull and the blade rusted, but it was still better than not having one at all. The dagger had belonged to Harcourt and that was the real reason she hung onto it. She found it by the side of a road the day after he was released from the dungeon. He must have been drunk as usual and dropped it. She had planned to give it back to him, but then they had their fight. The dagger had been with her ever since.

Jalanna unlocked the door to her apartment and entered the dark room. She shut the door quickly behind her and reached for the lantern she kept on a nearby shelf. It was not there. She jumped as the room was suddenly illuminated. A man sat in a chair next to her bed holding the lantern.

"Looking for this?" he said.

Jalanna did not personally know the man, but she knew of him. Randar. "Working long hours lately, eh?" he asked, but she did not answer.

Her hand crept closer to the dagger hilt. "Ah, ah. I wouldn't even dream of pulling a weapon if I were you," the Guild enforcer said with an evil smile.

She dropped her hands to her sides, doing her best to appear calm. "What do you want?" she asked, fighting back the tremble in her voice.

"Where's your boyfriend?" he got right to the point.

"I don't have a boyfriend."

"Don't play stupid with me," he said, standing up. "Where's that loser Harcourt hiding out these days?"

"I wouldn't know," she answered truthfully. "We had a fight some time ago and I haven't seen him since. Rumors say you guys killed him."

Her heart raced as the enforcer walked over and touched her cheek with the blade of a cruel-looking knife. "It wouldn't be good to lie to me, you know," Randar stared into her eyes. "And we have no reason to kill him. I just want to talk to him. I have a job for someone of his talents."

Jalanna fought hard to remain composed. "I told you the truth. I don't know where he is."

Randar was an expert at interrogation; he knew when someone was lying. This woman was telling the truth. One of his men swore he had seen Harcourt recently in the south district and Randar was positive he would have visited Jalanna. He figured now that he was wrong with that assumption.

"Nice place you have here. Must be difficult for a serving wench to afford on her own. Maybe I'll drop by again soon. Ta ta."

As soon as the thug disappeared into the night, Jalanna let out a huge breath of air that she had been holding, and slumped to the floor sobbing, her back against the door. As she wept, she thought of one positive thing that came from the encounter; Harcourt was still alive. If Randar was looking for him, then he must be alive.

"Harcourt, where are you?" she whispered.

*   *   *   *

The security guard approached the front gate of Kalandra Manor and gave a salute to the guard already on duty with a matching uniform. "Good evening."

"I wouldn't know," the gate watchman grumbled. "I've been stuck here all night. What are you doing here? There are already six of us working tonight."

"With Lady Kalandra away for the next few days, she wanted more security at night. I think there is one more guy coming as well."

The gate watchman unlocked the gate and pulled it open. "Alright, get in here then. I suppose the Lady is getting paranoid with all those recent burglaries going on. Belton is around back I believe, he can give you your duties."

The guard nodded and entered the manor grounds. Kalandra Manor was a very large, three-story mansion with a vast front lawn littered with stone fountains and statues depicting all sorts of animals and cherubs. The Lady of the house married into a wealthy noble family, but her husband had died several years past. By all accounts, the Lady was not too upset by this because it gave her more time to shop. And she loved to shop. Currently, she was away on a vacation.

The guard walked around the right side of the house and nodded to another guard he passed doing his perimeter patrol. Instead of going around the back to find Belton, the guard found a side door and tried the handle. It was locked. Glancing about, he slid two small strips of metal into the keyhole, played around with them, and then was rewarded with a familiar click. The guard slipped into the house, locking the door behind him.

He stood in the servants' hallway which would lead to the kitchen, he figured. A door to his right opened and out walked an elderly member of the cleaning staff carrying a broom. The little man stopped and looked at the guard quizzically. Guessing the man's thoughts, the guard said, "Ah, Belton said I should do an interior patrol."

"Someone just did an interior patrol. I thought it was every hour?" the old man said.

Thinking fast, the guard replied, "We are doubling up now. Can't be too careful these days with all the break-ins."

"Nobody would dare rob Lady Kalandra with all of you about," the cleaner said.

The guard just shrugged his shoulders. The cleaner wandered off and disappeared through another door. The guard entered the room the cleaner had just exited, a small room filled with cleaning supplies. Perfect, he thought. He undid his sword belt and dropped it to the floor, then stripped out of his guard's uniform. Underneath, he wore another layer of clothing, a very expensive set of matching black and blue pants and shirt. It was an outfit befitting a noble.

The dark-haired guard closed his eyes in concentration and his face became a blur. Seconds later, the man looked much younger and his hair was now golden in color. Harcourt pulled out a small mirror from a pocket to inspect his current disguise. Satisfied, he stuffed the guard's uniform and sword in the corner of the room underneath a pile of filthy rags. He was pleased to have bumped into the cleaner; now he knew he had about an hour before the next guard would do an interior patrol.

After some wandering around, the thief finally found his way to the grand staircase leading to the floors above. The house so far had been lavishly decorated. Paintings lined the walls of each hall, exquisitely-detailed sculptures were everywhere. Above the staircase hung the most elaborate chandelier he had yet seen. Lady Kalandra sure liked to spend he thought. He just hoped that she still had gold left to be found. His guess would be that she kept it all in her bedroom.

A tall and very thin man with graying hair dressed as a butler, appeared at the top of the stairs and stopped at the sight of Harcourt. He opened his mouth but the thief spoke first.

"There you are, finally! What does someone need to do to get fed around here?"

"And just who are you?" the butler asked.

"Who am I?? I am only Auntie Judith's favorite nephew, that's who. I would think that obvious. I was told to pop in and look in on the place while Auntie was on vacation. She doesn't trust the staff," Harcourt answered.

The butler stuck his nose in the air at the verbal jab.

In truth the thief had no idea if the Lady had a nephew, but he had learned from a drunk security guard the previous night that the Lady had a terrible temper and usually directed it at the staff.

"If I don't get something to eat soon, I shall have to tell Auntie her staff let me starve near to death."

Harcourt could tell the butler was angry, firstly, at being insulted, and secondly, for not being informed of the nephew's arrival. "Come on now, butler boy, get a move on. I want something meaty with some wine to wash it down with."

"The name is Normoon."

"Whatever. I am hungry. If I wait much longer, I shall pass out!" Harcourt shouted like a spoiled child.

The butler's face went red but to the man's credit, he kept his composure. He nodded to Harcourt and set off in the direction of the kitchen. When he was sure all was clear, the thief sprinted up the stairs. Judging from the veranda he saw from outside, Harcourt figured the Lady's bedroom was on the third floor facing west. He navigated his way to that spot and found two large oak double doors, locked, of course. Out came the lock picks and the thief went to work. The Lady really did not trust her staff; this lock was a good one, the expensive, sophisticated kind. Not good enough though, he thought, as he was rewarded with a click.

The bedroom was dark but there was enough moonlight shining in that the thief did not have to risk a candle. The room had many windows and a suspicious light source could be spotted by the guards outside. Harcourt scanned the large room and thought it might be the most elaborate he had been in. A gigantic four-poster bed, fur rugs, ornately-carved furniture, fireplace and more. The Lady spared no expense.

First, he searched the usual spots, her massive walk-in closet and all the dresser drawers. The woman had more shoes than he could count. The thief held no respect for people like this. Some of the kids in the south district wore no shoes at all and this woman could wear a different pair for every day of the year. She had not even raised a finger to earn this wealth, she married into it.

Harcourt guessed the Lady did not possess any imagination so he hopped on the bed and removed a portrait of her from the wall. He smiled as he stared at her secret safe. So predictable. The lock was even more sophisticated than the one on her door, but not a problem for a master thief.

The thief pulled his hands back quickly though, as he realized one other thing - it was trapped. Perhaps she did have an imagination after all, or more likely just paranoid. The thief could not tell what kind of trap it was but he could see what triggered it, inside the lock. With steady, practiced hands and patience, he managed to disarm it. The lock was defeated with not much effort shortly after.

Harcourt salivated at the collection of jewels he found inside the safe, especially the diamonds. Lady Kalandra was known for her diamonds. He scooped everything up and dropped it in what looked like a large white laundry sack. The jewels themselves were a great score, but where was her gold?

Counting on her predictability once again, the thief lifted up a bear skin rug at the foot of her bed and felt around for a loose floor board. He smiled from ear to ear as he lifted one of the loose panels and found a hole in the floor filled with gold coins and bars. Most likely, it was not even a fraction of her fortune, but it was more than enough for this job. If there was any more the thief would not be able to carry it out. He figured this haul might just give him what he needed to pay the priest for Jalanna's healing.

Harcourt arranged the room exactly as he had found it, even straightening the covers on the bed. There was only one exception. He took one of the Lady's vials of nail polish and painted horns and a devilish moustache on her self-portrait. He giggled to himself the entire time, trying to imagine her face when she saw it. It was childish he knew, but he could not resist.

Before he exited the room, he stuffed some of the Lady's clothes in the sack, covering the gold and jewels, then stripped out of his good clothes to reveal his last layer. Now he wore the uniform of one of the house's common staff members, such as one who might do laundry.

When the thief emerged into the hallway, he looked like an elderly man close to seventy and struggled to drag the laundry sack behind him. He got halfway down the last set of stairs when the butler burst into the foyer carrying a tray of food and looking frantic.

"You there, what's this about?" the butler said when he noticed the old man.

"Laundry," Harcourt replied.

"At this hour?" Normoon questioned. "Where is Andi?"

The thief pointed up the stairs. "If I were you, sonny, I would get up there with that food. The Lady's nephew is in a guest room cursing up a storm about how he has never had to wait this long for a meal and the Lady is going to hear all about it."

Normoon's face went bright red.

"You stay right here, I will speak with you in a moment," he said, storming up the stairs in search of a nephew that did not exist.

Harcourt moved as quickly as he could, dragging the heavy sack and retracing his steps to find the door he first entered. He found a small wagon near a tool shed at the side of the house and loaded his laundry bag on top. Shuffling along with the wagon in tow, he approached the front gate where the guard he spoke to earlier still stood watch.

"What ya got there, old man?" the guard asked curiously.

"That buffoon Normoon went and spilled a whole bottle of red wine on some of the Lady's good things. Now I have to go and get them cleaned before she gets back and hangs him from the veranda," the old man answered.

The guard had a good chuckle over that. "Better him than me," he said unlocking the gate for the old man.

By the time shouts of alarm erupted from within the manor grounds, a cloaked Lord Mornay was two blocks away pulling a shipment of goods home.

CHAPTER 14

"We have no leads whatsoever in the Kalandra Manor job?" Trascar asked in his usual miserable tone.

This time, he sat at a round table with six senior members of the Guild in one of their many hideouts.

"The city blames us again, of course, but does not have a single suspect in mind," said Jorold, a very dark-skinned thief. Jorold was born in Stonewood but his family originated from the jungles of some far away island. His kind was a rarity in this part of the world.

"Neither do we it seems, and that's the problem," Trascar shouted.

"We do know that the staff reported seeing at least three different people," Serdic added.

The silver haired Yanzul, the oldest member of the Guild spoke next. "So do you think we are looking for a small gang of thieves, or perhaps the rise of a rival guild?"

"Not a guild," Randar answered. "We would have known about that by now. It's too difficult to hide the dealings of a whole organization from our eyes."

"Oh? And we know so much about the demon cult, don't we?" Trascar said sarcastically.

"I am with Randar, it's probably just a small upstart gang," Jorold agreed.

"Or......I believe it is one person, a master of disguise," Zenod offered. "Remember the tales of Warden? It was said he was a master of disguise, and he was never caught."

"Hmmm, could Warden be back to his old tricks again?" Serdic asked.

"Don't be silly," Yanzul laughed. "I was around during the days of the One-Handed Bandit. Warden would be a very old man by now, and has long since departed Stonewood, I would have to say."

"But an old man was seen at the Manor," Serdic said.

"Might not be him, but possibly someone as good," Zenod reasoned. "None of us would have attempted Kalandra Manor on our own."

"Well, not without leaving a few dead bodies behind," the beautiful Feylane grinned. She was a blonde yet again.

"I don't care if it's one person or if it's three," Trascar said. "I want whoever it is found. I want more eyes on the streets and find out who was seen coming and going in the area that night."

*　　*　　*　　*

Harcourt lay back on his sofa comfortably, his arms behind his head. He was surrounded by piles of gold and jewels. It was funny to him, that he had gone from one extreme to the next in so little time. From having nothing, not even one lousy copper coin, to this.

He smiled when he thought about how the talk on the streets lately was of the One-Handed Bandit. Deep down he wished it was him that was getting all the credit, but he knew that would only put Jalanna in danger. For now, he would have to remain the mystery thief who had the whole city baffled.

The good news was that he only needed one more small job in order to pay the priest his fee. After he sold Lady Kalandra's diamonds to one of Filbur's contacts, he was just about there. He was keeping her biggest diamond aside though, to have a custom ring made for Jalanna.

As soon as it got a little darker, he planned to head down to the south district and give some more gold to Dahleene and the kids, then his mercenary persona would drop off another generous tip to Jalanna. After that, he would return home and rest up for a big day tomorrow. There was a large house he had been watching for days now that would be his next target. A lot of folk usually came and went but for the last several days there had been no activity at all. Perhaps the owners had taken a little vacation, he thought. Perfect time to pay it a visit.

The following night Lord Mornay was invited to a party. Harcourt had never been to a formal party before and he was interested in making an appearance. It would be filled with wealthy snobs, wealthy being the key word. He figured he would stay for a short time, relieve some partiers of their jewels and then depart. The people he dealt with as Lord Mornay disgusted him. He missed his friends at the Den, most of all Jalanna. Soon, he thought.

"Warden, wherever you are, thank you," he said to himself.

*　　*　　*　　*

Harcourt paused as he spotted Andil weaving through a crowd of people on a busy street. He was about to call out to his friend, then remembered he was wearing the guise of a skinny blond man. The thief had just finished his business at the orphanage and was on his way home. Positive that nobody was looking, he quickly removed his mask and caught up to his old friend. "Give me all your coins."

Andil spun, knife in hand, then paled as if he had seen a ghost. "Where in the hell have you been?" he said, concealing his knife back up his sleeve.

"I was thinking of asking the same question of you," Harcourt replied. "I've been by the Den a couple of times and have not seen you. I'd love to know what happened to you that night - the duke's gold was almost the end of me."

"You first, you've been gone for months. Jal is worried sick," Andil replied.

"Just been hiding out. I didn't want to endanger Jal since I figured there would be lots of people looking for me."

"Hiding where?"

"Not important. I was nearly captured that night, and nearly killed. Where were you? You were supposed to warn me if any guards were approaching. I ended up surrounded," Harcourt asked.

"I warned you that job was too dangerous from the start," Andil said. "I noticed Zorfal and a few others had shown up suddenly, but if I signaled you they would have been alerted to both of us. I was counting on your keen senses to spot them before it was too late. I am deeply sorry about that."

"Well, I escaped the guards, barely, only to run into Randar. Funny thing though, he said my name while I was wearing that skull mask. Somehow, he knew it was me."

"How could he have known?" Andil wondered.

"No idea. Did they coming looking for you?" Harcourt asked.

"Nope. Nobody saw me that night, thankfully. But I've been laying low just in case," the skinny thief replied. "Did you leave the city? How could you have eluded everyone for this long?"

"I've been around," Harcourt answered cryptically.

"Where? You can tell me. You certainly haven't been in the south district."

"I've been all over, my friend, and doing well for myself. Here," Harcourt handed the skinny thief ten gold coins. "What I've owed you, plus interest," he winked.

Andil looked astonished.

"Where did you get all this? And those clothes?" the other thief asked, finally noticing the expensive clothes and boots his friend wore.

"As I said, I've been doing well for myself. That streak of bad luck I ran into for years has vanished," Harcourt smiled.

"You've been thieving?" Andil asked.

"Well, I am not working for the King. There is only one thing I am good at."

"What about the Guild? They are furious with you," Andil said.

"I care nothing for the Guild. Let them be furious, I don't need them."

"It's not a matter of needing them. You know you cannot operate without their approval, and that you will never have. You, my friend, have a death wish."

"I am not worried about them finding me, let them search," Harcourt said confidently.

"This is a cause for celebration then. I'll drop by your hideout later for drinks? Sound good?" Andil slapped him on the shoulder. "Where is it?"

"I'll be in touch soon, my friend, I promise," Harcourt answered.

"I can help you, though. We can work together again. I won't screw up again, I swear it," Andil pleaded.

"I'll be in touch," Harcourt repeated and walked away leaving his friend on the street.

By the time he rounded the next corner, he was a skinny blond man yet again.

CHAPTER 15

Harcourt dropped down from the wall to land behind the stump of a large tree. He was dressed all in black with the hood of his cloak drawn over his head. Tonight, he wore the face of a dark-haired, middle-aged man with a crooked nose and several scars. He sat motionless, invisible in the shadows, before moving silently as a cat to the side of the house. For several days, he had watched this house and was hoping to find it currently unoccupied. There had not been any visible activity in that time. He found it surprising that given its location in a wealthy neighborhood, he had also noticed no staff members or security. The house intrigued him.

The yard was dark without any external lighting. Thankfully, there was no internal lighting that he could see either, and this place had a lot of windows. The eight-foot wall that surrounded the house offered the thief cover from prying eyes on the street while picking the lock on a back door. It was a surprisingly easy lock to defeat, considering the size of the house. They should have been able to afford something a little more sophisticated, not that the thief was complaining.

As he entered a living room, the thought suddenly occurred to him that he had not run into any bad luck lately. No guards had shown up unexpectedly. Nobody had returned home early. That puzzled the thief. Surely the magical mask made things a lot easier, but that should not have eliminated his bad luck entirely, though it was gone. He had met with success on each of his missions. That made him wonder.

Harcourt was not overly impressed with the décor in this house. The furniture was not up to the standards of what he came to expect from houses north of the river and the walls were devoid of any paintings or mirrors, or decorations of any kind. In fact, several of the rooms he passed were dusty and full of cobwebs. Odd, considering he had seen people come and go from this house before, and yet it appeared as though nobody lived here.

As he moved throughout the main floor of the house, he found all of the rooms were pretty much the same. None of them appeared lived in. He could not understand why someone would pay so much for a house like this only to let it fall into such disrepair. Perhaps the upstairs would be different, he thought.

Usually the stairs creaked in these houses when someone ascended them, but Harcourt's practiced steps made not a sound as he reached the second floor. Whispered voices from down the stairs caused the thief to whirl around and drop flat to the floor. Peeking over the top of the stairs, he watched two dark robed figures, one carrying a lantern, pass below him and disappear down a hallway. Good thing he had not been seen.

Harcourt lay there for another few moments, blending into the darkness, when another pair of robed figures passed by following the same direction as the previous pair. Now the thief was curious; who were they?

He waited another few moments and when no other robed figures presented themselves, he silently crept back down to the main floor. The thief could hear soft voices coming from a room branching off to the left of a long hallway and could see lantern light spilling out of the doorway. He was considering his next move when the voices went silent and the light disappeared. They must have moved on. For a moment, he wondered if they were thieves like himself, but then thieves did not use lanterns.

Cautiously, Harcourt crept down the dark hall and peered around the doorway where he had last seen the light, and found what looked to be a small library. Dusty reading chairs were spread around the room and book cases covered each wall from floor to ceiling. It took Harcourt a moment to finally notice one key thing; there was no other exit from this room. He was positive the voices and light came from this doorway, but where could they have gone? Footsteps could suddenly be heard from down the hall. Cursing to himself, Harcourt ducked into the library and found the largest chair to crouch behind.

A man clad in a similar black robe as the others entered the library carrying a lantern. The hood of his robe was pulled over his head concealing his face and he wore a strange-looking silver amulet around his neck. He looked like a priest. Harcourt watched the priest, or whatever he was, walk over to one of the book cases and scan the volumes as if looking for something in particular. When he found what he sought, he pulled on the book rather than removing it, and one of the book cases swung out like a door, revealing a dimly-lit stairwell that descended below the house. The robed man disappeared down the stairs and the book case closed behind him. The mystery of the missing men was now solved.

All common sense told the thief to leave the house now, especially since there did not seem to be anything worth stealing here. Curiosity was getting the better of him though, and he wanted to see what was hidden below the house. He told himself that he would depart at the first sign of trouble, and besides, he was not overly concerned about priests, if that is what the men were. They never came across as a dangerous lot. Delusional, but not dangerous.

Carefully listening for more approaching footsteps, Harcourt did his best to face the book case in the exact same spot where that man had stood. He knew the general area of the book the man had used but it took him eleven attempts to find the right one to open the secret door. A tome on the human anatomy was the key.

After ensuring that the stone stairwell was empty, the thief silently descended. Torches lined the walls which provided illumination, but stole Harcourt's cover. To his surprise, the stairs went down quite a ways before he reached the bottom. They led him to a very long and cold stone hallway which was similarly illuminated with torches. Other hallways branched off this one and it ended in a large room where many voices could be heard. Again, ignoring common sense, the thief crept to the end of the hall.

Peeking into the room, he noticed roughly thirty people all wearing the same black robes, and thankfully

facing the opposite direction. The room looked huge with
a very high ceiling and many stone pillars throughout.
Harcourt slipped in behind one of the pillars for a closer
look. Everyone faced a raised platform upon which stood
an obsidian altar. Behind that altar stood the robed man
with the silver amulet. When the man shifted to the side,
Harcourt spotted someone in a white silk gown chained to
the wall, a young woman by the look of it. Now he was
really curious.

He risked moving to the next closest pillar for a
better view. The girl was young, a teenager, probably about
the same age as Krestina, and she looked horrified. Eyes
wide with terror, tears streamed down her pretty face as
she sobbed and trembled uncontrollably. The thief could
not imagine what kind of place this was.

The man with the amulet started in with a speech but
Harcourt found it hard to make out all the words with the
humming that everyone else had begun. He thought he
heard "glorious" and "lord", yeah definitely priests. Then
"Lucy is heinous", who was Lucy? The girl chained to the
wall? No wait, Lucivenus! *Oh curses*, he swore to himself, he
was right in the midst of the thrice-damned demon
worshipping cult. How could he have been such a fool?
He followed those maniacs right into a nest of them. He
needed to leave, and now. *But what about the girl?* he
wondered. Damn his soft heart, he could not just leave her
here. Nobody deserved the fate that he assumed was in
store for her.

The thief peeked back around the corner and counted
exactly twenty-five people on the floor, plus the head
priest with the amulet. Not very good odds at all. Harcourt
watched the dark priest produce a red-bladed dagger from

within his robe, and to his horror, plunged it into the screaming girl's chest. Blood showered the demon worshipper. A scream of, "Nooooooooooo," escaped Harcourt's lips before he even realized he was doing it. All eyes turned on him.

Harcourt heard the next words out of the priest's mouth loud and clear, "Bring the intruder to me."

The thief sped off down the hall with twenty-five sadistic cult members right on his heels. Each time he passed a torch he snatched it from the wall and threw it behind him. Anything to slow them down. Visions of that poor girl flashed through his mind as he ran for his life. He probably would have gotten himself killed trying to rescue her anyways, but his conscience would not have allowed him to just leave without trying. Now however, she was dead, and he was likely to follow her into the underworld.

As he flew up the stairs he had descended earlier, he suddenly realized that he had no clue how to open the secret door from this side. He reached the top and did not see any levers or knobs of any kind. Desperate, the thief grabbed the last torch off the wall and threw it at his pursuers coming up the stairs screaming for his heart. The door behind him opened. Ah, the torch he thought.

Into the library he sprinted as he heard shrieks of alarm from cult members whose robes had caught fire. With all his strength, Harcourt forced the secret door closed causing a rain of books to fall down upon his head. He was hoping that without the torch on the wall the cult members could not open the door from the other side. Turning to leave, he froze in place as two more of the robed men entered the library from the room's other door. All three stood silent for a moment, staring at each other in surprise. These two men had their hoods down and the thief swore he recognized the tall gaunt one that was as pale as a ghost.

Harcourt reacted first, drawing both of his daggers and hurling one at each man. The first one struck home catching the cult member in the upper thigh, dropping him to the floor in a howl. The second blade missed the pale man completely, as if the dagger had been deflected off some invisible wall. Harcourt was stunned. The ghostly cult member mumbled some indecipherable words and for a brief moment his eyes seemed to glow a bright red. Then it felt as though the thief was hit in the head with a brick and the floor spiraled upwards to meet his face.

*   *   *   *

Harcourt's eyes opened and at first he saw nothing, until they adjusted to the gloom of the cell that he occupied. *Am I back in Stonewood's dungeon?* he wondered. No, this was no cell he recognized. It had a strange odor. The thief could not properly describe it, except that it smelled like fear. He had been stripped of everything but his pants and laid on a cold stone floor. The cell door consisted of a series of thick iron bars, and the only source of light came from a torch down the hall.

The thief rubbed his head, trying to recall what had happened. It took a moment before he remembered running into two of the cult members in the library. The pale one said something in another language and his eyes had turned red. Or did he imagine that part? Then someone must have struck him in the head from behind. He quickly examined his head but found no blood, no lumps, in fact he was not in any pain at all. How was that possible? The blow had knocked him cold.

With nothing to lose, he stood and shook the bars while shouting for someone. He could make out two other cells like his but could not tell if they were occupied or not. The thief was disgusted in himself for not leaving the house when he had the chance to do so. Then he heard the sound of footsteps approaching. Two people. The thief stepped back away from the door and waited.

Two men dressed in black robes, one with the silver amulet around his neck, stopped in front of the cell door. Upon closer inspection, the amulet was shaped in the head of a horned demon. "You animal!" Harcourt growled. "She was only a teen!"

"Our order does not discriminate," the man with the amulet replied in a calm voice. "Young, old, female, male," then he paused, "or thief. Every living sacrifice loosens the bonds that keep our Lord Lucivenus from returning to this world. Every heart taken makes him stronger."

"Fairy tales, fables, ghosts and goblins. You are a delusional lot. Sick and delusional," Harcourt spat.

The evil priest stepped closer to the cell door. "It is you who is delusional. It is unfortunate that you will not be around to learn the truth since our Lord requires your heart."

Harcourt got a good look at the man's face when he stepped forward and he could not believe his eyes; he knew that face. Magistrate Krommel. This man had sentenced Harcourt to the dungeon on several occasions. The magistrate was a demon cult priest? And a high ranking one at that? The thief was relieved that he was not wearing his real face, his captors had not realized he wore a mask. They might tear out his heart, but he did not want these maniacs targeting Jalanna or anyone else he knew.

"Why were you here, thief?" Krommel asked.

"Not very bright are ya?" Harcourt replied. "I thought that would have been obvious. I'd say I chose the wrong house to burglarize."

"Indeed you did," Krommel said disgustedly, walking down the hall. The other priest followed.

"Hey! When are meals served around here? And I'd like a little water please," Harcourt shouted after them, but there was no response.

He joked, but the situation was no joking matter. They were going to sacrifice him to some stupid mythical demon if he did not find a way out of this mess. The fact that a magistrate was a cult priest was very troubling. *How many others in the King's administration were also involved?* he wondered. He guessed this was the reason that very little had ever been achieved in eliminating the cult.

Then it suddenly struck the thief as to where he had seen the tall pale man with the red eyes. The night Harcourt had gotten very drunk and attacked Captain Dornell, earlier that man had given him the invite to one of their "meetings." Right from the start, Harcourt had felt that there was something very bizarre about the man. Bizarre was not even the half of it.

The thief sat on the cell floor and rested his back against the cold wall. There was most likely very little time remaining before his heart would be pulled from his chest. He let out a very long sigh of frustration and fell into deep thought.

*   *   *   *

Mellivan was patrolling the hallways when he heard shouts coming from one of the holding cells. They had captured a thief who was currently locked in one of the cells. He ran as fast as he could to investigate the noise and was shocked by what he saw. "Brother Jaspar, what happened?"

"Unlock this door, the prisoner has escaped," shouted an enraged Jaspar, a tall gaunt, pale man. "The damned thief used trickery to get me to unlock the door, then overpowered me."

"Hang on," Mellivan said running to retrieve the cell keys that were hung on the wall. He quickly returned and unlocked the door. "How did a common thief overpower you brother?"

"He is no common thief, I am afraid. There is magic about him. Perhaps a magician in disguise here to spy on us," Jaspar answered. "Now give me your robe, the trickster stole mine. We must find him before he escapes."

Mellivan removed his robe and handed it to Jaspar. "I will alert the others immediately," he said.

"Yes, do so. Make for the altar room, I believe he might have gone that way."

Mellivan nodded and ran as fast as he could to the altar room. As he entered, he had a flashback of the sacrifice that taken place only hours earlier. The scene had been intoxicating until the intruder had interrupted and spoiled the event. Two cult members currently occupied the room. They had their backs to him but Mellivan recognized High Priest Sarvin from the silver amulet he wore.

"Your highness," he called. "Forgive my intrusion, but the prisoner has escaped. Brother Jaspar was…" and his sentence was cut off as the two men turned to face him, Sarvin and Jaspar.

Mellivan's eyes bulged at the sight of the ghostly pale priest. "What were you about to say about me?" Jaspar inquired. "Speak!"

"I-I-I, well-you-," Mellivan stammered, trying to work out in his head what was going on.

Magistrate Krommel, or High Priest Sarvin as he was known here, smacked the lower priest across the face and shouted, "Where is the prisoner? What is this you speak of?"

Mellivan swallowed hard and spoke, "I found Brother Jaspar locked in the prisoner's cell. He told me the thief had tricked him into opening the door, and was then overpowered."

"And you unlocked the door for me? Is this correct?" Jaspar asked.

"W-well yes. I thought it was you."

"Fool! You are the one who was duped!" Jaspar shouted shoving him aside. "We must not let this man escape!"

The tall man ran from the room and only then did Mellivan realize the Jaspar in the cell was not so tall. How had his eyes deceived him? High Priest Sarvin stepped closer, "Tell me. The prisoner looked just like Brother Jaspar?"

"Yes, your highness I swear it. But now I think he was not as tall, or as thin. It was dark in there and I was not expecting a trick. He must have cast a spell on me that fooled my eyes," Mellivan said.

"Hmmm. Could we be dealing with a meddlesome wizard? Fezzdin perhaps?" Sarvin said more to himself than to Mellivan. "In any case, this house is compromised."

"I am terribly sorry, your highness. I am a loyal servant and I've pledged my life to the service of our Lord Lucivenus," Mellivan pleaded.

"I know you have. And now you can serve our Lord in another manner. You can personally do your part in increasing our Lord's strength by forfeiting your heart."

Before Mellivan could register any movement, Sarvin drove his red-bladed dagger into his chest. The blade pulsed inside him as if it were drinking his blood, and tugging at his very soul. He was dead before he hit the floor.

CHAPTER 16

She moved through the crowded ballroom with such grace, a glass of wine in one hand, a piece of cheese in the other. She wore a long elegant black dress that hugged her thin athletic body. Her hair was long and dark with golden streaks throughout, her nails a dark crimson. She was easily the most attractive woman at the party, and despite having received many offers to dance and converse, she seemed bored.

She stopped next to a tall, blonde woman in a dark blue gown who was taking a break from dancing and asked, "Are all the men here so stuffy and dull?"

The blonde woman laughed.

"No, not all, but those that aren't, are a rare find. New to Stonewood?"

"Why, yes. I am just passing through and an old acquaintance of mine invited me to this party. The food is excellent but oh, wait, who is that over there?"

The blonde woman followed her gaze to a very well-dressed handsome man standing alone on the far side of the room. "Oh, that's Lord Mornay. He is fairly new to the city as well. He is a very wealthy man from what I've heard. And single," she said with a wink. "Not very social though."

"Where does his wealth come from? Rich parents?"

"I don't rightly know, he is very secretive."

"Well enjoy the rest of your evening," said the woman in the black dress and made her way across the dance floor agilely dodging dancers and revelers.

Lord Plumburg always went all out at his parties and he spared no expense. The Lord made his fortune from buying and selling property. People joked that he owned the upper west district, and that was probably not too far off the mark. At least once a month, he threw a lavish party for no other reason than to show off his wealth. Only the rich and influential were ever invited.

The beauty in the black dress turned down three offers to dance by the time she reached the lonely-looking Lord Mornay. She sauntered by him to stand to his left side. When he made no acknowledgement of her presence, she let out a loud sigh - she was unaccustomed to not being noticed.

Harcourt, as Lord Mornay, leaned back against the ballroom wall. He was at the party and yet he was not at the party, not mentally anyway. He had not fully recovered from the previous night's events. The image of that poor girl being murdered by a city magistrate in front of a crowd of jubilant spectators would not leave his mind. It sickened him. Growing up in the south district, Harcourt was no stranger to violence and death, but that scene in the altar room would haunt him for a very long time. He wished he could have done something, but he knew there was nothing he could have done, not without dying along with the girl. He had barely escaped with his own heart intact.

The strange, magical mask had been his savior. The thief knew that his disguise as the pale priest Jaspar, or whatever the hell his name was, was far from perfect, but in the gloomy cell, it was enough to fool the other cult member. Slipping away while wearing the man's robe was easy after that. Harcourt wondered what happened to the man when the others found out he had opened the cell door, but oh well, he deserved whatever fate befell him. The thief was going to send a letter to the city guard informing them of the cult's house but then heard of a mysterious fire that had burned the place to the ground.

"I said, you look just as bored as I feel," said the extremely-attractive woman standing to his left.

"Pardon me, my lady, my head is not here, I am afraid. I have a lot on my mind lately and I am not much fun at a party."

"I don't think it's you," she said with a flirty smile, "it's this party. I find it a dreadful bore. I don't mean to sound insulting but I don't seem to fit in with these snobby types. Everything is always business."

"No offence taken. I feel the exact same way, to be honest," Harcourt replied.

"I am just passing through Stonewood, here for a few nights. I feel rather uncomfortable not really knowing anyone here," she said, sipping her wine.

"Well, a woman of your beauty can't have much trouble making friends, I am sure of it. But again, I feel the same as you. I've only been here for roughly three months now and I cannot say I've made too many friends. Not any that I care to spend much time with," Harcourt said.

The woman giggled. "You flatter me. I have had many offers to be 'friends' this evening. But none of them have interested me, until now."

Harcourt smiled. "Do you like brandy or whiskey?"

"I like a lot of things," the woman answered.

"Well, it just so happens that I have a collection of the finest drinks in Stonewood back at my home. It's not too far from here," the thief boasted.

"Are you asking me to leave this wonderful party and accompany you back to your place of residence?"

"It's much easier to have a conversation without having to talk over the musicians. Wouldn't you agree?" Harcourt asked.

She smiled ear to ear. "I completely agree. And I accept your invitation, Lord….?"

"Mornay. Lord Mornay. And your name my lady?"

"You can call me Feylane."

*   *   *   *

"You live very modestly, my lord," Feylane said, commenting on Harcourt's lack of décor.

The thief had very little furniture and not much else aside from his impressive liquor cabinet. All the walls were bare except for two paintings which he had stolen but not yet sold. "Disappointed?" he asked.

"Not at all," she answered. "Just not what I was expecting from a lord."

"I don't feel the need to show off my wealth like Lord Plumburg. People like him crave attention. And I also wasn't planning on staying in Stonewood for too long. I just visit here for business," Mornay said.

"And what is your business, if you don't mind me asking?" Feylane purred.

"Brandy or whiskey? I can assure you both are the best vintages available," Mornay asked.

"Brandy, please."

Mornay poured them both generous glasses and invited her to join him on the sofa. Feylane sat very close, her leg touching his, and she smelled very, very good.

"Diamonds," he said.

"Pardon?"

"You asked me what business I am in. I deal in diamonds."

"Ooooh," she smiled. "Women love diamonds."

"Precisely why I made that career choice," he winked at her, taking a sip from his drink.

"And how is that business in Stonewood?" Feylane inquired.

"Not bad at all. I acquired some recently and have been trying to find a buyer to offer me the right price."

"From a private collection?"

"As a matter of fact, yes. But I thought you didn't like it when people talked business," he teased. "I am sure we can think of something more interesting to talk about, or not talk about."

"You are right," she said, her face aglow. "Close your eyes and I'll get a little more comfortable."

Lord Mornay closed his eyes with an excited grin. Then the smile faded as something sharp poked into his throat. His eyes shot open and Feylane wore a wicked smile as she held a long thin knife.

"How long did you think you were going to get away with this?" she asked. "Oh, and I wouldn't move or shout if I were you."

"I beg your pardon, what are you talking about?"

"Don't play dumb with me, Mornay, or whatever your name is. You've made a lot of people very angry with your recent exploits," she said.

"Exploits? I don't follow."

"The Thieves Guild are not fools. A crime spree started about three months past by someone not within the Guild. You showed up in Stonewood about three months past. A private collection of diamonds was recently stolen from Kalandra Manor. You recently acquired a private collection of diamonds and you were seen near the manor that very same night. Coincidence?" Feylane pressed the knife tip a little harder drawing a trickle of blood.

"You cannot pin the diamond theft on me. One of your own people came to me with them," Mornay said.

"I am listening."

"Some thief approached me with the diamonds. Said he needed gold to pay the Guild their share. I swear it."

"What was his name?" she asked.

"He didn't tell me," he replied.

"An interesting story, but one I do not believe. For crossing the Guild, your punishment is death. You will die and we will take your diamonds."

"A shame," Mornay said. "And here I thought we hit it off."

Feylane laughed and downed a mouthful of brandy with her free hand. "Oh, and you pay too much for this stuff. Doesn't taste any better than the stuff I am used to. Waste of good gold."

"I've always said the same thing, believe it or not,"

Mornay said.

"Too bad that's your last drink of anything. I....I...,"she shook her head.

"Yes?" Mornay asked.

"What did you....?" Feylane's eyes rolled back and she fell to the floor, dropping the knife.

Harcourt could have caught her but did not bother. Her head bounced off the floor. He had known something was up with her long before she approached him at the party. She was good, but it takes a thief to know a thief. Suspecting trouble, he spiked her drink with some of his sleeping poison and luck was with him that she took a sip before things got ugly.

So the Guild was onto Mornay now, they were smarter than he thought. It was a good thing he had recently rented a new place on the other side of the city under a different identity. He took that precaution in the event of an emergency, an emergency that just revealed itself. This place was no longer safe. A shame, he liked this house.

"Now," the thief said to the slumbering Feylane, "What do I do with you?"

*   *   *   *

Feylane awoke as ice cold water splashed into her face. She found her wrists and ankles were tightly-bound to a chair and she could not move them an inch. She sat in a tiny dark room, probably underneath Mornay's house, and her head was throbbing. As her eyes adjusted to the gloom, she could see Mornay standing before her with an empty pail.

"You drugged me," she spat.

"Shut up you painted trollop. You don't have your knife to my throat now," Mornay shouted. "So I'd watch your tone."

"You won't get away with this," she said, her voice lower this time.

"You were so easy to ensnare, my dear," Mornay taunted. "After I captured the other Guild member, I knew it was only a matter of time before they dispatched someone to look into it."

Feylane looked puzzled. "What other member? I don't know who you are talking about."

"The one with the diamonds. I was telling the truth about that. He was trying to sell me the diamonds to pay the Guild."

Feylane had no idea who he could be talking about.

"The name Harcourt ring a bell?" he asked. "I was at least able to beat his name out of him. So far though, he has refused to give me any other names or information about your Guild even under intense torture. But, I don't need him anymore, now I've got you," Mornay said with an evil smile, causing Feylane to struggle desperately against her bonds.

Mornay laughed at her pitiful attempt to break free and backhanded her across the face, bloodying her nose. "You were gonna cut my throat were ya? Oh, I am gonna have so much fun with you. You will beg for death before the end."

Feylane finally knew how her victims felt just before the end. For the first time in her adult life, she knew true fear. There was no way out, and nobody even knew where she was. She had targeted Mornay on her own, hoping to impress the Guild with her catch. Now she was going to die a slow agonizing death. Tears welled up in her eyes.

"You are going to tell me everything I want to know about the Thieves Guild. Then I am going to rip out your heart in the name of my Lord Lucivenus," Mornay took her knife and gently caressed her leg with the blade.

"Now I have something to take care of. When I return, Harcourt loses his heart, then I play with you."

A shiver ran down Feylane's spine and Mornay left, closing the door and leaving her in pitch darkness.

*   *   *   *

A crashing sound from some room up above awoke Feylane this time. She had been drifting in and out of sleep for lack of anything else to do. Mornay had been gone hours, or was it a day already? She could not tell. Now she heard shouting and cursing but could not make out any of the words. She wondered if Harcourt had lost his heart yet to that vile demon worshipper.

She cursed herself for not suspecting a trap. If Mornay was telling the truth, then Harcourt was the thief they had been searching for all along. He stole Kalandra's diamonds. Pretty impressive. But what was he doing trying to get gold to pay the Guild? Was he planning to buy his life back? Feylane knew nothing of the thief except that Trascar was intent on seeing him dead. She felt bad for the renegade though; she might have been an assassin, and a good one, but nobody deserved to die at the hands of this cult, sacrificed to some disgusting demon lord.

Feylane had little time to worry about the thief though, she was next, and she could hear Mornay approaching. The fictional lord burst into the room out of breath and looking very distraught. He was holding her knife and staring at her intensely. Please god, give me strength to get through this, she thought. "Well," he said, "Your friend has escaped. How? I know not. I would imagine he is running back to your precious little Guild right now to bring them all back here to save you."

Feylane wanted to cry again. Harcourt was gone and there would be no Guild members coming for her. For some strange reason, it felt worse knowing she was now alone here. Mornay continued. "You got very lucky, pretty girl, that I do not have much time. I might not be able to play with you, but I will still have your heart."

Feylane screamed as he advanced. Mornay smacked her across the face again, "Shut up!"

The knife blade bit into her chest as she struggled but there was no hope. This was the end. Suddenly Mornay was distracted by a loud crash from upstairs. Feylane screamed for help and received a backhand in response. Mornay cut a strip from her dress and gagged her with it, then cautiously stalked out of the room closing the door behind him.

The right side of Feylane's face throbbed and she could feel the blood running down her chest. Her heart raced. She could hear more crashing sounds from above. A struggle? Did she just hear someone grunt in pain? Had someone heard her screams? Then silence. By all the gods, what was happening up there? She strained to hear to anything, then there were footsteps coming down the stairs. *This is it*, she thought, *now I die*.

The door flew open and she attempted to scream. Instead of Mornay though, a man she did not recognize staggered in clutching a blood-soaked wound on his right side. His other hand held a dagger, red with blood. "You must be Feylane?" the man said in obvious pain, pulling off her gag.

"Yes, yes I am. Please cut me loose. Who are you?" she said frantically.

"My name is Harcourt."

The thief cut the assassin free of her bonds. Feylane looked to the door with a worried expression and asked, "Where's that monster, Mornay?"

"Gone. He fled. We fought and I managed to injure him, though I fear not mortally. We are safe for now, but we should still leave quickly."

Harcourt suddenly collapsed on the floor in pain. Feylane, who was quite strong for her petite size, helped him stand and together they made their way up the stairs. She noticed all the signs of a struggle and blood was splattered on the walls and floor. When they reached the street outside, she finally allowed herself to relax a bit. It must have been the middle of the night, she figured, by the position of the moon and the fresh air was heavenly. They took a break for a moment while the thief ripped a fresh strip from his shirt to hold against his bloodied side.

"Why did you come back? Mornay said you had escaped?" she asked.

"I came back for you. Mornay told me he had another prisoner. A woman from the Guild," he replied.

"But the Guild has been hunting you. Why would you want to rescue me?"

"You are still a human. I could not let you stay a captive of that creature. Nobody deserves that. I have, unfortunately, witnessed the cult's cruelty first-hand and would not wish that on anyone. I had to get you out of there, no matter the consequences."

Feylane, still trembling a little bit, hugged him tight. "Thank you, thank you so much."

"Here, we part ways. I have a friend nearby who could see to my wound and I cannot be seen where you are obviously heading," Harcourt said.

Feylane nodded. "Seek me out tomorrow at the Blue Goose. Are you sure you'll be ok?"

"I'll be fine. You just get somewhere safe. Stay alert and warn the Guild about Mornay," Harcourt answered.

The assassin kissed the thief on the cheek and took off as fast as her bare feet could carry her. Harcourt half staggered down another dark empty street. When he was certain that Feylane was long gone, he straightened his body, casually walked over to a puddle and washed the pig's blood off his hands.

CHAPTER 17

Trascar sat at the table stewing. Everyone could tell he was furious but this time he was doing more listening than shouting. Jewel just finished inspecting a small pile of diamonds that sat in front of her. Jewel was called Jewel because of her skills in appraising precious gemstones and spotting fakes.

"They all look very good, flawless in fact. About three thousand in gold worth here," she said.

"And you say that Harcourt was planning on handing over all of these to the Guild?" Serdic asked.

"Yes," Feylane answered. It had been two days since her horrific ordeal and she still had some bruising on her cheek, but thankfully the cut on her chest had not been very deep.

"How can we be sure he would have? Maybe he lied," Randar reasoned.

"It was Mornay who told me that. Also, Harcourt had vanished for months. He could have easily just disappeared again after we escaped, but he met with me the next day and handed these over," Feylane replied.

"The Kalandra job was quite impressive," Zenod said.

"Indeed," said Serdic. "Given these circumstances, I think we should excuse his past offences against the Guild."

That brought Trascar out of his silence.

"Are you all mad? We need to make an example of him, lest every renegade in the city think they can get away without following our rules. Feylane, you need to set up another meeting with him, then eliminate him."

The assassin's mouth hung open for a moment before she could speak. "He saved my life! I was going to be tortured, then have my heart ripped out for a cult sacrifice, but he came back for me!"

"You dare disobey me, girl?" Trascar's eyes narrowed.

Yanzul cut in. "Not a wise decision, eliminating the thief now. Other thieves respect him for the jobs he has pulled off and word has quickly spread about his rescue of one of our own from a repulsive end."

"I agree," said Serdic. "He is looked at as kind of a hero right now."

"Not to mention he has struck the first real blow against that hated cult," Jorold threw in. "Something we have yet to accomplish."

Trascar's face was red with fury. He turned to Randar since the Guild enforcer had a personal grudge against the renegade thief but Randar just shrugged his shoulders with indifference. Randar would never openly admit it, but he had developed some measure of respect for the thief since their last encounter.

"How do you all expect to run a successful Guild

when you are all too damned soft?" and with that the Guild leader stormed out of the room.

"Perhaps we should reconsider his membership, he could be quite useful," Zenod said, and the others nodded in approval.

*　　*　　*　　*

Jalanna anxiously stood at the edge of the bridge watching the river flow swiftly by. A large white feathered bird sat perched on a rock looking for fish to snatch out of the water. Nearby, an elderly woman threw stale bread crumbs to some small, grey birds that had gathered around her. About an hour ago, a mysterious man had handed Jalanna a note telling her to come to this bridge. It was signed, Harcourt. She had gotten here as fast as she could. The last time they spoke, she had yelled at him and that was over three months ago. She missed him so much and not a day went by that she did not wonder and worry about where he was. This could also have been a trap, possibly set by Randar, but she decided she had to come anyway.

She spun as someone tapped her on the shoulder and her face lit up like the sun when she saw that her lover stood before her. He looked different she thought. The thief was wearing some very expensive-looking clothing, without any of the usual rips or tears. He stood tall with an air of confidence about him, something he had been missing for quite a long time.

First, she slapped him across his smiling face and then wrapped him in a very tight hug.

"Don't you ever disappear on me like that again, you

hear me?" she said, tears running down her cheeks.

"It was not by choice, believe me. It was for your own safety," he replied, hugging her back as tightly.

"I thought you were dead!"

"I almost was."

"What if someone sees you here?" she then asked worriedly.

"It's ok now."

Harcourt proceeded to tell her an abbreviated version of the last few months, leaving out any mention of Warden and the magical mask. He did admit to sending a mercenary by the Den a few times with some generous tips for her. That got him another big hug and kiss, and her tears flowed once again. He concluded his tale with his capture at the hands of Lord Mornay, how he escaped and rescued a high-ranking Guild member in the process.

"So the Guild has pardoned me. I am free to walk the streets again. I may even be accepted into the Guild," he said.

That was wonderful news, Jalanna thought, at least the being pardoned part. She did not like the idea of him being a member of the Thieves Guild, but she did not want to start another argument right now. They could discuss that later.

"But here is the best part of my story," he continued. "I have the five thousand gold pieces to pay that priest. So, what say you and I meet at the temple in two hours?"

She stepped back stunned, unable to believe her ears. "Y-y-you have what?"

"I have it all and more," he smiled. "You will never have to worry about working again."

"This is not funny, Harcourt!" she said with a serious

tone.

"I am not joking. I have it all. I swear to you. I am that thief everyone has been talking about in the streets lately."

"You…you are not kidding?"

"Of course not. I love you, Jalanna. I have done all of this for you."

Jalanna began weeping again and her body shook with joy. She wondered if she was going to wake up from a dream any second now. How could this be true? Never once had she ever allowed herself to believe that her scars could be healed.

"I have to make some arrangements to move that much gold," Harcourt said. "Give me two hours then meet me at the temple of the One God."

She gave the thief another giant hug then took off running.

*   *   *   *

Harcourt paced inside a room within the Temple of the One True God. The entire inside of the temple was richly-decorated, with many things made of solid gold. The god was not poor, that was for sure. The thief smirked and made a mental note that he should come back and visit, late one evening.

Half an hour ago, two priests had taken Jalanna into a special room and asked that Harcourt remain outside the door. The thief thought it funny that it did not matter what your station was in life, everyone's face lit up at the sight of five thousand gold pieces. Those priests could not usher Jalanna in fast enough. For her sake, and theirs, Harcourt hoped the priests were not frauds.

After obtaining the magical mask, he now knew that some magic did exist in the world, but whether these priests possessed any magical abilities at all, he could not say. It was said that the priests wielded divine magic, handed down to them from the gods themselves. Since he had nothing else to do, and he was in a temple, he prayed for her.

His prayer was suddenly interrupted as Jalanna shrieked from within the room. Harcourt drew his pair of daggers and kicked open the door. He marched into the room to find his lover standing naked in front of a long mirror. She turned to face him and tears of joy ran down her face, her perfect flawless face. Not one scar remained anywhere on her body. She was the old Jalanna once again.

Harcourt could see a spark that returned to her eyes, something that had gone missing for so long. *I did it*, he thought, *I actually did it*. A smile crept onto his face and he let out a long sigh. He grabbed a robe hanging from a hook and wrapped it around her.

"Show's over," he said to the priests, who were staring a little too much.

One of the priests huffed in disgust at the remark that he might have been staring, even though he had been. Harcourt approached the other priest, a man with a large protruding stomach and long brown beard.

"Thank you Brother Andolan."

"My pleasure. You see what happens when you put your faith in the One True God? Miracles can happen. Our Lord answers the prayers of his faithful and bestows upon us…"

"Yeah, yeah, great," Harcourt interrupted. He handed

the priest another bag of gold. "In case anyone ever asks, you did this out of the kindness of your oh-so-pure heart. Nobody paid you. Got it?"

The priest eagerly nodded.

*   *   *   *

A short time later, Harcourt and Jalanna strolled hand in hand down a busy city street. The thief proudly wore his own face and Jalanna proudly displayed hers. It was the first time in years that she had been out in public without her veil, which she had burned at the temple. Neither could believe this day would ever come and yet here they were.

"I can't thank you enough, Harcourt. That was a lot of gold you had to spend on me. Too much. And I don't want to even think of the dangers you would have been in to get it."

"I told you, I have plenty more where that came from. Besides, this was worth every coin to see your old smile return. I would have paid fifty thousand to see that again," he answered.

She squeezed his hand tightly and could not prevent the tears from streaming down her face again. "Now, how about I show you where you will be living from now on?" he said.

Harcourt led her to the new place he had been renting. It was a very cozy, three-bedroom bungalow in a nice and quiet area of the city. There was even enough room in the backyard for a quaint little garden. She cried again.

"Would you stop that? You are gonna make me join

you if you continue," he said.

"What about that evil priest who captured you? Won't he come looking for you?" Jalanna asked, concerned.

"Nah. My guess is nobody will ever see Lord Mornay again. Someone even burned his house down later that night. Probably the Guild."

"I just don't want anything to ruin this. This is too good to be true," she said.

"Nobody will ruin it. It only gets better from now on. Will you marry me?" the thief asked, pulling out a shiny gold ring set with a large sparkling diamond, Lady Kalandra's best.

Jalanna was rendered speechless again. Harcourt slipped the ring on her finger while her hand trembled. "Is it…..is it real?" she whispered in amazement.

The thief nodded.

"Yes, Harcourt, I will marry you!" she said, and the tears flowed yet again.

CHAPTER 18

Jalanna stepped out the back door of the Ogre's Den for some fresh air. The Den was packed to capacity tonight with everyone celebrating the announcement of her engagement and her miracle healing. Word spread quickly throughout the south district and folk from all over wanted to pass by and witness the miracle for themselves. The last few days seemed like a dream to her, just a fairy tale. She prayed she would not wake from a dream and find that nothing had changed. All eyes were on her tonight, which was why she thought it best to leave her diamond ring at home.

Even though it could be exhausting most of the time, she would miss working at the Den. Harcourt insisted that she not work there anymore and suggested they open their own business. She liked the idea of making custom dresses or importing exotic clothing. She also wanted Harcourt to focus his attention on a legitimate business and forget about a life with the Thieves Guild. She could not handle it if he were sent to the dungeon again and she just wanted them to live a good clean life together, never having to look over their shoulders.

"Well, I had to see it for myself to believe it," she jumped as she heard a voice from the shadows behind her.

"Trascar? Is that you?" she asked, straining to make out the man's face in the gloom.

"The one and only. And don't you look absolutely ravishing," the Guild leader said with a sly wink.

"My god, it's been so many years, how have you been?"

"Very well, thank you," he replied. "And very successful. I own a lot of properties in Stonewood now, as well as in other cities. I live in a large manor in the upper west."

"Wow, good for you, that's great to hear," Jalanna said, genuinely happy for the man.

"It is great. You should come by and visit," he said.

"Sure, Harcourt would probably be happy to see you again too," she answered.

"You are really marrying that drunken loser?"

"He is not a drunken loser," Jalanna replied very offended.

"Last time I checked, the man sleeps on the ground in an alley. Thirty years and he could never better himself. I came from the same neighborhood as him, and look at me now," Trascar boasted arrogantly.

"Well, that's good for you, but just because he wasn't as lucky as you were doesn't make him any less of a man," she said angrily.

"Jal, I can give you everything you need. I still love you. A successful man like me needs a beautiful woman like you by my side."

"You love me? You used to hang out here all the time. We used to talk, that's all. We were friends, so I thought. It's funny how after I was burned in the fire, you never came here to drink anymore. Not once. Now my scars are healed and look who shows up to flirt again? What a coincidence," she said.

"Oh and you think that lowlife Harcourt loved you with all those terrible scars? You think he enjoyed looking at those?"

Jalanna wanted to cry but fought to remain in control. "He has always loved me. He stayed by my side through everything!"

"He is a loser that cannot stay out of the dungeon. He is not even any good at the only thing he knows how to do. Don't waste any more of your time with him."

"You should stop wasting your time and leave. Maybe you could take some lessons from Harcourt on being a man!"

Trascar raged inside. He hated Harcourt more than anything. All through life growing up, Harcourt had always been better than him. He was a better climber. A better pick-pocket. A better lock-picker. A better fighter. Then Jalanna came to work at their favorite haunt the Ogre's Den and Trascar had wanted her very badly. Everyone did, she was so beautiful. But the trollop fell for Harcourt. Nothing he did could steal her away from that lowlife. After she was scarred in that fire of course, Trascar had no more use for her. She was hideous. He could have easily financed a priest to heal her but no woman was worth five thousand gold pieces, not even her. But since someone else had bought her a miracle, he figured he would drop by and try again.

"Stubborn wench. Those priests are not cheap. Where did you get the gold for that?"

"They did it for free," she answered.

"Like hell they did. Did you sleep with the whole temple? Or did your boyfriend pay? I wonder where Harcourt could come up with that much gold?"

Jalanna spat on the ground and stormed back inside the Den. There was a reason she never had any interest in this man. She could always sense the blackness of his heart. Where she could feel kindness from Harcourt, she felt cruelty and malice from Trascar. They were exact opposites.

So Harcourt has been a busy thief, Trascar thought. He was willing to bet that Kalandra Manor was not the only place the thief had hit recently. He was positive that Harcourt was responsible for the latest crime spree.

"You are not winning this time," the Guild leader growled to himself.

* * * *

Harcourt jogged down a dirty street on his way to the party at the Ogre's Den. The south district was not much to look at, but oh how he missed it. He had just dropped off another sack of gold at the orphanage and while there, he had bumped into the young girl Krestina. He wanted to ask how she was doing and give her a few more gold coins but she took off, seemingly very upset about something. Young girls were such strange creatures he thought.

From there he passed by old Kan's alley, filled his tin cup with gold and gave him a bottle of fine brandy. Kan could have talked for hours but Harcourt promised to return later.

A whistle to his right drew the thief's attention to an all-too-familiar city guard leaning against the wall of a stable.

"Captain Dornell, how are you?"

"Good," the captain answered in his usual serious tone. "Nice clothes. Where have you been lately?"

"Out of town. I was working for a merchant in Dulbard protecting caravans. The pay was good," the thief lied.

"Must have been quite good indeed. Fancy clothes, expensive ring for your girl, big party, getting married. I see Jalanna's scars are healed too," Dornell observed.

"Bless those priests and thank the lord for their charity," Harcourt said.

"Since when do the priests in the city do charity work?" Dornell asked.

"Go ask them yourself if you don't believe me."

"Maybe I will." The captain stepped closer to the thief. "You don't fool me. Working for a merchant in Dulbard? I know you would never leave this city. I've known you just about your entire life. Thieving is all you know. Now I've always wanted you to one day clean up your act and I've hoped that woman of yours would have helped you, but I am not buying any of this. I hope I am wrong, but I highly doubt it. I do not tolerate thievery, you know this and if I can prove that is what you've been up to, it's back to the dungeon with you. Your future wife will not be pleased with that."

"Sorry to disappoint you, my old friend, but I am a thief no more. The good lord has shown me the error of my wicked ways. Jal and I will open a shop, I think. I can see you are on duty now so I won't invite you to the party at the Den, but do drop by the wedding on the morrow at the temple of the One True God. Free eats and drinks," the thief winked at the captain and resumed his walk.

*　　*　　*　　*

"You know you are taking my best barmaid away from me," Wulfred said between huge gulps of ale.

"That's what the extra bag of gold was for," Harcourt replied with a smile. "I feel guilty."

"That was kind of you. That was a lot!"

"Well, you've given me a lot of free drinks and meals over the years. Just paying you back, big guy."

The thief spotted Andil entering the tavern. He thanked Wulfred again for hosting the party and headed over to speak with his skinny friend.

"Glad you could make it Andil. Nobody ever knows how to get ahold of you so I was hoping you had heard about this."

"You know I hear everything," Andil replied. "Congrats with Jal and all, but where did you ever raise that much gold? I heard you took credit for the Kalandra caper but come on, you couldn't have made that much from just that."

"No, it wasn't all from there. I'll explain it all to you soon I promise," Harcourt whispered.

"I don't know how you've been doing it. It would take the One-Handed Bandit himself to pull off some of the jobs that have been done lately."

"You don't know just how true that is," Harcourt laughed.

189

"I gotta know everything," Andil said. "When you plan your next job, please let me know. I can help you."

"I know you can, buddy. Like I said, I'll explain more soon."

Harcourt noticed that Jalanna had been looking a little distressed at the party. He excused himself from the other thief, made his way over to the woman he loved and pulled her away from some gossiping barmaids. When he asked about her mood, she explained that she was just overly tired with everything that had been going on lately.

"Come on then let's go home. I think we've mingled enough," Harcourt said to her.

"Yeah, I am ready leave but you can't come with me," she said.

"What?"

"We are getting married tomorrow. You can't stay with me tonight. You can't see me until we are at the temple."

"That's ridiculous."

"That's tradition."

"So we can break tradition."

"No we will not. Now you can walk me home but you can go find some nice inn to stay at tonight."

*   *   *   *

Harcourt was pretty exhausted himself and it was quite late already. Jalanna had told him to go find an inn to stay at but the thief had another idea in mind. He turned into his old alley and found his little shack just as he had left it many months ago. Only one difference; someone else was currently sleeping in it. The thief nudged the man with his boot. "Hey you, get up."

The man just grumbled. Harcourt nudged him a little harder. "Let's go, I said up."

Finally, the man rolled over and it was one of the beggars he shared the alley with. "This is my place now. Go away," he said.

"And you can keep it good sir, I only need it for tonight," Harcourt said dropping a handful of silver coins on the ground. "Here, go find somewhere else to be tonight."

The beggar could not collect the coins fast enough.

"Thank you," he kept repeating over and over then ran off into the night. Most likely to find a drink.

Harcourt kicked the filthy blanket aside. The night was mild enough that he would not need one. He climbed inside and lay down in his old home. He figured his back would suffer tonight, but for some reason, he found it fitting that he spend one more night here. Tomorrow, a whole new chapter of his life would begin.

Out of curiosity, he removed the loose board from the wall and found some of his old clothes still stuffed inside his little hiding spot. He smiled to himself, then placed his magical mask and coin purse in there for the night and drifted off into an uncomfortable but somehow satisfying sleep.

CHAPTER 19

Harcourt hurried along home. He slept in longer than he should have and had to rush over to the Siren's Retreat for a bath and a shave. Now he needed to get back to the house to change into something appropriate to get married in. Jalanna cared about things like that. She had stressed over picking out the perfect dress for this big day. Harcourt figured it was the least he could do to try and find something extraordinary to wear. Coordinating colors and styles though was not a skill he had ever perfected. Usually, he just wore whatever he could steal and preferably it was black. He did though have some idea in mind since his time as Lord Mornay had him dealing with all kinds of wealthy well-dressed folk. With a little luck, all attention would be on his beautiful bride this day and not him, he hoped, Harcourt never liked being the center of attention. Being a thief, he spent most of his life not wanting to be noticed.

The thief figured Jalanna would have left for the temple by now with her friends, so it would be safe for him to go home without being yelled at for seeing her dress too soon. He felt nervous. After all the adventures he found himself in throughout his life, he could not understand why this one made him so nervous. Perhaps it was the attention - too many eyes on him.

He ran up to their door and knocked loudly. "Jal? You still in there? Hello?"

He waited a few moments then tried the door and found it unlocked. She must still be home then, he thought. "Hello? Jal I need to change so go hide if you have to. Ok?"

No answer. "Hello?"

He was hoping that she hadn't just left the house unlocked, considering the amount of gold and valuables he had hidden away there. She should have known better. Suddenly feeling a little uneasy, he drew one of his daggers and silently entered the house. The hairs on the back of his neck stood on end as a strange feeling of panic washed over him.

As he entered their living room, he was greeted by a scene out of a nightmare. The thief's legs went weak and he wailed, "Noooooooooo," so loud the windows shook.

Jalanna, the woman he loved, lay sprawled on the floor in a pool of blood, a dagger buried in her heart. Harcourt ran to her, nearly slipping in the blood and dropped to his knees, his hands trembling. He sobbed uncontrollably, his mind reeling, unable to accept the scene before him. He screamed again in anger as loud as humanly possible, a primordial roar.

It was at that moment that city guards burst into his home led by the brute Zorfal but Harcourt was oblivious to their presence. The guard shouted, "Harcourt, you are under arrest for the suspicion of…" then he spotted the thief kneeling next to Jalanna's body.

"By all the gods, a murder! Weapons out, this one is dangerous."

Zorfal and the three other guards drew their swords and spread out to circle around and surround the thief. One of them blew their horn. Harcourt continued to sob, not even registering that the guards were there.

"Surrender yourself, thief," Zorfal commanded. "Don't make this any worse for yourself. Stand up and keep your hands where we can see them."

Harcourt did not move. Zorfal motioned for one of the guards to grab the thief. As the man put his hand on Harcourt's shoulder, the thief stood, turned and exploded into action throwing a surprising left hook that broke the guards jaw with a crunch. Fueled by unbridled rage, the punch sent the guard reeling back several feet into a wall.

Zorfal was there in an instant, slamming the hilt of his sword into the back of the thief's skull, sending him to the floor. "Resist, I dare you," the brute said.

Then, it was as if the life was sucked right out of the thief. He slumped onto the floor and sobbed, all fight having left his body. Still very wary of another attack, two other guards cautiously approached the thief, then lifted him up and shackled his wrists behind his back. They dragged his limp body out of the house as more guards arrived.

Zorfal stepped outside and gave a salute to Captain Dornell as he approached.

"I came as soon as I got your message. What in god's name happened here?" the captain asked.

"Gruesome scene sir. We received a tip from a

woman that Harcourt was involved with a lot of the recent burglaries and was stashing all of the loot at this house. We came here to arrest him and search the place. When we entered, we found that he had killed his girl," the brute answered.

"He what?" Dornell asked unable to believe what he had just heard.

"Drove a dagger into the poor wench's heart."

"You saw him do it?"

"No, sir. We must have arrived right after he'd done it. Unfortunately, we were too late to do anything for her."

A guard stuck his head out the door and called to Dornell. "What are your orders, sir?"

Captain Dornell was still in a state of shock. Something did not feel right about this whole thing. He was a guard captain but this was not his district.

"Leave the woman where she is until Captain Fallow gets here, I have sent for him. Search the house."

Zorfal shook his head in disgust. "How many times do we see these lowlifes get drunk and then go after their poor women. I should have just killed him myself."

Dornell ignored the comment. *Something does not seem right*, he thought again.

*   *   *   *

Harcourt was led into the courtroom with wrists and ankles chained by two very large guards. The room was full of people that had known both the thief and Jalanna. There were mixed emotions throughout. Anger and sadness at the loss of Jalanna, as well as shock over the deed allegedly having been carried out by Harcourt, of all

195

people.

Wulfred sat there grim-faced while the other barmaids cried. Andil sat tucked away in a corner, his face expressionless. Dahleene sniffed and wiped tears from her eyes with a handkerchief as a horrified-looking Krestina sat next to her. Even Feylane was there, today a redhead.

Captain Dornell and Zorfal stood at the back of the room along with several other guards. Dornell watched intently as the thief was brought before the magistrate's elevated desk, never once looking up from the floor. His body moved, but it was as if there was nobody home. A walking zombie. He had been that way since his arrest. He did not speak, he did not eat.

Harcourt was truly unaware of his surroundings, not even noticing that it was Magistrate Krommel that entered the courtroom, clad in the customary blue and black robes, and sat at the desk. The magistrate banged the table with a gavel silencing the room, save for those still crying.

"I must say I am not surprised to find this man standing before me once again. Harcourt's life has been a life of crime. A petty thief from the time he was a child. A disease upon our fair city. This time, he has gone too far, murdering an innocent woman. The very woman he was to marry. A woman who had trusted him. That trust would be her undoing. A dagger that was confirmed to have belonged to the accused found buried in her heart. The blade so dull that only anger and hatred-fueled strength could have driven it into her. A search of the thief's house produced many stolen treasures from a recent crime spree that took Stonewood by storm. The city guard received information that Jalanna was not pleased with her man's thieving ways. She was considering doing her duty as a citizen and reporting him. In a drunken rage, this lifetime criminal must have decided to silence her before she could speak to the authorities, proving that coins mean more to thieves than anything else. To our dismay, our guards arrived too late to save the life of this poor woman. I find it utterly repulsive when an innocent life is taken. Murderers cannot be allowed to get away with these heinous acts. Not in Stonewood. This is not some lawless city you may find elsewhere in this world. We here are civilized and must conduct ourselves in a civilized manner. Because the victim in this case was a foreign citizen, I will forego the punishment of execution. So Harcourt, of no known last name, I hereby sentence you to life in the dungeon. May you never pose a threat to this great city again."

He banged the gavel down loudly.

People shouted, people cried and never once did the thief look up. He might not have even heard a word the magistrate had said. The guards grabbed him and pulled him roughly out of the courtroom. He shuffled along without any resistance, without any spark of life.

"There is one more lowlife off the streets permanently," Zorfal said.

"I am not so sure about this one," Captain Dornell replied. "Harcourt was a thief, of that there is no doubt. But he was no murderer. It was not his style. Why now?"

"Who can say what runs through the minds of drunken madmen? Let's get something to eat, I am starving," Zorfal said leaving the courtroom.

Dornell stayed back until he was the last one remaining in the room. A known criminal had just been locked up for good, but the captain did not feel any satisfaction this time.

CHAPTER 20

Four Years Later

A pathetic-looking man sat securely-bound to a chair in a dark, musty warehouse. Blood flowed from his mouth and several of his teeth lay on the floor. Both eyes were purple and swollen nearly closed. In front of him, stood an imposing figure, the Thieves Guild's top enforcer, Randar. Randar had removed his shirt to avoid getting it messy, his chiseled chest splattered with the man's blood.

"Just give me a location. That's all I want. Then I'll let you go," he said.

The man spat out a mouthful of blood and replied, "Our Lord Lucivenus will punish you for this. An attack on me is an attack on our glorious Lord himself."

In one clean swipe, Randar removed the man's head with his short-bladed sword. He wiped his blade clean with a dirty cloth as he walked over to where Feylane was standing. The beautiful woman with her long blonde hair tied back in a ponytail looked very disappointed. Since her encounter with the sinister Lord Mornay, Feylane had given up her usual role as Guild assassin. For the last four years she led a small task force of thugs and assassins whose sole purpose was to find out everything possible on the demon worshipping cult. It was not going well.

In all that time, the headless man sitting in the chair was only the fifth cult member they had been able to catch. Randar was always brought in to interrogate, but every time ended the same way. They received nothing of value and the cult member lost his head. In return, four Guild members had been found butchered and missing their hearts.

"I don't understand it," Randar said. "They never talk, no matter what I do."

"This goes beyond normal brainwashing. It's like they are under some spell that does not allow them to reveal any secrets," Feylane guessed.

"Now you believe in magic spells?" the enforcer snickered.

"How do you explain it then?" she countered. "I am as loyal as they come, but you do some of those things to me and I'll tell you where Trascar lives."

Randar did not smile. "Let's hope they don't get their hands on you again then, eh? I'd keep that little admission to yourself if I were you. Honestly, I can't explain it. They obviously feel the pain but something prevents them from talking. Perhaps fear of what their priests would do to them if they talked outweighs the fear of me and my torture."

"I would guess from the faces on the two of you, this was another failure," Trascar said as he and the weasely Zenod entered the warehouse.

"He gave us nothing," Randar admitted.

"Wonderful," Trascar answered sarcastically. "While you two were here playing with him," he pointed to the headless corpse, "Harvad was found dead in his apartment this morning. We are now even again, five for five."

"His heart?" Feylane asked.

"Gone," answered Zenod.

Randar growled. He wanted to slaughter the entire cult. Harvad was a friend and a good fighter. "So it's an all-out war they want?" he said.

"Good," Trascar said. "Get mad. Do something about it. I want results. This game has gone on long enough."

"First things first. Randar, we need you to go to seventeen Adleton Road," Zenod said. "The merchant there has a package for us. Smack him if you feel like it, he's been rather difficult."

"What about that silver shipment due in tomorrow?" Trascar asked the weasely rogue.

"Taken care of. None of our boys. I've got some mercenaries that are gonna hijack it a few miles outside the city. No link to us, it'll just appear to be random highwaymen," Zenod replied.

Trascar nodded in approval. "Excellent, finally some good news today. Feylane, meet me at our lower west gambling house later tonight. And if you see him around, tell Andil I've got another job for him."

*　　*　　*　　*

Heavy boots descended down the dark narrow stairwell. One had to be careful with one's footing here, for it would be a long and painful tumble to the bottom. Torches sparsely populated the stone walls giving the corridors very little illumination. The shadows created by the flickering torchlight could play tricks with the mind down here. Loud footsteps and the jingle of chainmail armor echoed down the hallways as the man marched with purpose.

He counted doors as he went, ignoring the anguished wails he heard from behind many of them. Thirteen, fourteen, ah, fifteen. The man peeked through the tiny iron-barred window set in the middle of a heavy wooden door. It took a moment for his eyes to adjust, then he spotted the figure he sought. A dirty man sat huddled in the corner of the cold cell. His lean muscular body carried many scars, some old, some fresh. Some had come from the lashes of a whip, others appeared to be slash wounds. His long dark hair and beard showed some hint of silver.

The armored man in the hall took an iron key and unlocked the door. He drew a razor-sharp dagger and stepped inside the cell, shutting the door behind him.

"Been a long time," said the man with the dagger.

The other man did not reply, did not even move save for his eyes, which stared intently at the visitor.

"Have you been treated fairly?" the visitor asked.

With lightening quickness, the shirtless man jumped to his feet causing the other to step back and raise the dagger before him in a defensive stance.

"What's that for Captain? Nervous about being in a cell with a murderer?"

"I don't believe you are a murderer, Harcourt," Captain Dornell answered, but did not lower the blade.

"And yet you are visibly nervous."

"Who knows how four years in this place has affected your mind?" the captain replied.

Harcourt suddenly feinted in, causing Dornell to reach out and swing with the blade. The thief easily stepped back out of range of the swing, then darted in with amazing speed grabbing the captain's wrist and twisting his arm. Sharp pain caused Dornell to let go of the weapon, but Harcourt caught it before it fell. The guard captain reached for his sword hilt but the thief was on him instantly, holding the blade to his throat. There was a long tense moment of silence, then Dornell finally spoke. "What now?"

"Now," Harcourt replied, "You can relax, and tell me what you are doing here."

The thief flipped the dagger around and caught it by the blade. He held it out, handle first, to the captain. Surprised, Dornell accepted the weapon back and Harcourt went and sat on the floor with his back to the cell wall. Dornell did relax then. He sheathed the dagger and sat against the opposite wall.

"You are right, though, "Harcourt said, "I am no murderer. And I cannot explain how, but my mind is still intact. But has it really been four years?"

"Yes, I am afraid so," Dornell answered. "Tell me, what happened that day four years ago?"

Harcourt sneered. "Why did it take four years, four very long years, before someone finally asked me that?"

"Let's face it, you were no model citizen. When the city gets a chance to lock up a known criminal, they are not inclined to ask too many questions. Your own dagger was the murder weapon and you were the only one on the scene. Clear-cut to the courts. You know the King ordered a crackdown on the Thieves Guild, so they'd jump at any opportunity to lock up a Guild member. Whether you were a member or not, you were still a thief and it's all the same in our eyes."

"Oh, so let's pin a murder on a simple thief. Let's take away a man's life so he doesn't take a few coins from those who wouldn't even miss them."

"Stealing is a crime no matter who you take it from. It doesn't belong to you. You'll get no sympathy from me on that issue. I uphold and enforce the laws here. I ensure that justice is served. In this case, I don't believe justice was served. I believe there is still a murderer on the loose out there," Dornell said.

For a moment, Harcourt's eyes glazed over. "Of course, there is still a murderer out there. I loved her. I would never have done anything to hurt her."

"Who would have wanted to kill Jalanna?" the captain asked.

"Nobody. She had no enemies. You couldn't find a more decent person. Whoever did this wanted to get to me, it had nothing to do with her," Harcourt reasoned.

"I suspect the Thieves Guild most likely. Were you a member?"

"No."

"Be honest here with me. I need the truth."

"I wasn't. They never let me in. The Guild did want me dead not long before, but that had been cleared up," Harcourt said.

"Explains much, then. The Guild has strict rules against those who commit crimes not authorized by them. That string of burglaries you pulled off would have most certainly angered them. Usually though, it would have been you floating down the river. Framing you for the murder of your soon-to-be wife is not common practice. That is the act of someone that hates you. They were not looking to simply punish you for breaking their rules, someone wanted you to suffer."

"How are you so sure it wasn't me?" Harcourt asked.

"I see no motive for you to have killed her and I know you are not prone to violence. I've known you a long time, know you better than anyone else, I think. In all those years, I don't recall you ever starting any fights. Oh, you've hurt a lot of people, but always in defense of yourself or someone else. That's not the profile of a killer. I even remember a few instances where you would have been justified in the slaying of another and yet you still held your hand," Dornell answered.

"Why are you investigating this? Doesn't Stonewood have people for that?"

"Yes, and that's me," Dornell replied. "I am still a captain, but no longer of the south district. I am now the captain of the Investigations Unit."

"Why have you waited four years to begin?" Harcourt questioned angrily.

"I haven't, I started four years ago. It has taken me this long to get the city to agree to this," Dornell replied.

"Agree to what?" the thief asked curiously.

"Agree to release you into my custody, in exchange for your help in finding the killer and possibly toppling the Thieves Guild."

"Released? Me?"

"Yes, as long as you agree to help."

"Toppling the Guild? I can't…"

"Harcourt," Dornell cut him off, knowing where he

was going, "These people are not your friends. They have tried to kill you and someone did kill Jalanna. Someone or several people need to pay for her death. Don't you think she deserves that?"

"Yes. Yes, I do."

CHAPTER 21

Harcourt and Dornell quickened their pace through the dark city streets, cloaks pulled tight against the cool breeze and hoods drawn over their heads. The thief could not believe he was actually outside in the real world again. He wondered when he was going to wake from a cruel trick of a mind gone mad. But was he mad? The breeze felt real enough. He drank in the fresh air and savored every bit of it. He long ago accepted the fact that he was going to die in the dungeon. The first few months had been the hardest. Dealing with Jalanna's death and a life sentence simultaneously should have driven him over the edge, and quite nearly did. Harcourt was a survivor though, always had been.

It was impossible to track the passage of time in the dungeon but the thief guessed it took nearly a year of mourning before his mind snapped back to reality. He realized he needed all his wits about him to avoid all the dangers of the dungeon. He refused to meet his end at the hand of some other low-life prisoner. Harcourt spent most of the day alone in his cell but twice a day, the prisoners were allowed to stretch their legs and had meals in a common hall. It was there where you fought for your life against real murderers with nothing left to lose. Needless to say, the thief had not been idle the last several years. If anything, his fighting prowess had only increased.

Harcourt found it astonishing that Captain Dornell had actually petitioned his case all the way up to King Stonewood himself. The thief and the guard captain had been lifetime enemies. Strict rules came with Harcourt's release though, as Dornell had explained to him, the most important of which was that this remain top secret. Nobody must learn of Harcourt's release. The court system could not be made to look foolish and its integrity brought into question by admitting they possibly had made a mistake.

An obvious rule was that he was not to commit any further crimes lest he return to the dungeon for life and the investigation would be dropped. He was Captain Dornell's responsibility and was to be with him at all times.

What the thief found amusing was that he was now in the employ of the city. His food and lodgings were now provided for and he was for the time being, an agent of the Investigations Unit. It all felt very foreign to the thief but he would do anything to catch Jalanna's killer. After he did, he was not sure what life had in store for him.

The unlikely duo finally reached their destination. It would be a lie if Harcourt said he had not spent his life wondering what it was like inside this place. The entire city was full of rumors surrounding Fezzdin the Fantastic and his mysterious tower. Now here he was, in front of the tower's double doors with the stone gargoyle leering down at him.

Captain Dornell raised his hand to knock, but before he could, the doors swung inward as if on their own. Not a soul stood inside to greet them. The two men exchanged glances then Dornell entered. Harcourt reached up to touch the gargoyle sculpture and recoiled as it hissed back at him. Startled, the thief ran inside the tower.

"How does he make it do that?" he asked.

The doors slammed shut behind them causing both men to jump.

"That is beyond either of us. Wizards guard their secrets very closely," Dornell replied, a little unnerved.

"You don't actually believe in this whole wizard business do you?" Even after owning the magical mask, Harcourt still found it difficult to wrap his head around the concept of a wizard, a person who could cast mysterious and wonderful spells. "Parlor tricks, all of it."

"Believe what you like. I've seen a lot of strange things in my time. Magic has to account for some of it," Dornell reasoned.

They stood in a lobby of sorts, a large circular room with several comfortable-looking chairs and exotic plants. The walls were adorned with many paintings depicting bizarre creatures and scenery. There was one of a blue frog with the antlers of a deer. One had a green sky with trees that bore purple leaves. Yet another depicted a three-headed winged dragon fighting several individuals with pointed ears, elves as they were called in the fairy stories.

As the pair gazed around the room, a voice from nowhere spoke to them. "Please gentlemen, come up to my study. I apologize for not greeting you personally, but I am in the middle of something. Up the stairs there, all the way to the top."

The hairs on their necks stood on end at hearing the disembodied voice. Dornell walked over to the narrow winding stairwell and looked up. It stretched up as far as he could see.

"All the way up huh? Well let's get going if we want to arrive by dawn."

The captain, who was weighed down with his mail shirt and sword, did not look forward to climbing to the top of Stonewood's tallest structure. It also appeared to be taller from the inside than the outside which confused the captain. With a sigh, Dornell motioned for Harcourt to follow and began to ascend the stairs.

What appeared to be the mid-way point was where Dornell finally had to stop to take a break and catch his breath. Harcourt too, was a little winded but feared if they waited too long, then his legs would not co-operate in carrying him up the rest of the way.

The two men did eventually reach the study after what felt like an hour of climbing. Dornell wanted to appear professional but fell to his knees with exhaustion. Harcourt, who was not burdened with the same weight, was tired but not nearly as winded. "Bet he doesn't get a lot of visitors," the thief commented.

A wave of dizziness washed over Harcourt as he turned his attention to the room they now occupied. The room appeared much larger than it should. His mind struggled to accept what he saw. How was that even possible? When he finally got over the issue of the room's dimensions, he was awestruck by the state of its disarray. The thief was not even sure the word messy could properly describe it. There was clutter everywhere. Papers, books and little odds and ends were scattered over every inch of the study. The walls were lined with over-flowing bookcases. There were several tables and desks in the room with one long workbench in the center. The tops of the furniture could not be seen due to the sheer amount of clutter. The thief also noted two more stone gargoyles perched atop bookshelves watching over the room.

"Look at this place," he said to Dornell. "I've never seen so much rubbish."

"I can hear you," said Fezzdin, lifting his head up from behind a pile of books.

Harcourt had not even noticed the man sitting amidst the mess. Fezzdin looked just like a wizard taken right from the pages of a child's fairy tale. He was an elderly man with snow white hair and a long white beard. His robes were bright blue with a matching conical blue hat covered with golden stars and half-moons. Harcourt smiled at the spectacle but held back his laugh at how ridiculous he thought the man looked.

"No wonder this room is a mess, your maid couldn't make it up the stairs. I think we passed her skeletal remains somewhere on the way up," Harcourt said.

"Harcourt, I presume?" Fezzdin said without any hint of amusement.

"Yes, please don't mind him sir," Dornell said, finally standing and getting his breath back. "And I am Captain Dornell of the Investigations Unit. I was instructed to come here this evening and that you were informed of this situation."

"Indeed I am, good Captain. You'll find what you are looking for on that table to your left. The flask with the red liquid," Fezzdin said, then turned his gaze back to the thief. "Take one drop of that each week to maintain your alteration."

"My what?" Harcourt asked.

"You cannot be walking about Stonewood having people recognize you as the man who was sent away for life in the dungeon. One drop of that elixir will alter your appearance slightly. It will change your eye color, your hair color, and even remove those scars on your cheek and chin. Each drop lasts only a week mind you," Fezzdin replied.

"An illusion, eh?" Harcourt smiled. "I've heard talk of magical masks that can do similar things."

Fezzdin raised an eyebrow. "Have you now?"

"Of course, that's all just fairy tales to be sure," Harcourt said.

"Indeed," the wizard remarked, eyeing the thief curiously.

Harcourt spied a deck of playing cards on a nearby table and walked over to retrieve it. He shuffled the deck thoroughly then said, "I'll show you some magic, wizard. Pick a card, any card."

Fezzdin mumbled something and snapped his fingers. Harcourt yelped as the deck burst into flames and was consumed. One lone card remained and fluttered to the floor.

"The King of Stonewood," Fezzdin said.

Harcourt bent over to pick up the card, and it was indeed the King of Stonewood. "How did......"

"Come on Magician Harcourt, time to go," Dornell cut in. "We thank you for your help, sir. It's greatly appreciated."

"You are welcome, Captain. Keep me updated on

your progress and come and see me when that flask is empty," Fezzdin replied, still watching the thief curiously as the guard captain grabbed the flask of red liquid and pulled him away to the stairs.

Halfway down their long trek to the bottom, Harcourt asked, "How did he do that? Where did the flame come from?"

"He's a wizard, that's how he did it," Dornell replied as if that answer explained everything.

CHAPTER 22

Harcourt felt extremely weighed down by the chainmail vest. He had never worn armor of any kind and found it awkward. How could anyone fight effectively with this on, he thought. Dornell explained it was part of his new uniform. He worked for the city now and was no longer a thief.

"Surely I don't need to carry this?" the thief asked holding a long city-issued sword.

"Yes. It's part of the uniform so get used to it. Perhaps you should learn to use it too," Dornell answered.

"At least give me a short-bladed sword. This is not practical indoors or in narrow alleyways," the thief countered.

Harcourt had already selected two daggers from the south district guardhouse armory and figured that was all he needed. Dornell handed him a short-bladed sword and the thief strapped it to his belt with a shrug. The captain then went to hand over the horn that all guards carried, but Harcourt waved it off. "No thanks. I've had too many bad memories with those, if you don't mind."

Instead of wearing the blue tunic with Stonewood's emblem on top of the mail vest, Harcourt wore a dark cloak with the city's emblem sewn on the inside. This was the uniform of the Investigations Unit.

While Harcourt was getting outfitted, another member of the unit entered the room to replace his broken sword with a new one. He saluted Dornell as soon as he realized who it was. "Greetings, Captain."

"At ease, Melvon," Dornell replied with a nod. "What happened to your blade there?"

"A little mix-up with some mercenaries over on Barrel Way. Luckily, nobody was hurt, aside from a few of the mercs. We've been watching this group for days," Melvon told the captain.

"I am glad everyone is ok. A broken sword is easily replaced."

"Yes, indeed. Who is this? A new recruit?" the other guard said motioning to Harcourt.

"Ah, why yes, I apologize," Dornell was quick to answer. "Melvon this is Krathan, Krathan this is Melvon." Harcourt extended a hand to Melvon and gave him a nod. "Krathan here is our newest recruit. He has been an outstanding guard serving in the lower east for the last five years. His exceptional record and cleverness finally caught our eye and we decided to bring him aboard."

Melvon shook the thief's hand with a strong grip. "Welcome to the team, Krathan. We can use all the help we can get. But don't think that this promotion means you will be equipped with better weapons," he chuckled, holding up his broken sword. "Our funding is lacking just as much as all the district units."

Melvon swapped swords from a rack of weapons and gave Dornell another salute before leaving.

"Krathan, eh? An outstanding guard from the lower east, eh?" Harcourt said when the pair was alone again. "Why Captain Dornell, you are positively deceitful. You would have made a good thief, I think."

"Shut up," he replied.

"When do I get the training on how to tell such convincing tales?" Harcourt asked.

"That is training that you do not require," Dornell said. "In fact, you could probably teach that yourself."

Once they had finished their business at the armory, Captain Dornell led Harcourt into a room with a large table. Upon the table sat a small scale model of the south district. Within the model district were placed tiny, colored figures carved from wood. Dornell explained, "See the blue figures represent a single guard. The red figures represent three guards. The yellow figures represent five guards. The white figures represent a mounted guard and the purple figures are heavily-armored soldiers. Each time a guard leaves this post for patrol, they will place the appropriate figure near the area they plan to be in. When they return, they will place the figure back to the home-base position."

"What are the black figures with the devil horns?" Harcourt asked.

"Known criminals. They are placed near their last known whereabouts or where they dwell," Dornell replied. "And the buildings with red doors are suspected Guild businesses or hangouts."

"Interesting system," Harcourt commented. "Where are the suspected cult members and cult hangouts?"

Dornell paused for a long moment. "Well, we have no leads on them," he answered embarrassed.

"Then I've got a tip for you. How's Magistrate Krommel doing these days?" the thief asked.

"You mean Chief Magistrate Krommel," the captain stated.

"Chief?"

"Yes, Chief. He was promoted two years ago."

Before Harcourt could say anymore, two guards burst into the room out of breath. The one with long blond hair looked relieved to see the pair in the map room. "Captain Dornell, good timing, I was about to have someone fetch you. I think you should go to Nine Dandelback Street immediately, gruesome scene there, sir."

Dornell was out the door in a flash with Harcourt in tow. A few twists and turns down dusty streets brought them to the address they were given, a used clothing shop. At this late hour, the shop would have been closed. A city guard stood watch outside the shop door while a few drunks looked on curiously.

Dornell approached the guard and flashed the city emblem from inside his cloak. The guard saluted and stepped aside to allow him to enter. Harcourt did the same and the guard nodded, letting him pass. The thief wished he'd had one of these cloaks years ago; it would have come in very handy.

The scene before them was gruesome indeed. The other guard had not exaggerated in the least. The shop was small with only a few racks of clothing. There was a body on the floor in the middle of the room, its head over in a far corner. The man lay in a pool of blood, and it was splattered everywhere. The shop had a back room where they found a window left open, facing an alleyway.

"It was the shop owner," Dornell said looking at the head. He then nudged the body over onto its back with his boot. "And look here, his heart is missing. It was that vile cult."

"It's not missing," Harcourt called over, "It's here under a pile of clothes."

Dornell walked over to see for himself. "So we have a cult member that came through the back window, murdered the shopkeep in some disgusting ritual, then ripped out his heart," he said.

Harcourt shook his head. "I don't think so. Come back here."

The captain followed the thief into the back room.

"See this window? The glass is all intact but the locking mechanism is on the inside. It's a good window. It was opened from the inside."

"You are telling me that there is no trick for opening these windows?" Dornell asked.

"Of course there is, but it requires breaking or cutting the glass. This window is still in one piece." The thief motioned for Dornell to follow him to the front door. He opened the door to inspect the outside lock. "This lock was picked, and by an amateur too."

"How do you know?"

"See these scratches around the keyhole? That is someone fumbling with a lock pick. A skilled thief would not have left those marks."

"Couldn't the shopkeep have made those marks fumbling around with his own keys in the dark?" Dornell asked.

"The key would have made a thicker scratch mark.

These ones are too thin," Harcourt answered.

"So what are you saying? A cult member did this? Or the Thieves Guild?"

"You're most likely looking for a Guild member. Probably a thug not so skilled in break-ins, or a drunk thief who was sloppy. They broke in through the front and waited for this poor bastard. The conversation didn't go well and the shopkeep was beheaded. Possibly in a panic, the killer decided to rip out the man's heart and stage a cult murder. He opened the back window to make it appear that's where he entered."

Dornell rubbed his chin in deep thought. "Since his heart was ripped out, how do you know a cult member was not the one who picked the lock?"

"Ripped out, yes, but not missing. Have you ever found a heart at any other cult murder scenes? From my understanding, they use the heart in some sick ritual. It does not get cast aside like this one was. Our killer here had no knowledge of that detail." Harcourt walked over and crouched by the body. "And look here. Look at the cuts in his chest around his heart. A sloppy job. The person didn't know what they were doing."

"Good deductions," Dornell admitted, a little surprised. "I believe you are correct. And I also believe there was more than one attacker. See here? Two different-sized bloody boot prints."

Harcourt nodded in agreement. "My guess would be three. Two inside and one outside to keep watch."

Their conversation was suddenly interrupted by a woman's scream from somewhere outside. The pair ran out of the shop and a second scream told them the woman must have been one street over. Dornell pointed to the guard standing by the shop door. "Stay here. We'll investigate the screams. Let nobody enter aside from Captain Flannis."

Captain Dornell and Harcourt took an alleyway shortcut and had to jump over two homeless men and dodge an angry dog. They emerged onto a street that was lined with a series of warehouses and listened intently for any further clues to the woman's whereabouts. A female whimper, followed by a muffled laugh came from one of the nearby buildings.

Harcourt pinpointed which warehouse and the two men approached the front entrance. Muffled voices and laughter could be heard from within. "Wait here," Harcourt whispered. "I'll find a back way in."

At first, Dornell was reluctant to let the thief out of his sight, but something told him he could trust Harcourt. The captain gave a nod and the thief disappeared around the corner. Harcourt found a side door down a narrow alleyway and to his relief, it was unlocked. He no longer owned any lock picks. He drew his two daggers and slipped inside.

The inside of the warehouse was illuminated with several lanterns. It was crowded with stacks of wooden crates and Harcourt ducked behind one of them. Near the center of the large warehouse stood two bloodied thugs wrestling with a struggling woman whose dress was torn to shreds.

The woman did not appear to be wounded and the blood the men were covered in did not appear to be their own. A pale-faced, red-haired man laughed and taunted the poor woman, blowing her kisses. A stocky man wearing studded leather armor tried to hold her arms behind her back. The stocky man then said to the redhead, "Back off, Davdin. She's mine first."

That voice, Harcourt thought, *where do I know that voice from?* The woman's struggles turned the stocky man around for a moment and anger swelled up in the thief as he recognized the man. He would recognize Haig's ugly face anywhere. It was confirmed when Harcourt noticed the man was missing a finger.

The thief stepped out in the open, a dagger in each hand, and called out. "Hey, ugly. Remember what I said I'd do the next time you touched another woman?"

Haig and Davdin regarded the thief with shocked expressions at his unexpected appearance. Haig squinted but did not recall ever seeing the man standing before them. Fezzdin's elixir had done its job. "Go find your own whore, this one's ours," Haig said, not releasing his grip on the woman.

Harcourt took a menacing step forward then dropped to his knees, momentarily blinded. A third thug who had gone to relieve himself struck him in the back of the head with a long piece of wood. The makeshift weapon broke in half when it connected with the thief's skull. Haig and Davdin roared with laughter. The woman sobbed when her would-be rescuer fell to the floor in a daze.

The thugs then received their second surprise of the night when Captain Dornell appeared from the opposite direction, long sword in hand. "Who the hell are you?" Davdin questioned.

"Why don't you gentlemen tell me whose blood you wear? I see no wounds on anyone in here, aside from my friend's head," Dornell said.

"Give me one good reason why I shouldn't split open

both your skulls. Who are you working for?" Haig asked.

Dornell opened his cloak to reveal the emblem of Stonewood.

"Now, why don't you three start explaining where you were tonight when that shopkeep lost his head and his heart."

"That's right, you're that Dornell fella. I thought you looked familiar. I am afraid we were drinking in a tavern all night, until this pretty little tart came by and propositioned us. The blood is from some unfortunates who picked a fight," Haig said, his hand inching towards his sword hilt.

Taking advantage of his distraction, the woman broke free of Haig's grasp and sprinted behind a stack of crates. "He lies! They boasted about killing a man tonight who wouldn't pay them some tax. They grabbed me on the street and dragged me in here," she shouted.

Haig shook his head and drew his sword. "Shoulda kept your mouth shut, wench. Now you're gonna have to die along with these two."

Davdin drew a slender sword in one hand, and a dagger in the other. The third thug, who appeared to be only a teen, drew his short-bladed sword. Harcourt, who feigned being more injured than he was, jumped to his feet and side-kicked the teenage thug into a pile of empty barrels. Dornell reached for his horn then remembered in his haste, that he had forgotten it. Well he thought, we are on our own.

Davdin advanced on Harcourt while Haig engaged Dornell. Davdin flashed an evil grin and feinted a jab with his dagger, following it up with a sweep of his sword. Harcourt did not fall for the feint and leaped back away from the blade. He gave a feint of his own and Davdin backed off, flinching from a strike that did not come. The pair circled each other while the clang of steel on steel rang out as Haig and Dornell battled fiercely.

Harcourt used a favorite trick of his, glancing behind the red-headed thug and smiled. Worried about a possible attack from behind, Davdin risked a glance back. Harcourt rushed in, scoring a deep strike on Davdin's left shoulder. The thug cried out and stepped back with a wild swing of his sword. Harcourt ducked underneath and slid back out of reach, suffering a small cut to the top of his already bruised and bloodied head. He cursed the armor that Dornell had made him wear, it slowed him down and threw off his balance.

Just as the thief finished that thought, he was pushed forward with a thudding strike to his back. The teenage thug had thought to drive his blade into Harcourt's spine but lacked the knowledge that the thief wore armor, and lacked the strength to penetrate it. Davdin sliced Harcourt's right arm with his sword as the thief stumbled towards him. Harcourt countered with a quick slice across the redhead's cheek, then put some distance between himself and his two attackers. *Maybe the armor was not so bad after all*, he rethought; that attack should have been the end of him.

Haig stabbed forward with his sword and Dornell parried. Dornell countered with his weapon and Haig parried. Sparks flew as the pair went back and forth, neither finding an opening. They were about equal in strength but the advantage of youth was with Haig. His swings were a little faster than his much-older opponent. Dornell, though, had been doing this his whole life. He had fought countless men before and was always patient in battle, always looking for little mistakes.

Haig stepped in with a wide arcing swing. Dornell easily blocked the attack and tied up the thug's arm. The captain lashed out with his left fist and bloodied Haig's flat nose. Haig stumbled back a few steps and fell to one knee, blinking. Dornell foolishly fell for the trap and moved in. Haig drew a knife from his boot and sprang at a surprised Dornell. The blade penetrated his armor and slid into his belly. The captain gasped, then struck Haig in the nose with his forehead, knocking him backwards. Dornell swung wildly with his sword, catching Haig's left thigh and forcing him to one knee, then reversed his attack and removed Haig's head. The woman nearby shrieked at the sight and Dornell stumbled to the floor, holding the handle of the knife embedded in his stomach.

The teen jabbed with his sword and Harcourt deflected it with his dagger. Davdin did the same and Harcourt parried with his other dagger. The thief was now getting used to the feel of the mail vest and knew his limitations. He feinted an attack at Davdin forcing him back, then went full speed at the teen. The young thug brought his sword up in defence and Harcourt batted it aside with one dagger and drew a red line across the teen's chest with his other. He was rewarded with a cry of pain, then turned his attention back to the redhead.

Davdin would feint with his dagger then attack with his sword. It was the same pattern over and over and was very predictable. He was trying to force the thief back against a wall. On the fourth attempt of the same manoeuver, Harcourt dove straight in instead of retreating backwards. He slipped inside the reach of the sword and cut open Davdin's dagger hand, disarming him of the weapon. The thief nicked his neck as the thug desperately backpedaled away.

Harcourt heard the woman scream and from the corner of his eye, caught Haig's headless body crumple to the floor, followed by Captain Dornell who appeared to be injured.

The teen rushed Dornell with his sword raised for a killing strike. Harcourt did the only thing he could and threw one of his daggers, just missing the boy. He cursed then threw his remaining dagger, sinking it deep in the thug's right shoulder blade. The teen cried out then was silenced when Dornell sat up and drove his sword through his attacker's belly and out the other side.

Harcourt spun back to face Davdin and with no other choice, drew his short sword. Having lost his two companions, and knowing what Harcourt was capable of with just daggers, the thug had little stomach to face the man now armed with a sword. The redhead threw down his weapon and said, "I surrender."

Harcourt approached the man and slammed his jaw with a left hook, flattening him to the floor. "Don't move," the thief growled, then ran over to check on Dornell.

"I'll live, I've suffered worse," the captain said trying to struggle to his feet. "Take these, you know how they work. Shackle our prisoner."

Harcourt pushed the stubborn captain back down and told him to sit tight. He went over and chained Davdin's hands behind his back, then threw him back to the ground. The woman ran over to thank the pair for rescuing her. Harcourt handed her his cloak to cover herself up. "Go, girl. Run and find some guards. Tell them we need a priest immediately."

She left at a full run, not wanting to spend another moment amid the carnage. Moments later, two guards entered the warehouse. Harcourt gave them a brief explanation of what took place and they left dragging Davdin with them, saying that a priest would arrive shortly.

Dornell sat with his back to a crate holding his stomach in obvious distress. "Thank you," the captain struggled to say.

"For?"

"For saving my life. That little bastard there would have cleaved my head," Dornell rasped.

"Think nothing of it. The sword and armor saved mine, so thanks for making me wear them," the thief chuckled. He pointed to Haig. "What's it like to take someone's life?"

"Well," Dornell thought for a moment, "I don't really dwell on it. These men attacked us, tried to kill us. So it was us or them."

"Never bothers you?" Harcourt asked.

"The first time yes, it bothered me. I can still remember watching the life fade from his eyes. Something I'll probably never forget. But I was defending myself and justified in my action," Dornell took a deep breath before continuing. "Nobody would have questioned you for killing any of these men here tonight. We were in the right."

"I understand, but I still prefer not to," Harcourt said.

"Then you are a better man than most. Most people think brutality and killing first. Just comes natural."

"Speaking of brutality, what ever happened to your old partner, Zorfal?" Harcourt asked.

"Captain Zorfal is now the guard captain of the lower west district."

*   *   *   *

Randar jogged to catch up to Trascar who was walking fairly quickly down a lower west street. "I just confirmed it was Haig and his crew last night. Haig and Erwald are dead. Davdin was arrested and will most likely hang."

"Good riddance to those fools. They should never have killed that shopkeeper. Not yet anyways. I am sure you could have convinced him to pay our tax," the Guild leader said in his usual miserable tone. "A dead shopkeeper pays us nothing."

"In my opinion, that particular shop should never have been targeted. That was a hard-working man who made very little coin in return. He could not afford any tax," Randar said.

"Excuse me? He ran a business in our city. Everyone is fair game," Trascar replied angrily.

"If we tax every little shop, we'll run them all out of business. Where's the profit in that?" the enforcer asked.

"You don't get paid your ridiculous wages to think about how we will make our profits. Just stick to enforcing our rules," Trascar said. "Now, what news of the Guild in Hartlan?"

"Crushed," Randar replied. "King Stonewood hired out some of his troops to aid the Duke. The Guild was annihilated and survivors have fled the city."

"Ah, such a shame," Trascar snickered.

CHAPTER 23

Harcourt entered the south district alone. It was the first time since his release that he was out without Dornell's supervision. It was no easy task convincing Dornell, but Harcourt wanted to continue with their investigation. The captain was still recovering from his stab wound and it was the advice of the priests that he remain in bed and do nothing for at least another week. That was precious time lost, Harcourt had told him.

The two of them had decided that Harcourt should attempt to infiltrate the Thieves Guild. This way, he could search for Jalanna's killer while relaying important information back to the city to help them bring the Guild down. They were unsure how Harcourt could achieve this but two days ago, a plan presented itself.

The city of Hartlan was the next closest city to the size of Stonewood and lay about a two weeks' journey away to the north and east. Years back, there had been a failed assassination attempt on the ruler, Duke Ortol, by the city's Thieves Guild. Ortol went on a crusade to root out and destroy the Guild which controlled much of the city's activities. It was a long process but with the aid of extra troops hired from Stonewood, the Guild was finally smashed. The Guild leader's head now hung from the castle wall and surviving members had scattered across the countryside in all directions.

One such member fled right to the gates of Stonewood itself, where he was apprehended. It turned out this man was the second in command of Hartlan's Thieves Guild. He was brought to the Investigations Unit headquarters and Harcourt had been allowed to interrogate the man; he secured a wealth of information he could use to his advantage. The next day, the Hartlan thief had been secretly executed for the crime of fighting against Stonewood troops.

Harcourt's plan was to approach the Guild, posing as this thief fleeing from Hartlan. His only concern was that he was not too confident in the changes Fezzdin's elixir made to his appearance. He did not feel that it would fool anyone who really knew him up close - someone like Serdic. The thief's plan was to seek out Andil first and see if he knew another contact person he could go to instead of Serdic. The first real test would be to see if he could fool his old friend.

Harcourt did not like the idea of visiting the Ogre's Den; there would be no smiling Jalanna there to greet him. For the longest time, he stood like a statue across the street from the tavern, afraid to enter. Folk came and went and he found himself waiting for Jalanna to walk out for her break to get some fresh air. He had to remind himself that was not going to happen. Harcourt pulled the hood of his black cloak around his head, took a deep breath and finally entered.

The tavern was not overly-crowded this night, small groups were scattered throughout. Dee was bringing some ale over to Whitemane who was sitting alone, as usual. It was nice for the thief to see some familiar faces again. Wulfred worked the bar and looked exactly the same only a little greyer.

Harcourt scanned the room looking for his skinny friend but Andil was not to be seen. The thief decided to risk approaching the bar to speak with Wulfred, and made sure to keep his face covered as best he could. "Excuse me barkeep, a question if you don't mind," he said.

"Go ahead, stranger," Wulfred replied in his gruff voice.

"I am seeking a man named Andil. I was told he frequents this place."

"You were told wrong, then. He used to come here but not anymore. Been at least four years since I've seen that walking skeleton," Wulfred said.

"Four years? I thought my source was reliable. They told me he hung out here a lot."

"Like I said, he used to. His good friend got locked up for life in the dungeon and he hasn't been back here since. I've heard he still lives in the city, but you won't find him here," the barkeep answered.

"Life in the dungeon? What did that poor bastard do?" Harcourt asked.

"They said he murdered his girlfriend, who actually worked here for me. Pretty little lass and a hard worker too. Don't rightly know what motive he would have had. I think it was some kind of set-up. Poor girl."

"Who would want to murder an innocent girl just to

set someone up? Just kill him instead."

"Don't rightly know. The Thieves Guild in this city is capable of some nasty things. And I'd wager they had something to do with it."

"Sounds to me like you don't care for them much," Harcourt commented.

"And I don't. They send someone by here weekly to collect an operating tax from me. Each year, it goes up. Now I can barely make a profit. I can't stay in business like this for much longer. You stay in the south district long enough and you'll run into them eventually," Wulfred said.

"Well, thanks for your time barkeep. Appreciate it," Harcourt dropped a gold coin on the bar and turned to leave.

"What's that for? You didn't order anything," Wulfred called after him.

"It's ok. Keep it."

Harcourt had thought about ordering a drink, then decided against it. It had been over four years since he had drunk anything other than water. The cravings were gone. As he walked, he thought about what Wulfred had said. He was glad the man did not really think that he killed Jalanna. That was something that always nagged at him in the dungeon, wondering if his friends thought that he had really done the unthinkable.

He was also angry that the Guild would target a decent man like Wulfred, a man that was part of the community and gave so much to people who needed it most. Sounded like they were on their way to running him out of business. Disgusting, the thief thought. And what about Andil? Maybe his old friend could not stand to be in the Den without himself or Jalanna around. The place certainly did not have the same feel to the thief, despite a few familiar faces. The Den had been robbed of its heart and soul. Now, Harcourt would have to seek out Serdic and hope that he would not be recognized.

Harcourt left the tavern and shortly thereafter froze in place as he passed the entrance to his old alley. A million memories flooded into his mind. He noticed that the alley was completely empty, his shack along with all the other beggars' tents were gone. Whoever owned the buildings must have decided to clean it up. Over ten years the thief had lived in this alley and he felt an odd pang of sorrow to see it all empty.

He walked over to where his place had been and tried to imagine it as it was. Harcourt figured they must have repaired the wall; he kicked the spot with the loose board and it fell open. Curiously, the thief crouched down to peek inside and rocked back in shock when he saw his magical mask sitting atop a pile of his old filthy clothes. But how?

Harcourt's memory had always been cloudy whenever he thought back to that horrible morning when he found Jalanna. Everything was a blur. Whenever he did try to ponder the fate of the remarkable mask, he had always assumed that he was carrying it at the time he was arrested and it had been confiscated by the guards. He imagined it most likely being tossed away as rubbish since nobody would have known what it was. But now he could recall forgetting it, that morning, in his hiding spot. He put it there the night before and in his haste to get home and change, he forgot to retrieve it.

Harcourt picked up his mask and a smile spread across his face. His appearance problem had just been solved.

*　　*　　*　　*

"So tell me, Weldrick, why did you flee to Stonewood of all places, when it was Stonewood troops that helped destroy your Guild?" Trascar asked, seated behind his desk. The Guild leader noted how calm and relaxed the man looked sitting across from him.

Randar and Arnald, another tough-looking thug, stood cross-armed on either side of the office door. They had brought the thief Weldrick to the Guild headquarters in the dead of night with a sack over his head. Weldrick had claimed to be the number two man in Hartlan's Thieves Guild and escaped the massacre. Now, he was looking for work and a place to hide.

Weldrick was a fairly tall and muscular man with a shaved head and a thin, dark goatee. His nose was crooked, having been broken several times, and he had bright green eyes which stood out. When they had searched him, they found knives and razor blades hidden all over his body. On his left shoulder was a tattoo of a grinning skull smoking a pipe and a dagger with a serpent wrapped around the blade was on his right forearm.

"I had always heard that Stonewood was a beautiful and wealthy city, much bigger even than Hartlan. Sounded like the perfect place for me to come and disappear," Weldrick answered with an air of arrogance about him. "I fear none of Stonewood's troops."

Weldrick might have appeared calm on the outside, but inside was a different story entirely. Harcourt had still not recovered from the initial shock that his old acquaintance Trascar was actually the leader of the Thieves Guild. Trascar was older than him by a few years but the pair grew up in the same neighborhood. The man even used to frequent the Ogre's Den quite a bit. Harcourt never remembered the man as being a great thief, but he was always cunning and manipulative with a cruel streak. He must have swindled someone out of that position, or killed them, he thought. This made Harcourt very curious as to why he was never allowed to join the Guild. Trascar knew who he was and knew he was a capable thief.

"Our intelligence said that you were picked up by the city guards at the east gate several days ago. What was that about?" the Guild leader inquired.

"They were merely being cautious. Keeping an eye out for fleeing thieves. They asked me a few questions but this lonely traveler has never been to Hartlan before. They had no proof to hold me and I was freed," Weldrick said.

"Who was the leader of your guild?" Trascar asked.

"His name was Yuural Sloane. A good leader but too ambitious. Now his head decorates the castle as a trophy for the Duke."

"How was it that you escaped and he did not?"

"Pure luck is all," Weldrick said. "See, the Duke's first move was to eliminate all the corrupt guards and officials so we would have no prior knowledge of the assault to come. The story behind Stonewood troops in the city was that King Stonewood was coming for a visit. I just happened to be outside the city dealing with some smugglers from Benhollow when the extermination began. I came straight here."

Trascar sat silently taking it all in. According to all of their reports, everything Weldrick said seemed to fit. What a great asset he would make to the Guild, he thought.

"What are your expectations here?" Trascar questioned.

"Based on my previous experience and rank, I want full membership in the Guild and some position of power," Weldrick stated.

"You expect to show up here and take the number two spot just like that?" Trascar smirked.

"Something like that." Randar and Arnald laughed. Weldrick continued, "You're mistaken if you think I will come here as some lowly street hustler or thug. That is beneath my skills."

Trascar chuckled. "Well, your skills will be put to the test. Every person that joins this Guild performs a task to prove themselves worthy. Yours is going to be more difficult than most after your boasts."

"You name it and I'll do it."

"I like your attitude already," Trascar said. "Arnald, take our friend here out into the games room for a moment while Randar and I converse. Watch him though, don't let him steal anything."

When the door closed and the pair was alone, Trascar asked, "Well?"

"He wasn't lying as far as I could tell. I've spoken to a few of our agents that have dealt with Hartlan in the past and his story checks out. All of our information has matched and his description fits. I believe he is who he says he is," Randar replied.

"I am thinking of sending him out to bring back a few of Lord Enright's rubies, if he thinks he is so good."

Randar looked puzzled. "He'll most likely be killed or captured trying to pull that one off. You'll be wasting him if it comes to that result."

"Oh, well," Trascar replied, "If he is as good as he claims to be, then let him try. If he fails, we have lost nothing. If he succeeds, then we have a very valuable new member added to our ranks. All of our members must perform one task to prove their worth. I've just set the stakes a little higher for our boastful, new friend."

CHAPTER 24

Harcourt lay on the sofa drifting in and out of sleep. He was in Dornell's private office within the Investigations Unit headquarters. The thief was getting some much-needed rest and waiting for the captain to return. All of the recent events were running through his mind.

Trascar was a schemer, of that there was no doubt. Harcourt had known him long enough to know that part. He had never heard of Lord Enright before but Dornell filled him in on the gem dealer, who employed a private army. It was an impossible task for the average thief, or any thief for that matter. After all of the boasts he had made, Harcourt's guess was that Trascar wanted him to return and admit that he failed and could not perform that particular task.

Dornell strolled into the office stirring the thief from his thoughts. He tossed him a small leather pouch. "You better be careful with that. That was not easy to come by."

The thief pulled out a flawless thumb-sized ruby

which seemed to glow with a red radiance, and he whistled. Upon closer inspection, he noticed a tiny "E" etched into it. "So Enright agreed to the idea, I see."

"Not without receiving the full value of that gem in gold as a security deposit. Wasn't easy to convince the treasurer to give me that much gold for a scheme involving the Thieves Guild," Dornell said, sounding exhausted. The captain slowly eased himself into a chair, clearly still feeling the effects of his wound.

"Everything else a go?" Harcourt asked.

Dornell nodded. "By tomorrow morning, the word on the streets will be that Lord Enright was robbed and demands the head of the thief who did it."

Excellent, the thief thought, he would present the ruby to Trascar as proof of his success. That should be enough to impress him and the other Guild members, but Harcourt also had another idea to secure the Guild leader's full favor.

"Fezzdin's elixir worked well then, did it?" Dornell asked.

"So far, so good," Harcourt replied. "Nobody seems to have recognized me. If they do, you'll find me floating down the river to be sure. I can't believe this stuff actually works."

Dornell yawned. "Good. Now get out of my bed and find something to do."

"What? If you are that tired just go home and sleep. There are no pressing matters that require your immediate attention here," Harcourt said.

"This is my home," the captain stated.

"What do you mean? This office?"

"Yes."

"This is where you stay when you are off duty? This is where you live?"

"Yes."

"There is no Dornell estate somewhere? Where is your family?"

"There is no estate. There is no family. I am married to Stonewood and have dedicated my life to her protection."

"No woman in your life? That explains a lot."

"Shut up and go."

"Why have you never had a woman?"

"I didn't say never. I was in love once."

"Why can't I picture the great Captain Dornell, with his hair all neatly-combed, bringing a flower to his sweetheart? She broke your heart, huh?"

"You could say that. Now get out of here."

Harcourt finally stood. "What, don't tell me she left you for that charming lad, Zorfal?"

"She was murdered. A long time ago."

"Oh. I am sorry."

"They tried to rob her and my woman put up a fight. The killer was never found."

"Very sorry to hear that. At least you weren't imprisoned for her death, like someone I know."

"That is why I worked so hard to get your release. We may not see eye to eye on a lot of things, and I find your chosen career path despicable, but on this particular issue I know your pain. I never caught Zelna's killer, but we are going to catch Jalanna's."

Harcourt nodded.

*　　*　　*　　*

The first time Arnald guided a hooded Weldrick into the Guild's headquarters, he was very rough. This time however he was not. The thug did not shove the man even once, merely guided him. It was a show of respect already.

A group of the Guild's top thieves, assassins and thugs had gathered in the gambling room for a glimpse of the newcomer who had somehow managed to rob Lord Enright. When the hood was removed, Weldrick received nods of respect from the assembled members.

"Greetings, Weldrick," said a particularly weasely-looking thief. "My name is Zenod. How in the hell did you rob Enright? I must know. I've spent years trying to plan a way to pull it off. The man owns a king's ransom in gems."

"I can't reveal all my secrets, good Zenod. But I believe I've proven that I can back up my boasts. I am a master thief and much more," Weldrick replied, patting Randar on the shoulder as he walked by. The enforcer flinched a little.

"Much more, you say huh?" Trascar asked, walking out of his office. "What do you follow that job with? Do you shoot lightning bolts from your fingertips as well?"

"I wish," Weldrick laughed. "But in Hartlan, I've never been bested in combat. I could out-steal and out-fight anyone."

A laugh came from behind the boastful thief. "This is not Hartlan," Randar said.

"I take it that you think you are the resident tough guy?" Weldrick taunted.

Harcourt could feel the tension in the air around him. The room went dead silent. People were afraid to breathe. He felt that a few looked at him with pity in their eyes, thinking that this new thief was about to be killed right here in front of them.

"I am the one who is gonna wipe that arrogant smile off your face," Randar growled.

"I dare you," Weldrick said.

Randar charged forward with the speed of a lion tackling the thief around the waist. Weldrick looped his right arm around Randar's neck in a head lock as they crashed to the floor. *By the demons of Stonewood, Randar is strong,* he thought. Weldrick tightened his grip on the enforcer's neck and held on for his life as Randar thrashed about trying to break free. The enforcer's movements gradually became slower and slower until finally his body went limp.

Weldrick rolled the unconscious man over onto his back then pulled out a knife that he was not supposed to have and held it to Randar's throat.

"Were we anywhere else this man would be dead right now," he said. "I am a guest here and he is an obvious asset to the Guild, so I'll let him live," Weldrick said and scanned the shocked expressions of everyone present. "But know this. The next challenger will not be so lucky."

Trascar clapped. "Step into my office."

Weldrick let out a silent sigh of relief. That whole scene relied on perfect timing and it had worked beautifully. The thief wore a simple steel ring on this right hand where a tiny needle protruded from the underside. Weldrick had coated the needle with a mild sleep poison and stuck it in Randar's shoulder when he touched him a few moments earlier. Then he just needed to taunt Randar into a fight and get hold of him until the poison kicked in.

What everyone else witnessed was Weldrick choke Randar into unconsciousness within seconds, an impressive show. Between that and robbing Lord Enright, the thief had just ensured his Guild membership.

Trascar shut the door behind them and motioned for Weldrick to sit. "A man of many talents, I see. Do you have any rubies with you?" the Guild leader asked.

Weldrick tossed over the small leather pouch that Dornell had given him. "I offer that one to you as a gift and proof of my success. The few others that I took are dearly needed since I left Hartlan with nothing but the clothes on my back."

"Fair enough," Trascar said while inspecting the gemstone for Enright's mark and nodding with approval. "I don't suppose you want to tell me how you pulled that off when our best burglar Zenod had not yet found a way?"

"Nope."

"I expected as much. Anyhow, we could definitely make use of a man with your talents. Normally, I wouldn't just take in a member of a rival Guild, but since your former employer no longer exists, I don't see any problems and your story checks out."

"Thank you. But don't think that because I am the new guy in town, I'll be answering to just anyone around here. Remember, I was number two in Hartlan," Weldrick stated.

"Well, there are a lot of senior members here that would not be too pleased if you were positioned higher than them," Trascar replied.

Weldrick gave an evil chuckle. "Tell them to bring their complaints to me if they have any."

The Guild leader nodded and sat in silence, considering that for a moment. He liked this Weldrick very much already.

"Welcome aboard, number three. I already have a competent number two and you can learn a lot about our city from spending some time with him."

A knock came at the door then and Trascar bid them enter. In walked a skeletal man Harcourt knew very well.

"Ah, here is my number two now. Andil, meet Weldrick, our newest member."

"You're the talk of the Guild. It's a pleasure to meet you," Andil said.

It took all of Harcourt's best efforts to remain composed and not sit there slack-jawed and stunned. Andil, the number two man in the Thieves Guild? But how?

"You look fairly young. Are you only new to the Guild yourself?" Weldrick managed to ask, and he was most curious about the answer.

"Don't let my baby face fool you, I am much older than I look. I've been a member of the Guild for over ten years," Andil replied.

Did he just say ten years? Harcourt thought to himself. He did not know what to make of this. It did not make any sense to him whatsoever.

"Andil used to be an actor for a group of travelling performers, so don't believe a word he says sometimes," Trascar chuckled. "You never know when he is acting and when he isn't.

"I suppose he must be very good at that, then," Weldrick said without any hint of humor, his eyes locked on the skinny man.

"He can show you around and teach you what's what in the city. I'll give you a few weeks time to get yourself settled and oriented before I pile on the responsibilities and there will be many. Now bugger off both of you while I tend to Randar's ego," Trascar said.

Andil opened the door.

"Go get some sleep if you can. We'll get together in the morning and take care of something I have to see to. Then I'll show you our map-house. I'll bet you didn't have anything like this in Hartlan."

CHAPTER 25

It was early morning when Andil and Weldrick met up and set out on Guild business. Shops were just beginning to open and the streets were still devoid of much activity. Even the beggars were still asleep. It took a lot of effort for Harcourt to keep from staring at his old "friend," trying to figure out who he really was. Never once had he ever doubted anything that Andil told him, but there was a lot more to the skinny man than Harcourt ever imagined.

They zigzagged through the streets of the lower west district and Andil finally broke the silence.

"The Guild is made up of hundreds of members, though most are never aware of the identities of the others, especially senior members. Lower level thieves will work through one contact and even that contact will not know the identities of very many others. For example, last night I had three low-ranking thieves rob a caravan as it left Stonewood. Those three were given the orders from a man named Gensen. If they were to be caught, he would be the only person they could provide if forced to rat out on someone. Gensen was given his orders from a woman named Taryn. Now, if Gensen was ever caught and forced to talk, Taryn would be the only Guild member he could rat on. Taryn works directly with me and me only and, well, she would know better than to ever rat on me."

"And what exactly keeps their tongues still under city interrogation?" Weldrick asked.

"Fear," Andil replied.

"Obviously, it's fear. But fear of what, specifically?"

Andil remained silent as a man passed them by pulling a cart and continued when he was far enough away.

"Torture. Torture of loved ones. The death of loved ones. Trascar has made examples of rats in the past, so we don't have that problem very often. Fear is a wonderful tool as I am sure you are well aware."

"What if an individual has no family? They are looking at a lengthy prison sentence so will have no fear of being caught by the Guild?" Weldrick asked.

"Our reach does not just stop on the streets. We have plenty of members inside the dungeon. Someone's stay in the dungeon can be made a lot more miserable than it would normally be, if we wish it," Andil answered. "There is no safe place to hide within this city."

"I've already heard whispers of a cult that operates in the city. To my knowledge they have done a fairly good job of hiding," remarked Weldrick.

"Yes, well, that is a special case. There is indeed a cult of vile demon worshippers that have operated in Stonewood for quite some time. So far, they have proven to be quite elusive but they cannot hide forever. Our lovely Feylane is heading a team that is actively seeking them out."

"What a body on that one, huh? She is incredible," Weldrick whistled.

"Look, but don't touch," Andil warned. "She might be a pretty flower on the outside, but she's a cold viper on the inside. She is the head of the Guilds' assassins. Once Feylane gets you in her sights, there is no escape."

Weldrick chuckled. "I'd hate to be the one who unknowingly invites her back home for a drink."

"Yes, not wise. So Feylane heads the assassins. Randar, whom you've met, deals with the thugs and enforcers. Zenod is our master burglar and deals mostly with those types of jobs. Serdic is the Guild treasurer and a good businessman. He looks after the purchasing of Guild property and managing our many fronts. He would actually be quite successful without the Guild, but understands there is more coin in working for us."

"So where do you and I fit in to all of this?" Weldrick inquired.

"We oversee everyone else and have our hands into a little bit of everything. Like right now. We are going to talk to an armorer about his operation tax. Because we are dealing with a larger amount of gold here, I don't want to send over just the average thugs. I thought I'd pay Wendall a personal visit. Since I am not an intimidating force, I've brought you along."

Andil led the other thief through a shop door and a wave of heat hit them both. They stood in the shop's display area, where the armorer hung items for sale and showed off examples of his work, but the heat from the forge in his work area filled the entire shop. Sweat started to form on Weldrick's forehead. He was no expert on armor and metal working but Wendall's work seemed to be of very high quality.

Andil paid the wares no mind and rang the little bell that sat on the armorer's desk. When there was no response, he impatiently rang it again.

"I'm coming, I'm coming. Relax out there," came a deep gruff voice from the back workshop.

Wendall walked into the room and his face slightly paled at the sight of Andil and his partner, though it was hard to tell as his face was almost completely covered with hair. He had big, bushy, black eyebrows and a long, bushy, black beard, though the top of his head was balding. What took Harcourt by surprise was the man's size. He was about half the height of the thief. He didn't think that deep voice could come from such a short man. Wendall might have been short, but was as solid as stone. He wore a white sleeveless shirt that was drenched with sweat which revealed an extremely hairy chest and back. His hairy arms bulged with muscle and he looked as though if he planted his feet, nothing could knock him over.

Harcourt in his life had maybe seen two or three men of Wendall's size; they were not very common. He had heard others refer to them as "dwarves." The thief recalled a tavern tale which spoke of entire cities of dwarves across the western sea. They were said to be masters of stonework and metalwork. Harcourt never really believed the tales, and never actually met someone who had been across the sea to confirm it. It did seem though that Wendall was indeed a master of his craft.

"What can I do for you, gentlemen?" the armorer asked eyeing them both suspiciously.

"Just stopping by for a visit," Andil replied.

"I doubt that," Wendall remarked. "I am busy so just

state your business and don't play any games."

"Oh yes, I've heard you've been quite busy lately," Andil said. "With that mercenary company giving you that juicy contract, I would imagine your forge runs day and night."

"I was fortunate to win that contract. They were impressed with my work," Wendall said.

"Of course they would be. Look at this stuff," Andil motioned to the items on the walls. "The best armor in the city. No, I correct myself, the whole region. Were I a soldier or mercenary, I would definitely want to be outfitted in famous dwarven-made armor. And since Wendall is the only dwarven armorer in Stonewood, naturally I'd be here giving my business."

"Get to your point," the dwarf demanded.

"Mind your manners. Don't forget who you are speaking to," Andil answered with an annoyed tone, something Harcourt was not used to hearing out of the skeletal man.

The thief could see that the dwarf seethed inside at being talked to like that from someone he could probably tear in half and could not blame the man for being angry.

"Alright then," Andil continued, "Let's not play any further games. That contract you just got was a substantial one. Naturally, we'll have to raise your operating tax as a result."

Wendall's face, what could be seen of it, turned red. "That is unfair! I've paid you back every coin I borrowed, with interest! And I've been paying your stupid tax. Now I am to be punished for running a successful business?"

"My dear Wendall," Andil said casually, strolling around the room. "It wouldn't be fair to smaller businesses if they had to pay the same tax as you. If you are making more, then you will have to pay more. Surely you can see the sense in that?"

"No, I do not see the sense in any of this. I work hard for my coins and you are just going to walk in here and expect a cut from everything?" Wendall replied raising his voice and advancing on the skinny thief.

"Ahhhh, Weldrick?" Andil said with a hint of concern.

As much as it made Harcourt feel sick inside, he had to keep up his charade. He drew one of his daggers and stepped between the dwarf and the other thief.

"Stand your ground, little man."

Harcourt could see the dwarf sizing him up and considering his chances against the two thieves, he backed off.

"That's a good boy," Andil said. "See, you do have some sense. You would do well to always remember who it is that you are dealing with here. Now, considering that business is booming, I would say fifty gold a month would not be too unreasonable."

With a growl, Wendall attempted to dive past Weldrick to grab ahold of the skeletal thief. Weldrick intercepted him, grabbing his sweat-drenched shirt with his left hand and holding his dagger to the dwarf's face with his right. Wendall grabbed Weldrick's right arm and he felt the strength that the dwarf possessed. For such a short man, he had a grip as strong as Zorfal's.

Weldrick stared Wendall in the eyes and shook his head no. He was silently pleading with the dwarf not to make another move. Harcourt had no desire to hurt the armorer and was not sure how he would handle this situation if he did not calm down. The thief held the advantage since the armorer was unarmed, but did not want to try and match strength with the dwarf.

"Now Wendall, do behave," Andil said. "I know you would never want anything to happen to that lovely little lass of yours. Or your boy. Am I correct in assuming this?"

Harcourt was relieved when Wendall released his arm and stepped back, his shoulders slumped in defeat. The thief wanted to grab Andil by the throat for those threats but kept his anger in check.

"I see that got your attention. I don't want to see anything happen to them either, Wendall, so just co-operate and everything will be fine. Word is spreading about the great dwarven smithy, soon you'll be overrun with orders and fifty gold a month won't seem like so much. Unfortunately, though, I will collect that today," the skinny thief said.

"I don't have that much. I've only thirty gold pieces here to my name at the moment," Wendall replied.

"That will have to do then. Someone will have to come around next week for the remainder," Andil shook his head, disappointed.

"You can't take it all now, that is all I own."

"Better get out there then and stir up some more business. Or get another advance from the mercenaries."

"How can I survive if you take all my coins?" Wendall asked.

"You are a dwarf. Aren't you people used to living in the ground or the mountains? I am sure you'll think of something. Now, pull out that strong box you've got underneath the floorboard over there and let's see what you've got for us."

Wendall reluctantly lifted a loose floorboard and with both hands, pulled out a heavy metal chest. He laid the chest on a desk and produced a key to open the padlock. Andil loomed over his shoulder while the dwarf opened the lid and counted out exactly thirty gold coins.

"Allow me to keep 5 pieces of gold at least. I need something for the next week to eat and keep things running here," Wendall pleaded.

"Sorry, I am afraid I cannot do that. Weldrick, collect the coins please, we must be off," Andil ordered, then stepped outside for some fresh air. The heat inside the shop was getting to him.

Harcourt tried not to make eye contact with the dwarf while he filled three small bags with the coins, but could feel the armorer's icy stare. He could not fault Wendall at all. Were the roles reversed, Harcourt probably would have fought them both and worried about the consequences later.

The thief paused on his way to the door, then against his better judgment, turned and dropped five gold coins onto the table. He then left the shop as Wendall stood there with a perplexed look upon his face.

Once outside, Harcourt tossed the coin bags to the other thief and wiped the sweat from his forehead. He felt disgusted to have been a part of what just took place in the dwarf's shop.

"Why take every coin the guy has? Do you want these businesses to eventually fail?" Weldrick asked as the pair walked down the street.

"Wendall is going to be a very successful armorer in this city. He can afford it," Andil replied.

"You keep raising his taxes and he won't be able to.

Either that or he'll turn you in to city agents when he finally gets fed up," Weldrick reasoned.

"Nah. Wendall owes me. He came to Stonewood with his family without any coins. I heard that he was inquiring about a loan and paid him a visit. He wouldn't even have that shop if it wasn't for the Guild's help. We gave him the loan to get started. Dwarves have an odd sense of honor. I am positive he wouldn't want that bit of info getting out, plus he wouldn't want anything to happen to his family either," Andil said.

Weldrick shook his head. "I just don't agree with that type of business. A guy like Wendall works very hard and eventually, you'll bankrupt these small businesses with those taxes. You cannot collect a tax from a shop that is no longer there."

"Agreed, but that is Trascar's way of doing things. He thinks of the now, and doesn't worry much of the later."

"Why doesn't someone advise him differently?" Weldrick asked.

"We've tried. He doesn't tend to listen to others, really. And if you press him too much, you risk angering him and you don't want to cross him. So, it's just best to do as you are instructed. The Guild is wealthier since he took over."

It seemed to Harcourt that many members of the Guild did not like all of Trascar's decisions, but fear kept them in check. The Guild could be wealthy without exercising this stupid tax on the poor business owners of the city, but the Guild leader was extremely greedy. *Why would you want to make an enemy of the average person?* he thought. Eventually, when people get pushed far enough, they will rebel. That could be the downfall of the Guild in the future.

"Now wait 'til you see our map-house," Andil said. "This is impressive. Follow me."

*   *   *   *

Andil just finished explaining what all of the colored figurines on the model of the city represented. Harcourt could only shake his head. It was the same city model the guards used with all the same colored figures. The only difference was that the table was huge and the model was of the entire city, not just an individual district. "But how do you know when and where to place the guard figures?" Weldrick asked the skinny thief.

"Ah, perfect timing," he responded. "Zorfal here can show you."

Just then, that ugly brute of a city guard, Zorfal, walked into the map room in full guard uniform. Weldrick reached for a dagger and Andil laughed. "Don't worry, Weldrick. Zorfal works for us."

"That's Captain Zorfal," the brute grunted.

"Yes, Captain Zorfal. He is the captain of the lower west district. He'll come in here frequently and place the guard pieces for the lower west and south districts. So for the next few hours we'll know roughly where the patrols will be in those areas," Andil said

Harcourt stood there stunned as he watched Zorfal position different colored figures onto the city model. First Andil, and now Zorfal are Guild members? Who is next? he wondered. Fezzdin? King Stonewood? The thief felt like this was all some crazy dream where nothing made sense. He wondered how many city guards actually worked for the Guild and was Dornell aware of any of this? Did he even suspect? Harcourt had always got a strange feeling from the brute. Something just seemed out of place with the man. Now his feelings made sense.

Captain Zorfal finished his task and left without a word. "Who places the rest of the figures?" Weldrick asked.

"We have a guard for each of the remaining districts. They will come and update our map as is necessary."

"Guards cannot be easy to buy, especially a district captain," Weldrick said.

"No, they are not cheap at all. Zorfal costs a small fortune, but he is well worth the coin."

"So tell me, Andil, how long have you held this position of Trascar's right hand? Took me many, many years and hard work to rise to that rank in Hartlan."

"Took me quite some time as well, but Trascar finally promoted me four years ago."

Suspicion rose in Harcourt. He was not sure why Andil had lied to him all those years but now wondered if he had anything to do with his "friend's" promotion.

"What happened four years ago?" he asked.

"Firstly, a lot of Guild members were upset with Trascar's decision, only it's not always wise to voice those opinions. I used to do a lot of personal projects for Trascar, and not all of them were Guild-related. He paid me well. When I had completed one such project, he was exceptionally pleased. Thus, my promotion."

"What kind of projects are we talking here?"

"Ok, for example, that last one took me years. There was this lowlife thief from the south-side that Trascar hated. My job was basically to make his life miserable,"

Andil laughed and Harcourt raged inside.

"How? Bully him?" Weldrick asked while fighting to remain calm.

"Do I look like I could bully anyone? Nah, this guy would have ripped me apart. I befriended him and hung out with him. Actually, in truth, the guy was one of the best thieves I've ever seen. One of the best in this city for sure. But I used to get him to tell me where he was planning his next job, then tell Zorfal so the guards would suddenly show up at the worst possible time and arrest him," the skinny thief laughed again. "He used to think he had the worst luck in the world, but honestly they'd probably never have caught this guy without me."

Harcourt's hands clenched tight and shook. He felt sick inside as if he had just eaten spoiled meat. It took every ounce of willpower he possessed to keep from reaching out and strangling the living skeleton right then and there. He knew he would not escape the Guild house alive if he did. The thief burned with such fury he did not even hear what Andil said after that.

"Hey, you there? Everything ok?" Andil asked puzzled, noticing a change in the other thief.

"Yeah I am fine, just a flashback of a similar experience in Hartlan," Weldrick said, finally gaining some measure of control. "How could you turn on a fellow Guild member like that? That's against the code."

"No, this guy was never a Guild member. Trascar never allowed it. He was just a renegade thief I was supposed to torment," Andil answered.

"Sounds like he would have been useful to the Guild if he was that good of a thief. Why did Trascar hate him so much?"

"Stupid jealousy, but that's just between us. They both wanted the same woman but she fell for the other guy instead. One thing you don't do is cross Trascar. So he decided to make that other guy pay."

Harcourt was finding it difficult to breathe, suddenly feeling that the walls were closing in on him. He was not sure how long he could keep his composure and needed to leave very soon. He was almost afraid to ask, but then did.

"So what, then? You finally just killed this guy and finished with all the games?"

Andil's face took on a pained expression. "You could say that. He's as good as dead. A life sentence in the castle dungeon for murdering his girl."

"Why would he murder his girl?"

"He didn't."

"Ah, you sly fox. But you killed an innocent woman just to punish a lowlife thief? Even I wouldn't stoop so low."

"Wasn't me. I wanted no part in that. That was between Trascar and Zorfal. Like I said, don't cross him. Either of them, actually."

Harcourt was now finding his legs were feeling weak. He needed to get out of there and sit. He quickly changed the subject before he did something foolish without thinking it through.

"So what happened to the previous second in command? Surely he wasn't too pleased about your promotion."

"He was always butting heads with Trascar over issues of Guild business. The guards happened to raid his place one day and found a lot of stolen goods. He is locked up for a long time," the skinny thief replied.

"How convenient for you," Weldrick said.

"Hey," Andil smiled, "I don't know how the guards knew exactly where to look."

CHAPTER 26

Harcourt stared up at the stars as he lay in the grass of a large empty field. There was a cool breeze and crickets chirped all around him. He had left the city and ventured a short distance away to find a quiet spot to calm himself down and to think. It was the first time in awhile that he had not taken any of Fezzdin's elixir and was not wearing the mask, he was just Harcourt. His head swirled as he tried to make sense of everything he had discovered. He had never felt this angry before and it scared him.

When sitting in the dungeon thinking that he was there for life, he was angry, very angry; he just did not know where to direct it. He did not know who to be angry with. Most of his life, he directed his anger back at himself. He blamed himself for all his bad luck and troubles. He blamed himself for not being able to protect Jalanna. Now though, he had a target for his anger. Or rather, targets.

Trascar or Zorfal had killed Jalanna. It did not really matter to Harcourt which one did the act since both were a party to it. As far as he could tell, they were the only two involved. Andil though, was guilty of a lot of other things. The skinny rat had also known what Trascar was planning to do and stood by, allowing it to happen. Jalanna had considered Andil a friend as well, she trusted him. He fooled them both.

Harcourt knew his magical mask made thievery much easier, he had always been expecting his bad luck to come into play at some point, only it never did. Once Andil was not involved in his life, his bad luck had vanished. "That rat!" Harcourt yelled out loud to himself. Only the glowing eyes of a night bird peered down from a nearby tree at the outburst.

All those times he sat in the dungeon in despair. All those times he was whipped or beaten. All those times he had been separated from Jalanna. That skinny rat had been the cause of it, every time. Standing behind the rat was Trascar the puppeteer, pulling the strings.

Now, Harcourt thought, *what do I do about them?* The thief had never killed anyone before and was always proud of that fact. He was not so sure that he was going to be able to hang onto that claim for much longer. That trio deserved death and Jalanna was owed some form of revenge. Yet the thief could almost hear her voice in his head telling him that murdering them was not the answer. She whispered that he should not stoop down to their level and it would be something he might live to regret. There was also the problem of Trascar's bodyguards who were never far away.

Then came the thought about what he would do when this was all over. He did not think he could continue working with Dornell and the city. Catching Jalanna's murderers was one thing but arresting thieves like himself was another. They were just people trying to survive in an unforgiving city.

He also could not remain in the Guild after taking care of three senior members, one being the leader. Suspicion of a rat would fall on him, being the newest member. Harcourt had spent most of his life dreaming about being a member of the Guild and now that he technically was, he wanted no further part in it. He always envisioned a group of thieves like himself, getting together and coordinating jobs, sharing information, gambling and hanging out. Now, he realized most were conniving murderers who extorted hard-working people who could barely survive on their own. That was not the Guild of his imaginations.

Fortunately, he still had his magical mask. Fate had smiled on him in one of those rare moments. He figured he would probably leave Stonewood when this was over and start fresh somewhere else. Perhaps he would even go down south and visit old Warden, see how the One-Handed Bandit was faring. There was nothing left that tied him to this place. First things first though; he had business to take care of in Stonewood.

*   *   *   *

"Zorfal? Captain Zorfal? Are you sure?"

"I saw him there with my own two eyes," Harcourt replied, sitting in Dornell's private office.

"This is not some ploy for revenge, seeing as how he was on the scene for your arrest is it?" the captain questioned.

"I swear to you."

Dornell slumped back into his chair with a defeated look on his face. "How are we ever to fight crime when those of us who are charged to fight it are working with the criminals? No wonder we have been fighting a losing battle all these years."

"I didn't see any others, but I was told that the Guild has at least one guard per district in their pocket," Harcourt added.

"Words cannot express my disappointment at this news," the captain said. "These men took an oath to protect this city and enforce our laws. To combat evil."

"If you think that's bad, remind me to tell you a tale about Chief Magistrate Krommel when this is all done."

"Pardon? He is a fine upstanding citizen. An example for all to follow."

"Let's deal with one thing at a time. We'll discuss Krommel later, I promise," Harcourt said.

"Where is the Guild headquarters?" Dornell asked.

"Not sure yet. I am still blindfolded when they take me there," the thief replied.

"Who is their leader?"

"I haven't seen him yet either, I only know his voice. They still do not fully trust me."

"And Fezzdin's elixir is still working?"

"Yes, they think my name is Lindon and I am a low-ranking thief who escaped from Hartlan. Not a threat to them at all," Harcourt lied, not wanting to reveal his full plan just yet.

"Good. I will need you to get me some evidence against Zorfal, then we can have him arrested as soon as possible."

"Not yet. Let me gather some more information first.

If Zorfal is arrested now, they may suspect a rat. Give me a little more time. Meanwhile, though I would suggest that your unit provide false information on the patrol maps. Let Zorfal bring the Guild the wrong patrol routes."

"An excellent idea," the captain said. "Try to hurry though. It makes me sick allowing these corrupt men to continue working for the city. Find out who the other guards are as well."

"Soon Dornell, it will be over soon," Harcourt said.

*　　*　　*　　*

Iaglen, "the Owl," waited for the last person to disappear around the corner at the end of the street before turning back to his work at hand. He used his trusty diamond-tipped tool to cut a fist-sized hole in the shop's window. The thief carefully removed the cut piece, then stuck his arm through the hole and unlocked the window latch.

He quickly climbed through the window and went straight for the shop's safe located in a closet in a back room. The Owl made short work of the safe's lock and filled a satchel full of coins. He went out the same way he came in and froze in place when he heard someone say, "What's this all about then?"

Two city guards stood nearby staring at the thief who was halfway out the window with a heavy satchel.

"Looks like a filthy thief to me," the other guard answered.

Iaglen had nowhere to go. If he went back into the shop, he would find himself trapped inside. The two guards grabbed him and roughly yanked him the rest of the way out of the window and onto the ground. One of them shook the satchel. "Let me guess, you were making a deposit, eh?"

The Owl did not understand what happened. There were no scheduled patrols on this street for two more hours.

*   *   *   *

Arnald dragged the middle-aged wagonmaker into the dirty south district alley with Cerdol following close behind. Two men having a whispered conversation scattered at the sight of the two thugs and the poor man being dragged along with them.

"You know today is payday and yet we had to find you hiding out in the Dragon's Tale. No coins for us then?" Arnald asked.

"I-I sold no wagons this week. I have nothing to pay you with," the panicked man answered.

"That doesn't concern me," Arnald said, kicking the man in the ribs. "You are not taxed on your earnings, you are taxed on being open for business. You were open for business this week, were you not?"

The man grunted in pain. "Y-yes I was, b-b-but how can I pay you if I didn't sell anything at all?"

Arnald kicked him again. "Allow me to repeat myself. Not my concern."

"I have nothing, I swear it," the man pleaded.

"Then we'll just have to make an example out of you," the thug said, pulling out a cruel-looking knife from his dark overcoat.

"No please don't! I beg you!" screamed the terrified

wagonmaker.

"Shhhhhhhhh. Keep him quiet will ya? Ya want the guards to hear him?" Cerdol said annoyed.

"Stop worrying, the nearest patrol is three blocks away," Arnald replied.

Arnald sliced the man's cheek and he yelped. He then grabbed him by the hair forcing his head back exposing his throat when somebody shouted, "Stay your hand, murderer!"

Arnald looked back to find a city guard pointing his sword at Cerdol's back. The thug let go of the wagonmaker and began backing up towards the other end of the alley. "Go no further," said another guard, blocking Arnald's only exit with a loaded crossbow aimed at his chest.

Arnald was young and foolish. He thought he was close enough to reach the guard before he could fire off his shot. Arnald was wrong.

* * * *

Zorfal stuffed his mouth with his favorite beef and onion sandwich as he trudged along Valorn Road. The sun had just dropped from sight which meant he still had a few more hours left on his shift. *I should have gotten two more sandwiches*, he thought to himself.

A horn sounded from a few blocks over to the north of where he stood. A quick glance in that direction revealed the orange glow of a building on fire. The fire did not surprise the guard captain, since he had played a part in that plan a few hours earlier, but the guards should not have been there so quickly.

The brute picked up his pace to a light jog and made for the source of the alarm. As he got closer, panic-stricken people ran about yelling "Fire! Fire!"

Suddenly, a man clad in dark clothing flew past him at great speed with a city guard trailing very closely behind. As the guard passed by, he shouted, "Captain! I was pursuing two of them but the other just split up and made for Blade Alley." Then he disappeared around a corner.

Blade Alley, huh? Zorfal knew a short cut that would bring him to the alley on the opposite side of the street from where Blade Alley exited, which was most likely where that individual would be heading.

The big man could move quickly when he put his mind to it and soon stood with his back to the wall of a dark alley. It did not take long before he heard the sound of someone running in his direction. As the man ran into the alley, Zorfal stuck out a boot tripping him and sending him sprawling to the ground. The guard captain drew his sword and advanced.

"Captain Zorfal! It's me!" cried the man after he rolled over to see who it was that had tripped him.

"Nalo, you fool, what happened?" Zorfal said angrily.

"W-we did just like you said. The Ferret refused to pay so we torched his store. B-b-but in no time, we found ourselves surrounded by guards. They grabbed Nix and shot Jon with a crossbow. Me and Alun ran for it, then split up," Nalo replied. "I thought you said there was a special meeting tonight and there would not be any guards around for hours?"

Zorfal rubbed his chin in thought with his free hand. "There was supposed to be. That is what I was told. This should not have gone down like this."

"It was n-not our f-fault, sir. But the guards, they got a good look at me. Y-you gotta do something. They are gonna come looking for me," Nalo stammered.

Zorfal was silent for a long moment, deep in thought, weighing his options. "Draw your weapon," he then said.

"Pardon?"

"I said draw your weapon."

"But…"

"Just do it," the captain growled with impatience.

Puzzled, Nalo got to his feet and pulled out the long, curved dagger that hung from his belt. "Who else knows that I put you up to this?" Zorfal asked.

"N-nobody! I swear it. I told nobody. Only y-you and I know."

"I hope that's true," Zorfal said, then ran the man through with his sword.

Nalo had a confused look on his face as he slid off the end of the sword and crumpled silently to the ground. He looked as though he had a burning question on the tip of his tongue, but lacked the ability to ask it. Zorfal stood over him and watched him die.

After Nalo had drawn his last breath, the guard that had been chasing him earlier arrived in the alley. "Captain, are you alright?" he shouted upon the seeing the bloody mess.

"I am fine. This fool thought to fight me," Zorfal answered.

"That will be his last mistake," the guard chuckled. "Him and three others set fire to the Ferret's place."

"For what purpose?" the captain asked.

"At the moment, we know not. One is dead and we have the other two in custody."

"Do we know who might have put them up to this?"

"We do know that this one here," the guard pointed to Nalo's lifeless body, "was pulling the others' strings. They did as he told them. I have a feeling that any valuable information may have just died with him."

"Curse his stupidity," Zorfal spat. "The fool left me no choice."

Nalo had always been useful and loyal to Zorfal, but the guard captain could not risk having the man captured and interrogated. Something went wrong tonight and that troubled Zorfal. Somehow, he had received the wrong information and passed that down to those working for him. He may have dodged an arrow this time, but he meant to get to the bottom of this to ensure it did not happen again.

CHAPTER 27

Weldrick was about to knock on Trascar's office door when a woman's voice from behind said, "I wouldn't go in there, he's in a bad mood." It was Feylane, with long fiery-red hair.

"I care not," he answered.

"Suit yourself, you were warned," she said while shooting him a flirty wink.

Weldrick watched her walk away and remembered how charming she could be in one moment, and terrible the next. He wondered which side of her was the real side and which was the act. When the beautiful assassin was gone, he ignored the bodyguards standing nearby, knocked on the Guild leader's door and entered. He found Trascar seated in his chair looking even more miserable than usual.

"What are you doing here? I didn't call for you!" the Guild leader barked.

"Well, I've heard about the recent troubles and thought I might discuss them with you," Weldrick said.

"And what do you know of Stonewood and our

operations already? You haven't been here long enough. Apparently, one of our city guards is not doing his proper duties."

"I think I might know which one," Weldrick said.

Trascar sat up straight upon hearing that. "Do tell."

"I told you when I first entered the city, the guards brought me in for questioning. I overheard bits of a conversation that didn't mean anything to me at the time. Something about a project going well and I am sure I heard that the Guild doesn't suspect a thing. The man doing the talking had an unforgettable face."

"Who?"

"Zorfal."

"What?"

"Yes. I couldn't forget the mug on that guy. I didn't pay that conversation much mind at the time but when Andil introduced him to me the other day, it all came back to me."

"I find it hard to believe that Zorfal is working against us," Trascar said. "He has been a loyal member for many years and he is paid quite well."

"But it certainly makes sense with all the recent activity. There is definitely a rat in the Guild and it has to be one of the guards. Based on what I've seen and heard, it's Zorfal," Weldrick reasoned.

Trascar looked distressed.

"Perhaps I could investigate further? Find out for sure," Weldrick suggested.

"How?"

"I am new here and the least recognizable. Plus I know a thing or two about disguises," Weldrick smiled. "I could keep an eye on him, see what he is up to. If I am wrong you've lost nothing. But if my suspicions are correct, this rat needs to be dealt with as soon as possible before he brings the whole Guild down."

The Guild leader sat in silent contemplation for a few moments, then nodded his head. "Alright."

*   *   *   *

Zorfal stepped out of the tavern and into the warm afternoon sun. His belly was full and he had just downed two mugs of ale. He felt satisfied. The tavern fed him for free; it was good to be a captain.

Now, after a good meal, he had a lot of work to do. One of the city guards was a double agent working against the Guild. He needed to find out which one it was and remove his head. He suspected Aldis of the upper west district so decided to pay him a visit first.

The brutish guard heard someone call his name and he turned to regard a long blond-haired man in a dark cloak approaching. He did not recognize the man.

"You are Captain Zorfal, I presume?" he asked.

"I am. Who's asking?" the captain inquired suspiciously.

The man opened his cloak to reveal the badge of Stonewood. "I am Uktavio of the Investigations Unit. I work under Captain Dornell. I've come with urgent news."

"Spit it out then," Zorfal insisted.

Uktavio pulled the guard captain off to the side of the road out of earshot of passing citizens. "As difficult as this is to believe, someone has escaped the castle dungeon."

Zorfal wanted to laugh but he could see that Uktavio was dead serious. "How in the hell did that happen? And who was it that escaped?"

"You know the man," Uktavio answered. "A thief named Harcourt. He feigned an illness. When a guard went to his aid, he killed him with a sharpened stone. Then he vanished."

"Vanished? How does someone just vanish in the dungeon?"

"That is a mystery to us all. For certain he has escaped. A sweep of the entire dungeon revealed nothing. Remember, he is a master thief skilled in escaping places unseen."

"He'll flee back to that dump he calls home in the south district and be caught in no time," Zorfal said.

"We have reason to believe he's coming for you."

"Me? Why would he be coming for me?" Zorfal asked amused.

"We've interrogated some of the other prisoners. Seems he has been telling everyone who would listen that he was set up and that you were the actual one behind the murder. He said that you were going to pay for that crime."

"I did it? How ridiculous. He is angry because I was there to catch him."

"I know," Uktavio agreed. "Four years can make a man go mad. We'll capture him soon but in the meantime, keep a watch over your shoulder."

Zorfal laughed. "I don't fear that dirty beggar. Let him come. I welcome the chance to run him through."

"Oh and don't mention this to anyone. The King himself has ordered this to be kept silent. It would look bad on us if word got out that a prisoner escaped the dungeon."

Uktavio bid Captain Zorfal farewell and left. *Phase one complete*, Harcourt thought to himself as he walked away.

* * * *

Weldrick navigated his way through the underground labyrinth of tunnels that connected various Guild hideouts to one another. Weldrick was now trusted enough to come and go as he pleased. He did not share that bit of information with Captain Dornell, though. Harcourt had a plan to administer his own brand of justice and he was sure Dornell would not approve.

The thief was impressed at how well the Guild blended into the city. The entrance he had just used to enter these tunnels was located inside a temple of all places. One of the high priests was a Guild member playing at being a priest.

A short time later, the thief arrived at one of their many gambling houses and found Trascar playing cards at a table with four others.

"We need to talk," Weldrick whispered in the Guild leader's ear, motioning to a dirty sack he carried.

Trascar excused himself from the game and the pair found an empty room to converse in. "What's in the sack?" Trascar asked.

Weldrick pulled out a bloodied black cloak and tossed it over. "Ahh, what are you giving me this for?" the Guild leader asked, disgusted.

"Look at the inside of the cloak," Weldrick said.

Trascar carefully turned the cloak inside out trying not to get any blood on his hands and found the badge of Stonewood. "What's going on? Where did you get this?"

"You are not going to like what I dug up," Weldrick said. "I've been following Zorfal around and he's been having secret meetings with members of the Investigations Unit. I managed to get close enough to one conversation to make out the words 'Guild' and 'patrol routes.' When Zorfal left, I decided to ask his friend a few questions."

"His friend being the owner of this cloak I assume."

"The previous owner. That cloak no longer has an owner," Weldrick said with an evil grin.

"I hope the body of that city agent will not be found anytime soon?" Trascar asked concerned.

"It won't be found at all," Weldrick replied. "I think you'll like to hear what he told me, before he expired. The King has launched a massive crackdown on corruption within the city. It was first sparked by some prisoner that had been doing a lot of talking and people were starting to listen. A thief of some renown who was blamed for the murder of his girl a few years back."

"Renown?" Trascar interrupted. "That thief was a homeless lowlife and nothing more. And he did murder that woman. He was found guilty for the crime and locked up for life."

"All I know of this is what that guy told me. Apparently, Zorfal was being investigated as part of that crackdown since someone had placed him at that murder scene hours before. During an interrogation he cracked and confessed to knowing who the killer was, but his life and the life of his family were threatened if he talked. He told them that the leader of Thieves Guild was the killer and he could help bring the Guild down. He is the one who has been giving false patrol information."

The blood drained from Trascar's face and his hands

shook. Weldrick continued. "Since Zorfal had confessed that the thief was not the real killer, the city secretly had the man released. Zorfal met this guy, I think his name was Harcourt, this morning. I followed them to a warehouse and listened in on their conversation. Harcourt wants you dead and will stop at nothing to achieve that goal. Zorfal plans to set you up."

"That is almost too crazy to believe. Harcourt released? I will have to see this with my own eyes."

"I have an idea. What if Zorfal confessed his betrayal to you himself?" Weldrick offered.

"And why would he be fool enough to do that? He knows he would be a dead man."

"If he didn't know that it was you, then he might. What if he thought that you were Harcourt?"

"And how would I pass as Harcourt?" Trascar asked annoyed.

"Do you believe in magic?"

*　　*　　*　　*

Andil was waiting to meet with an associate on a street corner when he was approached by Weldrick. "Good day to you," said the skinny thief. "Learning your way around the city, are you?"

"I still get lost occasionally, this city is like a massive labyrinth, but I am getting it all figured out," Weldrick replied.

"Was this just a chance meeting or were you looking for me?" Andil asked.

"Actually, I was looking for you. Zenod told me I could find you somewhere in this neighborhood."

"What is it?"

"I thought you might like to know that an old merchant contact of mine is in town. I've dealt with him many times in Hartlan when I had to move Guild merchandise. He is discreet, trustworthy and very wealthy. With Hartlan's Guild destroyed, he is looking for new business."

"Ah, sounds interesting," Andil said with a raised eyebrow. "I should very much like to meet this individual. Just so happens I have a few things I need to move."

Weldrick nodded. "I'll arrange a meeting this week and let you know when and where."

"Excellent," Andil replied. "Oh, one other thing while you are here. Remember that day we paid our dwarven friend Wendall a visit?"

"I do."

"I seem to recall he handed us, under protest, thirty gold pieces. I remember seeing it when he opened the chest."

"I believe you are correct about that."

"Yeah but the funny thing is, when I handed the gold over to Serdic, there were only twenty-five pieces. I may have to have someone pay a visit to that sneaky dwarf and teach him a lesson."

"That won't be necessary," Weldrick replied, looking at the ground in shame. "It was I who took the gold."

"You?"

"Yes, me. I fled Hartlan with nothing. I needed a few coins to last me until I sold Enright's rubies."

"I would be surprised if you didn't attempt to skim gold from time to time. We are all thieves, after all. Just don't let me catch you doing it again. Trascar would not like that very much. Be more discreet for god's sake," the skinny thief scolded.

"You won't ever have to worry about that again," Weldrick said.

*   *   *   *

Captain Dornell found Harcourt in the guardhouse map room. "The King is wanting a status report on our progress. He has been pleased with all of our recent arrests but is anxious to deal with the corrupt guards and the Guild's senior members."

"I am very close to finding out who the Guild leader is, as well as Jalanna's killer. I believe they are one and the same. Get two of your most trusted men and meet me at One Hundred and Thirty-five Pond Way tomorrow just before sundown. Do not be late, I beg you. Also, have Captain Flannis and some of his men raid the warehouse at Forty-two Hamols at about the same time. I think you'll be pleased with the results," Harcourt said.

"Good work, Harcourt. You've really done well. You know, we actually make a good team," Dornell said feeling very pleased.

"Who'd have thought that, eh?" the thief laughed.

"One other thing. There have been some major break-ins the last two nights. Small fortune in jewels was stolen from the upper east. Very tough places to get in or out of. I'd almost suspect your handiwork if I didn't know better. Have your heard anything in the Guild?"

"Oh yes, I certainly have."

*   *   *   *

"Ah Uktavio, have a seat. What news?" Zorfal said while stuffing his mouth with breakfast at a table in the Portly Bard.

"Much has happened since we last spoke," said the blond-haired investigations agent. "We have located Harcourt. He lurks about the south district as you suspected and spends each night in the same warehouse. Every night, I keep watch. We've been hoping he might lead us to some Guild hideouts, but so far nothing. Captain Dornell is impatient and doesn't want to risk losing him so he is to be arrested tomorrow morning. When we arrest him though, it's expected that he will be doing a lot more talking and pointing the finger at you again. Dornell believes we may be forced to run an investigation on you. That doesn't look good on the city. If someone were to eliminate the thief tonight, then he could not cause any further trouble. Thieves and murderers like him deserve no less."

Zorfal stopped chewing. "Interesting."

"He returns to One Hundred and Thirty-five Pond Way every night, two hours after sundown. If someone was to arrive an hour earlier and wait, they could surprise the thief and shut his mouth permanently."

"Yes, they could," Zorfal agreed.

"I will be the only one watching the building tonight. I could take a walk at that time. I wouldn't be able to see who enters or leaves the building," Uktavio said.

Captain Zorfal smiled an evil smile.

CHAPTER 28

Trascar stood in front of the mirror for the longest time. He could not believe his eyes, the magical mask really worked. It worked exactly as Weldrick had said that it would. The Guild leader could not even fathom what the value would be on such an item, it was priceless. He had known that magic existed, he had come across the odd magical trinket before but nothing like this mask. Oh, the things he could accomplish with this mask.

The Guild leader had to leave a fifteen thousand gold piece deposit here in this apartment to borrow the mask from the merchant that Weldrick knew. The gold would be returned on the safe delivery of the mask, only Trascar had no intentions of returning this mask. Randar and some of his boys would be dispatched to retrieve the gold and make the merchant disappear. Trascar also did not want to use his own coins, so he emptied most of the Guild treasury to use as a deposit. After all this was Guild business and he would replace the gold once he got it back.

Trascar still found it difficult to believe that Zorfal was working against them. He had known the man for a very long time and never once questioned his loyalty. In a few hours though, he would have the truth. He planned to show up at a south-side warehouse to meet the guard captain wearing the face of that wretched Harcourt, courtesy of the magical mask. Weldrick had explained that the illusion would not be perfect when trying to imitate someone known, but in poor lighting, a person should not be able to tell the difference. Trascar was given a detailed description of what the thief looked like today and had to concentrate hard on making the illusion believable.

The Guild leader spoke the command words aloud to remove the mask, then put it back on. He did this three times to be sure he had everything figured out. He was told the words needed to be spoken aloud for it to work. Weldrick had even left an elixir behind with a note that said drinking the elixir would also alter his voice, so as not to raise any suspicions.

Trascar could not believe his luck. This Weldrick was like a gift sent down by the gods. He may just give him Andil's position after this night, he laughed to himself.

*   *   *   *

Andil entered through the back door of the old store house. Half of the building was made up of black, charred wood, from the great fire. The other half had been rebuilt.

"Hello? Hello?" he shouted out.

No reply. He was to meet with the wealthy merchant that Weldrick had dealt with many times in the past. The skinny thief had some bars of gold and some gemstones that he wanted to move outside the city, but did not want to get robbed over the price. Weldrick had assured him that this merchant had deep pockets and vast resources for moving just about anything.

"Hello?" he called again.

Perhaps he had arrived too early, he thought. Lanterns were lit around the building so he figured someone must have been here not too long ago. He was looking about for signs of life when he found a small office illuminated with another lantern. Inside, he found several leather satchels piled on top of a desk with a sack lying on the floor. He pulled out a dagger and used the blade to gently lift open one of the satchel flaps for a quick peek. The unmistakable glitter of jewels caught his eye. Surprised, he stepped back out of the office and called again. "Hello? Anyone here?"

Still there was no answer. The thief went back inside the office and opened each of the satchels to find a small fortune in jewels. *Why would anyone be foolish enough to leave this lying around?* he thought to himself. Then he heard several heavy boot steps approaching. Alright, so they did not go very far after all. He turned and said, "I was beginning to wonder where you….."

The thief's sentence was cut short as his jaw dropped open in surprise. Standing before him was Captain Flannis of the south district guard, along with two other guards who were pointing loaded crossbows.

"What do we have here?" Captain Flannis asked.

"Ummm, this isn't mine," Andil replied for lack of anything better to say. And for once, it was in fact the truth.

"Oh, sure it ain't," one of the crossbowmen said.

Captain Flannis walked over and dumped the contents of all the satchels onto the table.

"Would you look at that. The missing jewels from those recent robberies. And what were you doing here? Just treasure-sitting these for someone?"

A panicked Andil replied, "I just got here, I swear. These were already here. They belong to some merchant. I was just supposed to talk to the merchant. I was told this is where I could find him. I am sure if we wait a short while, he will come back and you can ask him."

"Chain him, boys," the captain ordered.

Flannis then picked up the sack and dumped out two city guard uniforms onto the floor. "Impersonating guards as well? Is that how you pulled off these jobs? That is a major offence as I am positive you are well aware," he said with a raised eyebrow.

"Do I look like I could pass for a guard? None of this is mine! Please, this is all a mistake, someone is setting me up," Andil struggled as one of the guards chained his wrists behind his back.

"Tell it to the magistrate. Andillison Wulmcot, you are under arrest ," Flannis said. Real fear set into the skinny thief.

"Please, I'll pay you. I have a lot of coin. You could pretend you never saw me. I'll make you rich, I swear it. Just please, let me go!"

Captain Flannis shook his head in disgust.

"Theft from nobles. Theft from city guards. Impersonating city guards. Being a member of the Thieves Guild. Bribery of a guard captain. I am guessing you are going to spend a very long time in the dungeon."

Andil's cries of protest could be heard a block away.

*　　*　　*　　*

"You three hide in here," Harcourt said, motioning to a large crate pushed up against the back wall of a poorly-lit warehouse. "There are three peep holes. Just be silent and watch."

Captain Dornell just stared at the crate. "Do you plan on explaining what we are doing here and what we intend to watch?"

"You are about to witness a confession," the thief replied. "I have discovered much in the last day. I've found out that the leader of the Thieves Guild is someone by the name of Trascar Havholt. Somehow he caught wind that Zorfal was being investigated for having dealings with the Thieves Guild, and the story is that he emptied the Guild vault and fled this afternoon. As we speak, Captain Flannis is rounding up the Guild's number two man, Andil, who was responsible for all the latest major break-ins. The Guild has suffered a major blow this day, my friend, and shortly they will suffer another here. Just be silent inside there and observe. When you are satisfied that you have heard enough, you can spring out and make your arrest."

Part of Dornell wanted to find his own hiding spot, thinking that he should not be climbing into a crate at the request of a career criminal who had spent his entire life hating him. He could not deny, though, the good that Harcourt had done since his release. So he would place his trust in him once more.

Dornell and his two best men climbed into the crate and kneeled down inside. Harcourt lowered the lid then quietly slid an iron bar through a loop in the latch locking it in place. He crouched down in front of Dornell's peep hole and said, "Remember, not a word. The show should begin in less than an hour. I have to see to something then will return soon."

Captain Dornell watched as the thief disappeared out of view. The crate was positioned in such a way as to offer the best view of the warehouse's large store area. It was poorly-lit but still bright enough to see in.

Time passed and the three guards were beginning to get restless. It was certainly not comfortable in their cramped quarters and Dornell began to worry that something may have gone wrong. Then he heard the footsteps.

All three men held their breath as Captain Zorfal made his way cautiously through the warehouse with sword drawn, apparently looking for someone. Dornell had been hoping that Harcourt was wrong about Zorfal. He did not want to believe that the Guild could get to a district captain. Dornell always knew the brutish guard had a cruel streak and did abuse his power from time to time, but never suspected him as an outright traitor to the city. It made Dornell sick to his stomach to think of such corruption.

Captain Zorfal appeared to relax when he was satisfied that he was alone and sheathed his sword. He found a spot behind a pile of crates and sat down. The waiting continued. One of the other guards almost blew their cover when he attempted to keep from coughing, but Zorfal did not seem to notice.

Not long after that, Zorfal's head popped up as if he had heard something. It was then that Zorfal and Dornell spotted Harcourt inside the warehouse, appearing to be unaware of anyone else around. The thief was wearing different clothes and a different cloak from what he had on earlier. When Dornell shifted his gaze back to Zorfal, the man was gone.

Harcourt looked like he was about to get comfortable sitting on a crate when he heard heavy footsteps behind him and turned to face Zorfal.

"I've been waiting for you, thief," the brute said with a smile. "Nice of you to finally show up. Don't think about running, I've just barred all the exits."

Dornell noticed a puzzled look that crossed Harcourt's face that appeared genuine. The man was a good actor. "I thought I was on time," the thief croaked in a hoarse voice.

Harcourt then attempted to cough and clear his throat, continuing with that puzzled expression.

"You are on time for your own execution, you scum," Zorfal said. "I understand you've been doing a lot of talking lately. Telling everyone that I am to blame for killing that whore of yours. Sadly, though, I cannot take credit for the deed. Your old friend, Trascar, drove your own blade into her heart. I did watch her die though, then waited nearby for you to show up."

Harcourt attempted to say something but choked on his words and nothing came out.

"What's that? You'll have to repeat that. Guess you are a little upset, eh?" Zorfal taunted. "She was pretty, alright, but I don't know why Trascar was so taken with her. Just another south-side tramp if you ask me. But if he couldn't have her, then neither would you."

Harcourt rubbed his throat, struggling to say something, then he finally spit it out. "You are a traitor to the Thieves…," then his voice went silent again.

Captain Zorfal laughed at the distressed thief.

"I've been very loyal to the Thieves Guild, I am no traitor. I have no idea who the rat in the Guild is, but I'll deal with that nuisance next. I just heard that your tales scared Trascar into fleeing the city. Maybe I'll run the Guild now, in his absence."

Harcourt tried to shout something at the brute but nothing came out. That same strange look returned to his face and he shouted again. Still nothing.

"So frightened you lost your voice? A pity. I wanted to hear you beg for your life when I gutted you," Zorfal said drawing his sword.

That was all Dornell needed to hear. "Let's go boys," he said to the other two guards.

All three men attempted to stand, pushing upwards on the crates lid, but it did not budge. "It's locked," one of the guards shouted.

"Can't be, push harder," Dornell commanded.

In unison, the men pushed with all their strength. Kneeling as they were it was difficult to get good leverage. One of the guards positioned himself onto his back, and began kicking the lid, but to no avail.

Fearful for Harcourt's safety, Dornell tried one last time using every ounce of his strength and failed. He collapsed back down exhausted and turned his attention back to the peep hole where he was expecting to witness a murder.

*   *   *   *

An enraged Trascar attempted to shout at Zorfal but

nothing came out of his mouth. He tried again, and the result was the same. His throat did not feel sore at all, but he could not make a single sound. That elixir Weldrick gave him was supposed to alter his voice, not steal it completely.

"So frightened you lost your voice? A pity. I wanted to hear you beg for your life when I gutted you," Zorfal said drawing his sword.

What is going on here? Trascar thought. He was told Zorfal and Harcourt were conspiring together, not wanting to kill each other. Yet the ugly troll advanced with edged steel in hand. Banging noises and muffled shouts coming from a large crate against the wall startled the two men.

"Eh? What trickery is this?" Zorfal said, glancing suspiciously at the crate. Zorfal laughed when he realized whoever was in the crate was trapped. "Have you graduated to kidnapping now as well?"

Trascar was just as surprised as Zorfal that someone, or several people, were locked inside a crate. He had no clue what was going on here and wanted no further part in any of it. Zorfal turned his full attention back to the thief and fixed him with a murderous glare. Trascar again tried to shout at the guard captain to tell him he was not really Harcourt. Still not a sound would come out.

He suddenly tore at his face trying to rip off the magical mask but it held tight. Watching the thief claw at his own face made Zorfal pause a moment. "Damn, you really lost your mind in that dungeon didn't you? Just hold still then and I'll end your suffering for you."

Trascar desperately tried to speak the command words that would release the mask but they needed to be spoken aloud. So caught up with tearing at his own face, he barely ducked in time as the guard captain stepped in with a mighty swing of his sword. Trascar ducked, rolled, and jumped back to his feet. Fury and panic combined inside the Guild leader. He backed up while continuing to tear at his face and speak the words of release. Zorfal shook his head at the bizarre spectacle and lunged in with his blade but Trascar easily side-stepped out of the way.

*   *   *   *

Dornell winced as Zorfal nearly took Harcourt's head off with a powerful swing. The thief just managed to avoid the attack at the last possible second. Harcourt was behaving very strangely. He seemed to have lost his voice and he kept tearing at his face like a deranged madman. The thief seemed perfectly fine a short time ago. Dornell could not imagine what he was up to, Zorfal had already confessed. He was trying to figure out why the thief had locked them inside the crate. The captain came to the conclusion that Harcourt had wanted them to witness Zorfal's confession, to prove finally that he had nothing to do with Jalanna's murder, then planned to deal out his own kind of justice without them interfering.

A very bad idea, Dornell thought. He knew Harcourt was a good fighter, highly-skilled at close quarters combat, especially with a dagger or two. At a distance though, with an experienced foe wielding a sword and wearing armor as Zorfal was, he did not believe the thief had a chance. On top of that, Zorfal was an incredibly strong, brute of a man. Even Dornell would not relish the idea of having to fight him.

Oddly, Harcourt was not even fighting back, which

made Dornell wonder if this was all some sort of strange suicide plan. He winced again as the thief narrowly avoided another attack, then watched as he turned and ran for an exit.

*   *   *   *

The last swing of Zorfal's sword nearly opened Trascar's stomach but the thief's amazing agility saved him. He gave up on the mask and ran for the door that he had entered from. Zorfal could be heard laughing behind him. "Where do you think you are going, thief?"

Trascar's heart sunk when he found the door barred and padlocked from the inside. Zorfal had not been kidding about that. The Guild leader would have jumped through a window if there was any around but they were all too high to reach. The guard captain closed the distance and swung his blade again. Trascar rolled away to the side but not without a line of blood being drawn across his back. He made a silent gasp as no sound could escape his lips.

With no immediate alternative, he drew the two daggers he brought with him as part of his Harcourt disguise. Trascar was no stranger to fighting, and had killed many people in his climb to reach the top of the Guild. He had even killed a few city guards in his younger days although they had not been the size of Zorfal and he had not attacked them head on.

"Ah, excellent," the brute said with a smile. "Make a sport of it."

*   *   *   *

Amazingly, Harcourt avoided another fatal attack, but suffered a cut across his back this time. Captain Dornell clenched his fists tight, cursing all the gods above for his current predicament. The other guards continued to kick and punch at the crate's lid but made no progress.

Dornell nervously watched as Harcourt finally drew his weapons, having nowhere to run. Zorfal only appeared amused by that. The thief was looking for a way inside the brute's defense, but his sword was long and kept the thief at a safe distance. He feinted a few times but the experienced warrior never fell for the ruse.

Zorfal charged and swung for the thief's chest. Harcourt had just enough time to raise both daggers in an attempt to block the deadly strike. He was successful, but the force of the blow sent him back hard against a wall. Zorfal spun in a three-sixty turn and came in with a decapitating strike. Harcourt ducked and rolled as the guard's sword momentarily became stuck in the wooden wall. The thief slashed at Zorfal's side before retreating back out of reach, but caused no damage as the brute's chainmail turned away the blade.

*　　*　　*　　*

Trascar silently grunted in anger as his blade did not find flesh. Zorfal pulled his sword free and spun back to face the thief. It occurred to the Guild leader then that he had been set up. Weldrick must have been behind this whole thing. It also occurred to the thief that Weldrick was most likely not Weldrick at all, but someone who had used this very same magical mask to alter their appearance. But who? Could Harcourt really have been released from the dungeon to exact his revenge? *If I survive this*, Trascar thought, *I will spend years torturing Weldrick, or Harcourt, or whoever it was.*

His thoughts of revenge were interrupted as he was forced to backpedal away from another attack. Trascar knocked an empty barrel over in front of him but Zorfal shattered it with a powerful swipe and kept advancing.

The brute was backing the Guild leader towards a corner, looking for a way to end this little game and Trascar realized that he would be trapped. Before his back touched the wall, Trascar launched one of his two daggers at the large guard then dove into a roll. Zorfal had anticipated that. He dodged the flying dagger then drove the pommel of his sword into the thief's back with a sickening crunch as he tried to tumble past. Trascar was flattened to the floor with the wind knocked out of him, his remaining dagger slid across the floor out of reach.

Zorfal used the toe of his boot to roll the thief over onto his back. The brute sheathed his sword, placed his left knee on the thief's chest pinning him to the floor, then struck him in the face with a massive fist. Trascar's nose exploded sending blood spurting into the air. A second punch blackened one eye, a third blackened the other, and a fourth cracked a cheekbone.

Trascar's left hand desperately came up and shattered a tiny glass vial against the side of the guard's head. Zorfal howled and stood up as acid splashed all over his neck eating away at his skin. Battered and dazed, the Guild leader miraculously climbed to his feet. Zorfal drew his sword again and swung at the thief in anger. Trascar held up his left arm in a pitiful defense and the blade sliced off his hand at the wrist. He opened his mouth in a silent scream of agony and Zorfal was amazed that he made not a sound.

The guard captain glanced back over at that strange crate which began shaking violently again with shouts being heard from within. Even though Trascar was in agonizing pain, he managed to take advantage of Zorfal's distraction. The Guild leader activated a knife blade which now protruded from the toe of his boot, and kicked Zorfal in the groin area with all of his remaining strength. He was rewarded with a shriek from the brute as the blade sunk into flesh.

Screaming in rage and pain, Zorfal chopped into the thief's thigh opening a wide gash and sending the thief to the floor. Zorfal still could not understand how the man rolled around in pain and yet made no sound. "End of the line for you," the guard captain said through gritted teeth, in obvious pain.

Zorfal drove his sword straight down catching the thief in his side pinning him to the floor. Trascar's eyes bulged in horror and still continued with his silent scream. "What are you?" the brute said, twisting his blade around and still not getting a sound from the thief. "That must hurt so much!"

The beaten Guild leader had one last trick up his sleeve, literally. He raised his right arm and activated a fairly new device he wore strapped to his wrist. It looked like a thick bracelet and fired a spring loaded blade that traveled at great speed. It was particularly deadly at close range. The blade flew straight into Zorfal's throat and out the other side.

The guard let go of his sword and grabbed his throat

in a desperate attempt to keep his blood where it belonged. He made sickly gurgling noises as he tried to draw breath, then collapsed atop the Guild leader. Moments later, both bodies were still.

*   *   *   *

Both men lay unmoving in an expanding pool of blood. Captain Dornell fell back against the wall of the crate in great despair. His gut instincts had always told him that Harcourt was innocent of that murder. He spent four years of his life battling the system to see to it that the thief be freed. Now Harcourt had gone and thrown his life away unnecessarily. If he had only let him help, Zorfal would have hung for his traitorous crimes, and the thief would still be alive. "You fool," Dornell cursed. "Why did you have to try and fight him alone?"

A loud crashing noise drew the three guards back to their peep holes. They watched as city guards broke down one of the doors. Five men rushed in with weapons drawn, Captain Flannis following behind. "Sir, that one looks like Captain Zorfal," said one of the guards pointing to the bloody scene.

All six men turned to regard the large crate that began making noises. "I think someone is locked inside," said another guard running over to investigate. He removed the iron bar and lifted up the lid. "Captain Dornell?" he said with surprise.

"'Tis me," the captain replied, finally standing up and stretching his sore limbs.

"What a mess. What in the name of our good King happened here?" asked Captain Flannis.

"A tragedy," was all Dornell answered.

Captain Dornell took one last look at the two bloodied bodies on the floor and turned to leave. "Sir?" Flannis called after him.

"It's a long story, Captain. First I need some air."

CHAPTER 29

A dark figure flitted from shadow to shadow then slipped in behind the guardhouse, approaching a large shed. Deft hands worked the padlock on the door until it clicked open, then the near-invisible figure disappeared inside. The shed was devoid of any light until the man lit a small lantern he had brought with him. The illuminated room revealed three long tables, two of which held bodies. Thankfully, it was too soon for them to smell of decay, but the flies were everywhere.

The body on the right was that of Captain Zorfal. The disgraced guard had been stripped of his uniform. His body was caked in blood and flies hovered around his throat which was a disgusting mess.

The body on the left was unrecognizable, unless you knew who it was beforehand. The man approached the second body and leaned over with his lantern for a better look at the face, which was battered, bloodied and grotesquely swollen. He spoke the words "Argon Dol," and the face on the body shimmered, then became completely featureless.

Harcourt lifted the magical mask from Trascar's face, and found that he was still unrecognizable. The Guild leader's left eye was swollen shut, but suddenly his right eye shot open giving the thief a start. After a moment, Harcourt smiled and leaned in very close. "Well, well, how are you still alive? I just came to get my mask back. You were only to borrow it, you know. I am afraid I cannot give you your deposit back though, but it's going to good causes I assure you. Let's see, half of it is going to the orphanage. Some of it will go to the Ogre's Den, they are in need of some renovations. Some of it will go back to the small south-side businesses you stole from. Hmm, and the rest is going towards getting Jalanna a proper grave marker. One she deserves."

Trascar's mouth opened, but like earlier that evening, nothing came out. "Oh, still lost your voice I see. I am glad that you drank up all that elixir like a good little boy. I stumbled across that recipe purely by accident many years ago. I couldn't speak for a whole day. Luckily though, I never found myself in the situation that you found yourself in today. Gee, you didn't fare so well, did you? I am glad to see that you didn't die as quickly as your roommate over here. It was important for you to know fear and agony before you died, much like Jalanna. You know, even after all the horrible things you did, I still refused to stoop down to your murderous level. I truly did want to be the one to cut your filthy throat, but I talked myself out of it. I figured I would let you two devils cut each other to pieces. I want to thank you for being fool enough to carry out my plan to perfection. The word in the Thieves Guild is that the cowardly Trascar stole from the Guild treasury and fled. From now on your name will only be spoken with disgust."

Trascar's one good eye closed and Harcourt knew he was dead. Having retrieved what he came for, the thief extinguished the lantern and walked to the door. Before leaving, he turned back to the dead thief. "You should be happy. In the end, you still won and proved yourself the better thief. You stole Jalanna from me and I can never have her back." Then he faded into the night.

*　　*　　*　　*

The fog this morning was very thick. It gave an even creepier feel to the already eerie cemetery. Typical weather for a funeral, most thought. A fair-sized crowd had shown up, about thirty people all gathered around a small and very ordinary headstone. Some had not even known the thief buried there, but felt his story was a compelling one. People were always drawn to a good tragic tale.

First, the priest took everyone through a lengthy prayer and then said a few words regarding a better life that awaits after death, and how two lovers were now reunited in the gardens of heaven for eternity.

When the priest finished, a representative of the King stepped forward to say a few words.

"I would like to announce that King Stonewood has granted a full pardon to the man known only as Harcourt. The King would have liked to inform Harcourt of this in person, but as we are all aware, a tragedy has taken place. Harcourt had dealt in shady work for most of his life, a career thief. He redeemed himself, though, in the end. After a lengthy investigation, he was released from the dungeon to aid city agents in tracking down the real murderer of Jalanna Ezralys. He died in the service of Stonewood. Harcourt had uncovered the truth about a traitorous city guard who also died as a result of a battle with Harcourt. The real murderer was also discovered, a vile thief who is now on the run, but will be hunted down and brought to justice. My deepest sympathies go out to those of you who knew Harcourt and cared for him. Thank you."

When the speech was finished, people approached the grave one by one to say their own private goodbyes. The first one up was Dahleene, who ran the orphanage, and she cried hysterically. Behind her was a glassy-eyed Wulfred, followed by three of the Den's barmaids who laid flowers down on the grave. A middle-aged priest, with a protruding belly and a dark, bushy beard stood next to Captain Dornell who was in a full ceremonial guard uniform. His superbly-polished armor gleamed, even without the presence of the sun. The bearded priest looked to the grim-faced captain a few times before finally speaking.

"A strange sight to find a city guard and captain mourning the death of a south-side thief. People would not believe me if I told them."

"I knew the man fairly well, better than most I think," Dornell replied. "Harcourt and I go back a long way, when he was a boy of ten and I was a rookie guardsman. 'Tis true I spent most of that time arresting him and lecturing him, but I tried to set him on the right path. I knew inside that he was not a bad man, life had just dealt him a bad hand. I wish things had turned out differently, but alas, we know how this tale ends."

"Indeed. It is comforting to see that some compassion exists in the city guard. It was touching to hear you admit how you felt about the thief," the priest said.

"These last few weeks, I did not see the thief that he had been, only the good man that he was. I fear in the end he may have still borne a deep hatred for me and the role I played for much of his life. I only wish he understood it was for his own good," Dornell said with a defeated sigh.

The bearded priest put his hand on the guard's shoulder. "Fear not, good fellow. For we know that Harcourt looks down from above and thanks you for your kindness and your belief in him. He thanks you for giving him the chance to right a terrible wrong. He realizes that you were the father figure in his life, that he did not believe he had. He thanks you, good captain, more than you could ever know."

Captain Dornell smiled and nodded. The priest watched him take his turn kneeling at the grave to say a silent farewell. Harcourt was truly touched by it all. He had always wondered that if he died, would anyone even care or notice that he was gone. He had stood there as the pot-bellied priest, surprised at how many people had shown up. In a way, he felt badly for his deception, but it was necessary. With the deaths of Trascar and Zorfal, he closed that chapter of his life. Harcourt was gone. Now he planned to begin anew; a fresh start with the aid of his magical mask.

Originally, he had not planned on attending his own funeral but could not resist once he was here. He had only come to the cemetery to inspect Jalanna's new headstone, which was the talk of the town. Rumors swirled about how some anonymous person had recently purchased it and it was the tallest grave marker in all of Stonewood. That upset some nobles, but oh well, she deserved it.

Harcourt then watched as a raven-haired Feylane stood in front of "his" grave. The assassin shed no tears, but gave a nod of respect, then walked away. One-legged Kan hobbled up next. The old beggar was wearing some decent clothes for a change. It was good to know that he was not just drinking away all his gold that Harcourt had been leaving him. Whitemane passed by and gave the grave a salute. He had probably dug it himself the day before.

With all the mourners now having disappeared into the fog, save for an orange street cat that sat nearby washing its face, Harcourt finally turned to leave. Surprisingly, one last person ran past to kneel at the grave. It was a very attractive young woman who could not stop herself from crying uncontrollably. She struggled to breathe between sobs. Harcourt tried to position himself for a better look at her, without appearing too obvious. She seemed oblivious to his presence and just kept crying like someone who had lost somebody very dear to them.

He squinted his eyes. The beautiful woman looked to be in her early twenties, he thought. She was tall and thin, with long brown hair. She pulled something small from her pocket, kissed it, then buried it in the ground. Still sobbing, she stood and ran into the fog.

Curious, Harcourt walked over to the grave, and when he was sure he was alone, he dug up the spot to see what the girl had buried. He was puzzled to find a fifty-piece gold coin and now the mystery deepened. Who would leave such a valuable coin at the grave of a thief?

It suddenly hit him as he was inspecting the coin and

found teeth marks embedded in it. He then recalled giving that very same coin to the orphan Krestina many years ago as a gift. The thief was absolutely stunned that the young girl had kept that coin all this time and had not spent it. That was a lot of gold for an orphan. It was a lot of gold for anyone, actually. It must have meant a lot to her to have hung onto it for this long.

Harcourt felt flattered. He had never clued into how the girl might have felt about him, but then she was only young then anyways. All of sudden, the thief did not feel much like leaving Stonewood just yet.

EPILOGUE

The sun was at its highest point when the thief entered the secret Thieves Guild headquarters located beneath the streets of Stonewood. The place was empty, as he had expected to find it. Normally, it would be dead at this hour of the day anyway, but more so lately. News of Zorfal's treachery had spread fast and the Guild had no idea just how much information the city had on its members and secret locations. For the time being, everyone was laying low. All except one.

The thief found the door to Trascar's personal office unlocked and he entered. First, he searched the cabinets but all were empty. He then sat in the former Guild leader's chair and searched all the desk drawers. Empty. The thief had hoped to loot anything left of value before leaving the Guild for good.

"You won't find anything in here," a voice said, startling the thief. "I figured you would have abandoned Stonewood days ago, fearing a repeat of what happened in Hartlan."

Weldrick looked up to find the senior Guild member, Serdic, standing in the office doorway.

"Nah, I don't believe it will be as bad here. I believe you guys are good at hiding away and we'll regroup soon enough," Weldrick answered.

"We do not know what Zorfal told the city agents before he was killed. He could have given over all of our names and where to find all of our hideouts," Serdic said.

"Zorfal was a rat, of that there is no doubt. But I don't believe he would have given away much or the city would have already swarmed our buildings. I suppose it is wise, though, to keep a low profile, for a little while anyways," Weldrick reasoned.

"That chair suits you," Serdic pointed out.

"Pardon?"

"I said, that chair suits you. The Guild is without a leader and technically, the position falls to you."

"Oh? How so?" Weldrick asked, amused.

"Well, Trascar turned out to be a coward. At the first sign of real trouble, he emptied our vault and fled. There is a hefty price on his head right now. Bounty hunters and assassins are already searching for him. Our second in command was Andil and he was just given ten years in the dungeon. Trascar did appoint you as the number three man, so as I said, technically the position is yours. While others may disagree with that, I think you'll find them fearful to oppose you, if you were to accept the role."

"What about more senior members like yourself or Zenod?" Weldrick inquired.

"Myself and Zenod would be likely candidates, however neither of us wants the role. We would both endorse you as the leader though and act as trusted advisors. True, you may not be familiar with the entire city yet, but I trust you know the business of the Guild quite well. What do you say?"

This turn of events caught Harcourt completely by surprise. He had basically spent his entire life wishing he could be a member of the Thieves Guild and now he was being offered the position of Guild leader. It was true he did not like a lot of the Guild's practices, but as leader, he might be able to change the way they did business. He also liked the idea of sending Randar and a group of assassins to pay a visit to Chief Magistrate Krommel. Maybe he could finally eliminate the demon worshipping cult from Stonewood with a small army of thieves, thugs and assassins at his command.

"I accept."

ABOUT THE AUTHOR

Jeremy was born in Scarborough, Ontario, Canada, in 1974. He started creating his own characters and writing his own stories by the age of 9. He is a boxing fanatic having been an amateur boxer and is now a professional boxing judge. In his spare time when not watching boxing, or reruns of Lost in Space and Rocket Robin Hood, Jeremy tries to find time to write some of the many stories floating around in his head.